A COSMIC CHANCE

In a small corner of the universe, a young woman's life would be forever altered by prophesied events.

And she couldn't have predicted any of them...

A story by Sacha Kurucz

When reality
fails to write
the perfect
ending, your
imagination can
take you there.

Inspired by true events

Predestined Prologue

An unbound emotion burst through my chest as I stared at the little photograph in my hand. Like a spinning compass, I couldn't quite figure out where the feeling wanted to take me. For a moment, I laughed, remembering the time that it was taken and how I never was a fan of impromptu selfies. And then my smile fell into something more sombre, as I remembered everything that lead up to that night and everything that happened thereafter. My heart suddenly yearned to recapture that moment - a simpler time before anything else unfolded - but it was impossible.

Though, the longer I sat there with the little picture rested between my finger and thumb, gently being brushed by the whistling autumn breeze, I felt gratitude. Despite all that had happened, I was lucky to have those memories. Even the ones that seemed small or the ones that pained me to recollect, they all helped craft the binding to the pages of a very special life story.

And just like a row of dominoes, or a ripple from a butterfly's wings, what started out as a sequence of understated moments, eventually became a memory so powerful that it changed everything...

PART 1

The Family Portrait

'Hey Mum,' I groaned, knowing the conversation I was about to invite was one I really didn't want to have, 'you okay?'

For a brief moment before this, I'd wrestled with my thoughts. *"To answer, or not to answer? That is the question."* But the incessant buzz of my phone on my work desk successfully guilt-tripped me into the former. No doubt I already knew what she was going to say though, and the sniffle-ridden greeting she gave me only confirmed my suspicions.

'I just thought I'd let you know that I've done it, Simone,' she gibbered, a lump well-lodged in her throat, 'I've signed everything. All the documents are with the court office now, ready to be finalised. It's officially over.' There was a brief pause before she revealed her most prolific action yet.

'I even took him off my Facebook,' She confessed, with great liberation, 'as if I want to see that little green circle every day telling me he's online. The cheating swine!'

After twenty-five years of marriage, I could only imagine the pain Mum felt signing the divorce papers from Dad. They'd been in each other's lives for so long, erasing those memories would be near impossible, especially with two children serving as permanent reminders. Nevertheless, hearing her theatrical tenor reiterate the same story from its new stage of development on what felt like an hourly basis was becoming rather exasperating. To be honest, working for the MI5 is probably a less intense job than this was.

'You've done the right thing, Mum,' I softly reassured her, trying to speak with conviction on a subject I'd already heard a million times. 'Now you can finally begin to move on.'

From the corner of my apartment's kitchen, I could hear the chorus of a song playing on the afternoon radio. The infectiously catchy riff began to trickle its way into my ears and saturate my mum's words.

Air guitaring would be so much fun right about now...

Shaking my head, as if to rid the song from clutching my attention, I drew my focus back onto what she was saying.

'Isn't it ironic that the last time you'll ever see our names together will be on the Decree Absolute? No more, *Mr Ian and Mrs Fiona Hartley*,' she said with derisive inflection, 'stupid dirtbag. Well, good riddance to you, Ian Hartley. Good riddance to you and your stupid classic car toys, to your tidal wave splashes that ruined my bathroom walls and to your stupid inability to keep your stupid penis in your stupid trousers!'

It may make me sound like a bad daughter, but I'm pretty sure that was where I lost focus. Mum's conversation usually followed the same pattern, anyway. Stage 1: Self-pity. Stage 2: Reflective Sorrow. And Stage 3: Anger. This was Stage 3, and it could go on for a while.

'Mhmm, you're better off without him,' I replied whilst turning down the radio and discreetly tearing open a tea bag, ready to make myself a cup after she'd gone, 'Oh, I know!' I said effusively; the light bulb in my head suddenly shining brighter than ever. 'You should go on a holiday. I bet that'll cheer you up.'

6

By this point, I was desperate for my mum to see the light at the end of the tunnel. As much as I empathised and agreed with what she was saying, I really wanted to talk about something else - anything else. Plus, I knew this story of old.

Dad's infidelities began over three years ago. It was only with one person – his secretary; *cliché much?* Nevertheless, this news was hardly a surprise. He'd told Mum not long after it happened, as she'd become increasingly suspicious of the sneaky late-night texts and the unusual grin permanently stitched on his face. Oh, and the fact that they didn't seem to have sex anymore.

'Hmm, I don't know,' she whined, dejectedly. 'I've never been anywhere alone before.'

Back when I lived at home, my little brother Seb and I listened to both sides of this story multiple times. To be honest, it didn't matter whose side we were on, it was simply time to accept that their marriage was dead in the water. It still makes me shudder to recall those times. The tension in our household was pretty hard to bear. We both had problems we needed to keep a secret, because neither of our parents could cope with any more stress. So, we reluctantly plodded on, piling secrets on our backs like mules up a mountain. That seemed to be the definition of *"adulting"*- maintaining an outside face that didn't expose any inner-emotions. On the plus side, all of my parents' craziness made the previous focus on my introverted disposition seem pretty small fry. Unlike my parents, at least I was independent.

'Well, now's the time.' I reassured, pacing my apartment, and looking out the window for some kind of view that'd inspire a new topic of conversation. 'Going abroad will make you feel confident again, Mum.'

Unlike my family, I could keep my privates under control. I didn't need anyone else to define my existence or choices and, furthermore, I didn't care about being single. Not that anyone ever commended me for that, mind you. To be honest, I often thought my parents would be happier if I put less effort into my winged eyeliner and more into finding a "nice boy".

'I'm not sure, Simone.' Mum uttered, whimsically, her little sniff disrupting my brief reminiscence. 'I don't think I'm ready yet. Oh, why did that wretched man have to knock so much stuffing out of me?'

As Mum then began to reverse the conversational cycle back to Stage 2, it reminded me of my own reflective sorrow. It wasn't that long ago that I'd dated my very own brand of "stupid dirtbag." called Jake. He was also a complete nightmare (sorry, Dad) and reminiscing about him isn't something I like to do, so I'll keep it short.

Our relationship was about as calm as the Great Storm of 1987. Simply put, I had no other choice but to end things. Jake's fluctuating behaviour and compulsive lying drove me crackers. One minute, he'd be buying me flowers and would check up on me night and day (which was cute, yet simultaneously irksome). The next, he'd disappear for days on end and would tell me to "*eff off*" if I even did as much as send him a text message (which wasn't either cute or irksome; just downright bizarre). In the end, I couldn't hack it. He had to go. He'd stolen nearly two years of my life already and God forbid I was going to let him steal anymore.

With this thought in mind, I searched for a teacup and also responded to her previous rhetorical question, without thinking of the consequences.

'*Because,* some men are dicks?'

'Oh,' she scoffed, suddenly fuelled and ready for round two of "*Let's Slag off Your Father*", 'you're not wrong.' *Ding-Ding!*

While reeling off her never-ending list of why my Dad was utterly useless and that his penis was about the only thing of value, I laid out a selection of teacups whilst recollecting how my own affectional pandemonium had made me see the world.

Back when my romantic life went pear-shaped, I decided that, as much as I enjoyed throwing darts at a paper cut-out of Jake's face, I needed to make more positive changes in my life. So, at the ripe age of twenty, I moved out of my childhood home in scenic Nott's (Or, Nottingham, as you may know it) and made a fresh start in the capital. London was on all the fancy calendars, so I figured that there must be something intrinsically life-changing about it. Thus, maybe it would be a good place to start anew?

Back in the room, I tried my best to interject the conversation about holidays again with Mum. It proved useless. Her jabbering was on full-throttle. I had no hope of kyboshing that blame-train. So, I continued to stare at London's city skyline, which, in the midst of her chatter, made me realise something.

There I was, practically coercing my mum into travelling, profusely explaining how it'd be good for her, and yet, I still hadn't ticked off one of the biggest places on my own bucket list yet - Japan. If there was anywhere in the world I needed to visit next, it had to be the Land of the Rising Sun.

I'd succumbed to temptation a few times and googled capsules to stay in, watched programmes scanning the city views from above, and looked at stunning pictures of Sakura season in full-bloom. I'd envisaged myself staring up at the Sumidagawa fireworks from a boat, slowly sailing across the Sumida River and watching the psychedelic display of colours above me reflect in the surrounding waters. To me, that was a perfect dream. And so far, that's how it remained.

Alerting my already withered attention, the distant *click* of the kettle sounded from the corner of the kitchen. Mum was still talking about Dad's embarrassing miniature car collection as I quietly wandered towards it. It seemed rude to interrupt her monologue, so I took it upon myself to pour myself a drink.

Embracing my inner-Pink-Panther, I inconspicuously placed my mobile on the counter and popped Mum on speakerphone, freeing myself to pour out the boiled contents of the kettle onto my teabag. At that point, my discretion was going well. She most certainly had no clue that I'd missed at least ten minutes of her conversation to reverie. Until, I burned myself.

'*Shit...!*' I silently expelled, trying to ignore the stinging pain in my hand as Mum rambled on. Everything was against me that day, I swear. *Productivity; meet annoying distraction. Annoying distraction, meet A &E.*

'Did you say something, sweetheart?' I heard her say, all sweetness and light. You'd never think this was the same woman that once tore up Dad's posh shirts and then threw them out of the window in black bin bags, yelling, "*OUT GOES THE RUBBISH!*"

Oh, how the neighbours must have loved us that day...

'Nope,' I lied, running my hand under cold water and skewing my face like I'd just trodden on a mousetrap, 'just listening to you.'

'Okay,' she briefly paused, as if she knew something wasn't right, but chose to ignore it in place of continuing her monologue instead, 'well, as I was saying...'

Point proven.

Towel now wrapped around my throbbing hand, I walked back over to my open laptop which screened the unfinished manuscript I'd been thoroughly enjoying typing before she'd called. Trying to complete it had been pretty hard of late. Especially with this divorce business and both Mum and Dad calling me every five minutes to sound off about it. Sometimes, I wondered if my role as a daughter was a charade. They blatantly treated me as if I was their own personal agony aunt. However, even with their frequent distractions, I was pleased to say that I'd nearly finished writing my first ever book.

You'd think I'd have told mum about this little achievement, just to redirect the redundant chatter. But instead, for the sake of sanity, I said nothing. My friends and family would've had a field day, dissecting my twist on a romantic fiction. This was one of my closely-guarded secrets. If anyone had ever found my many notebook scribblings or flipped open my laptop, the interrogation would most certainly have been relentless. I'd spent so much time rejecting love in order to get over the past hurt; the last thing I wanted was for anybody to know there was even a tiny part of me that cared about it. However, coming from a girl who'd not been in, or surrounded by good, honest love, it seemed fairly ironic to write about it. But this was how I wanted to fill my spare time. It was quite therapeutic in a way - my means of believing that true love still existed, even if it was only vicariously through fiction. With hopeful ideals serving as my inspiration, I'd spent evening after evening, noting and typing into the night. Hoping that, one day, maybe my efforts would come to some kind of emotional osmosis. If not for me, then for others who needed hope where there was none. After all, there's still so much beauty to see in the world, it just helps when someone else shows you the right places to look.

Suddenly, as if by remarkable coincidence, a word I'd written earlier jumped out at me from the radiating computer screen. It was as if that word acted as a door, finally opening up to a world of stories that I simply had to explore right there and then. Why that always happens after an endless bout of writer's block, I am yet to understand. But with my attention now caught, my creative juices were sent into frenzy once again. An excitable rush of adrenaline coursed through my veins. I had to get Mum off the phone before this new flow drifted away.

'Do you remember those odd socks he'd wear?' she eagerly babbled, just as I'd readied my inhalation for a well-timed exit dialogue, 'Oh, and the embarrassment he brought on me that night at Aunty Brenda's charity ball. As if I had to introduce him to the Mayor wearing socks that informed others about returning him to a pub if found. *Oh*, the humiliation!'

Finally, she paused for breath. My chance was nigh.

'I know, Mum, those socks were terrible. Look, I'm sorry but someone's at the door, I've got to dash.' The laptop screen began to dim, so I quickly chucked off the towel nursing my free hand and shook the mouse, bringing it back to life. 'We'll catch up soon, okay?'

She didn't even sound disappointed, 'Okay, sweetheart,' she replied, 'off you go. I'll call you later.'

Ah, that's why - because she was going to call me again later.

'Love you.' She ended.

And, as if on autopilot, I answered with, 'Love you, too, Mum.'

Still staring at the screen, I placed my mobile back onto the desk, face down this time. Now the flow was back, I couldn't afford to lose it again. However, hearing yet another guitar-filled track the radio waves nearly got me distracted. I was determined though. Nothing was getting in the way of me and my manuscript again. Not this time.

…Well, after that song, anyway.

The Pushy Posse

Within a few seconds of venturing my way out of the underground, I was greeted by the familiar tunnel breeze that blew my hair onto my lips. No matter how many times I told myself to apply lipstick after I'd got to work, I'd always manage to somehow forget. So now, thanks to the pesky wind and my own absent-mindedness, I had no choice but to wipe off the remnant red streaks that marked my face with my fingers, hoping that no tube germs were being carried on the tips of them.

My iPod wires weren't disturbed by the unforgiving wind, thankfully, and remained firmly in place behind my windswept black hair, still playing the Joker's Ashes new album into my ears as I ventured up the flight of steps towards Oxford Street; piercing vocals and speedy guitar solos accompanying me as I walked.

It was busy that day. The last traces of summer calmly floated in the September sky above. And with such inviting weather sweeping the city, many excitable party guests would soon follow. Thus, amongst the rush-hour crowds was also a horde of eager tourists, each armed with a selfie stick as long as a cane, ready to take a picture of London's best attractions at any given moment. This was the first time I realised that the blue "Oxford Circus Station" sign I saw nearly every day was considered an "attraction". Quickly but carefully, I tried to weave my way through the flurry of matching people wearing sunglasses on sunburned faces, and just like a swimmer coming up for air, as soon as my feet hit the pavement and I was out of the sticky masses, I released a triumphant breath of freedom.

I checked my phone briefly. 8.46 am – I was still early. But, before I could return my phone safely back into my pocket, it let out its familiar recurring buzz. Rolling my eyes, I looked at it again and saw a few notifications pop up, each one demanding my attention right this second. I squinted as I tried to make out what they all said. The morning sun shone on the screen too brightly for me to see, so I tottered towards the towering buildings on the roadside and used their height for shade. Obviously, most of the notifications were crap and got swiped away; like Twitter or Pinterest telling me not to miss out on so and so's tweet, or to show me a pin of someone's interior decor I may like, as if it was *Breaking News*. However, one message did catch my eye.

It was Harry, an old college friend of mine who, thankfully, still shared the same love of rock music as me. Friends like him were few and far between these days. Since everyone "*grew up*" they also grew out of enjoying metal. Harry, however, remained ever passionate about it, which was why - on this very bright morning - he'd sent me a screenshot of a VIP package available for Joker's Ashes. He was seeing them at Rock City in Nottingham next week, and was raving about how cheap the meet and greet with the band was. To be fair, he had a point. Even with the free poster, signed CD and photo, it still cost less than two days of travelling on the pesky underground. Temptation had taken hold of me. I was already seeing them at the Koko this weekend (hence, binge-listening to their new album en-route to work) but did I really need to meet them too? I quietly pondered this thought. And then someone grabbed me.

'Boo!' The unannounced voice boomed.

I jolted, pulling the iPod wire free from my ears, 'Katrina!' I shrieked, relieved at the sight of her and not some stranger trying to rob me. 'You scared the shit out of me.'

'Sorry, sweets,' she said, keeping one arm around my shoulder and the other free to sip her on-the-go cappuccino, 'I couldn't help myself. You should stop being so fun to sneak up on.' She cheekily winked at me before animatedly taking a glug of her coffee, and for the second time that morning, I rolled my eyes.

As we walked along, I took the opportunity to fiddle with my tangled wires and put my phone away, eyeing up my best friend's excitable grin as she strode beside me, arm still over my shoulder, face like a Cheshire Cat.

'*So*,' I reluctantly began, 'do I even need to guess why you didn't make it back to the apartment last night, or is the oddly giddy smile affixed to your face already telling me the answer?'

Smile even bigger now, she peered over to me and cheerily uttered, '*Maybe*.'

I raised my eyebrows at her, voicelessly asking for her to dish the dirt on her date with Julian last night, the bartender from our favourite nightclub in Camden.

'Let's just say,' she began, 'we got to know each other *pretty* well.' The second wink confirmed my suspicions.

'Eww…' I mocked, scrunching up my face as hideous images infiltrated my mind. 'You filthy wench.'

'Ah, you're just jealous because you're not getting any,' she teased, before bending down slightly and placing her free hand straight beside her mouth, 'isn't that right, mini-Simone? You need some TLC from a sexy man to dust off them cobwebs, don't you?'

'Lordy Kats,' I squawked, pulling her up to eye-level once again, 'you're shameless.'

'And that's why you love me,' she smirked, before tossing her now empty eco cup into a nearby bin, 'now c'mon, hop to it before *Miss Trunchball* gets her baggy pants in a twist over us being late for work.'

I rolled my eyes at the prospect of moving any faster so early in the morning. 'Alexandra's not *that* bad...' was all I replied, hoping that it would get me off the hook.

She shot me an opposing glance as if to say, "*now that's a load of BS*" before swiftly leaping in front of me and running down the pavement. She was always running. I never could understand where she got all her energy from, especially when the majority of the time she was too busy out partying to get much sleep. All I could think was that those cappuccinos she drank on a daily basis must have been laced with something illegal. Or, knowing Katrina, blended with some weirdly named superfood no one had ever heard of. Nothing else could explain where her endless buzz came from.

She stopped a few yards ahead, quickly turning back around again to holler at me.

'Come on, Sims, shake a tail feather,' she called out, all smiles as she continued to sprint down the asphalt path, 'cobwebs aren't that heavy.'

Sweeping rebellious strands of hair off my face and hauling my handbag back over my shoulder, I feebly attempted to run after her.

'Damn it, Kats,' I grumbled, 'don't you ever just walk?'

***

'You're late.'

Katrina strode ahead of me into the open shop and smiled boldly at Alexandra - our now very chagrined manager, who stood at the front of the tills with her arms folded and right foot tetchily tapping away.

'Sorry, Alex,' she apologised, still baring her perfect pearly whites, 'the underground this morning was choc-a-bloc with tourists. I nearly had my eye taken out by one of those selfie sticks.'

'She's not wrong,' I agreed, following closely behind, still trying to catch my breath after the run to work. 'There must be some special event going on.'

'Hmm,' Alexandra groaned, unconvinced.

We stumbled into the back room and hurriedly placed our belongings in a locker, swiftly re-emerging in a tangle of our aprons and lanyards. Katrina flicked her long brown hair out from under the restrictive strings and allowed it to wave freely over her chest.

'Miss Stevenson,' Alexandra snapped, 'how many times have I told you that it's Botanique's policy to tie your hair back? No one wants your brown strands floating in their essential oils.'

'I'm on it.' Katrina saluted whilst pulling an elastic band from her wrist, placing it between her teeth and smoothing her hair to shape a high ponytail, ready to be locked in place.

'Good. Now, Simone, I want you at the front on skincare, and Katrina, I have some jobs for you to do out back. Our audit is coming up soon and I need this place looking spick and span, so there'll be no more messing about today. I want you both on your best behaviour.'

'When are we ever anything but angels, Alex?' Katrina declared, her green eyes glistening with innocence.

Alexandra's unimpressed expression remained as she made her way to the other side of the tills.

'That remains to be seen, Miss Stevenson. Now come along. Chop-chop,' she clapped insistently, 'let's get to work.'

With our orders given, Katrina outstretched her hand dramatically and mouthed, "*I miss you already*" before wandering out back. Laughing to myself, I sauntered to the front of the shop, show-face smile fixed firmly in place, ready to greet anyone who'd walk in at 9am. Mind you, no one usually came in first thing with such urgency for Ayurvedic skincare. So you can imagine my surprise when not just one person, but two, came in.

First was an elderly lady. I greeted her kindly, but I don't think she even knew where she was. And second was the quick-paced entrance of winklepicker-clad feet, running with jitter through the doors and clip-clopping their way straight into the elderly lady.

'I am so sorry, lovely,' He professed, taking hold of her purple anorak with apologetic grip, 'are you okay?'

She nodded silently, realising him for the excitable teenager that he was.

Typical Seb.

I walked over to him, cocking my head as I did so. Seeing him come rushing into my place of work first

19

thing in the morning wasn't the most standard move for my brother. It must have been important. Either that or he was going to show me another hilarious photo of a man he'd seen on some dodgy dating app. They did take some terrible shots, sometimes.

'Shouldn't you be studying?' I queried, staring at him, observing his clothing choice of tight white skinny jeans and electric blue shirt with the top few buttons undone. His highlighted hair was sprayed within an inch of its life and his skin was unnaturally bronzed. There was obviously a reason he'd made such an effort to look like a glow stick so early in the morning.

After hearing my question, he screwed his face up at me, as if the mere word "studying" made him want to heave.

'Urgh, you sound just like Mum,' he grumbled. 'No, it's freshers' week – no one has studying to do in freshers' week, you daft mare.'

'Charming,' I retorted, waiting for a further explanation that clearly my silly eighteen-year-old brother wasn't going to provide without further questioning. 'So…what are you doing here then?'

He went towards the shop window and began to peek out inconspicuously from behind our Indian herbal display at the passers-by on the street.

Growing impatient and concerned that Alexandra would come out and see him, I gestured a guttural cough to gauge his attention again, to which he merely flapped his hand at me.

'Oh, for God's sake, Seb, why are you here?'

Taking a sigh of relief, he unclenched his shoulders and walked back over to me, his puppy-dog blue eyes filled with worry.

'Chick calm down. I'm just making sure he's not here yet.'

'Who's not here?' I asked, even more confused than I was ten seconds ago.

'Tariq.' He replied.

'...*Tariq?*'

'Oh, my God! I'm going on a date with Tariq from uni and he's meeting me for doughnuts and coffee at double B's in like, thirty minutes? And I just needed somewhere to do my hair before he sees it looking like I've fallen in a bush.'

Noticing our decadent mirror hanging above a tower of spearmint body lotions, he went over to it and began to preen individual strands of blonde hair into place.

'Are you serious?' I remarked, ogling his rock-solid strands, 'Your hair's got so much spray on it that I'm surprised the sunshine alone hasn't set it alight yet.'

If only the expression he'd cast me then could be put into words that weren't profane.

Soon after the glowering daggers were thrown, Katrina popped through the door with a roll of bin bags in her hand, ready to deep-clean the till area. But as soon as she saw Seb, she instantly dropped them on the floor and ran straight over to give him a hug. Despite our derisive comments, we were all actually pretty close. It was just the way we were. Life had thrown so many spanners in the works that sometimes, the best thing to do was to simply take it on the chin and ridicule the bump it left behind.

'Baby Seb - what are you doing here?' she asked excitedly before admiring his vibrant get-up, 'Oh, my God, I love this look...Who is he?'

After two years of knowing my brother was gay, you'd think that I'd be more used to him going on dates with guys. But to me, he was still my little brother. The one I used to cook chocolate cornflake smarties cakes with and plaster up his knees after he'd fallen over from running around outside. Maybe, I was like Mum, in some ways. I just missed the innocence of childhood - the naivety of enjoying the simpler pleasures. Plus, from my experience, men were certainly not the be all and end all in life. And besides, we were all still young. Love could wait.

'His name's Tariq, apparently,' I answered obtusely, staring straight ahead.

'Ignore her, Kats.' Seb flatly stated, 'she's playing at being Mum today. Talking of which, have you heard from her, Sims? She sent me a right cryptic text last night and I didn't know how to respond.'

I furrowed my brow at him, 'What did she say?'

Seb shrugged his shoulders, 'I can't remember exactly. It was at like, 11pm last night. All I remember was thinking that she sounded proper sad.'

A pang of guilt surged through me. It was probably my fault for cutting her off the day before. Sometimes it evaded my thoughts that she was all alone now. Although I was aware she was going through the divorce, I forgot that she had no one to really talk to. What with me in London, Seb recently following suit to study at UCL nearby, and Dad obviously booted out, there was no one else at home, bar the company of our seven-year-old cocker-spaniel, Lizzie. Saying that, she had Andrew; her squeamishly servile colleague at the bank. He always seemed willing to keep her company. But then again, I wasn't sure that his company came without an ulterior motive.

Whilst I stood there in deep thought, both Seb and Katrina had returned the conversation to Tariq. Seb had whipped out his phone and started showing her pictures of him. From a distance, he looked quite lanky, but handsome, in a Bollywood type of way. It was just a shame that he'd dotted so much of his face with piercings. Not that I'm against piercings by any means, but his were just so tackily done - the symmetrical ones on each nostril being most distracting. Apparently, Tariq and Seb had first met during freshers' week and happened to be living in the same halls of residence. This, and the fact that Tariq was an Aries, according to my brother, meant that they were fated.

'Oh, yes,' I jeered, 'I'm sure that the cosmos know *all* about the needs of your D, bro.'

Hand on hip, Seb looked over at me with immovable conviction, 'Look, Sims, just because you don't believe in the stars doesn't mean that it's not true. Maybe you could do with looking into it. You certainly live up to your stubborn Capricorn name and even we mere mortals here can see that you have needs for the D, too.'

I tutted. 'Rubbish. I have no needs for the D.'

'Lesbian.'

Aware our bickering was nearing a crescendo, Katrina stood in-between us both, separating the tension with her well-manicured nails.

'Alright, break it up, you two,' she ordered, 'you're ruining the Zen of the store. Plus, we don't want *you know who* to come out of the office and call time on this little get together, do you?'

We both shook our heads like naughty schoolchildren.

'Good. Now, Sebastian. Go and have a brilliant date with Tariq. Eat lots of doughnuts and don't forget to lick the sugar off his lips! As for you, my darling Simone - chin up. We're going out tonight so we can find you some overdue D then.'

I sighed – D (the polite abbreviation for the male appendage, in case you hadn't quite figured it out) was definitely not on my agenda. It irked me how everyone scrutinised my love life – or lack thereof. No one seemed to care about the things I actually did love; like music or travel, or the book I was writing, not that anybody knew about that particular passion. But then again, I had been single since Jake, and even though I'd had some offers, I'd turned them all down.

There was a small part of me that thought my friends and family had a point. Having someone to share these things with would be nice. But even so, I didn't feel ready. The guys that liked me didn't have "it" – that spark, the *je ne sais quoi* you look for when it comes to finding romance. And in my eyes, there's no point settling for anything less.

A flurry of customers suddenly rushed in, and judging by their enthusiastic faces, they were most undeniably tourists.

Regaining my professional stance, I adjusted my apron and lanyard, ready to assist them, but not before wishing my brother luck on his date – Simone style.

'Enjoy your date, Seb,' I said, patting him on the shoulder, 'just make sure you keep away from any shop doorways, eh? You don't want Tariq's face setting off the alarms.'

Unamused by my joke, he tilted his head and glared at me.

'Oh, ha-ha. Very funny. Well, you have fun on your outing tonight too,' he replied, adjusting his hair one more time before making his way to the entrance door. 'And um, do send my regards to the poor fellas who end up contracting frostbite from the ice queen. *Ciao.*'

Katrina laughed as he spat out his tongue at me from the other side of the glass, and whilst no one else was watching, I flicked up my middle finger at him.

The Unexpected Message

For all the feminine parts of me, I loved hanging with the girls. For the way they could listen to a problem and find the answer in a bar of chocolate and a chick flick, and the fact that they were always there no matter what. You'd call them, they'd answer; armed with clever conversation and an ear to bend. However, in spite of this, the thought of meeting up with everyone at our apartment, in order to attend some gimmicky psychic event, made me realise that hanging with the girls was the last thing I wanted to do that night.

Selfishly, maybe, I grabbed my nearby notepad and began to jot down more ideas for my book, using the fantasy of Mr X as the object of the protagonist's affections. He was a perfect figment of my imagination, created as a means to not only escape the doldrums of my reality, but, by which, it could also be somewhat *re*-created.

I began to daydream about a scene at a coffee house, where both characters would rebelliously order a matcha latte instead of the conventional cappuccino, and they'd sit in awe at the revelation of their shared dreams and passions - wholly fascinated by the endless journey their conversations could take.

Upon this fantasy's dissolution, I realised that no part of me wanted to sit in a room with some charlatan in a headdress reading prettified cards to me. It seemed stupid. But, then again, sitting there envisioning a person who didn't exist was probably no less ironic. Plus, it's not like I wanted a boyfriend - not really. I just wanted someone I could connect with differently; someone who shared and valued the same things that I did and could teach me something new about the world. Unbeknown to those around me, though, I kept this dream to myself.

Perhaps it was silly of me, but I didn't want anyone else to know that there was a measure of me that cared about finding love. All they'd do is harp on about it, anyway. No, I'd made a silent pact: to abstain from such trivial nonsense. I was far too young to settle down. Plus, what would be the point in being with someone when I still had so much to see and do? They'd only get upset that I wasn't there to eat pizza and watch Netflix with them every Friday night. With so many things on my list to complete, there'd be no time for such trifling distraction. And besides, I already had plenty of people in my life who provided me with an ample amount of conversational enthral.

'Skirt or dress?'

I stand corrected.

Turning out of my trance-like state, I looked at Katrina in the doorway of her bedroom as she held up two hangers against her.

'What?' I responded, barely listening.

She rolled her eyes and bobbed her head between each hanging option.

'*Skirt* or dress?' she repeated.

'Does it really matter?' I replied, folding my notepad shut and picking up my buzzing mobile from the arm of the sofa. 'It's only some local psychic event.'

It was Dad, doing his usual competitive parenting thing and dropping me messages about having a great time tonight and how much he was looking forward to meeting up with me tomorrow. Ever since he and Mum officially split he'd been like this. When they were together he barely took notice of my interests. But now, well, let's just say that if being an awesome parent was a marathon, then he was sprinting for his life to win first place at the finishing line. It was so weird. If this had happened when I was six, then it would have been in the form of weekends filled with days out at a theme-park, eating ice cream and going to bed ridiculously late – just to prove that he was *the best*. This adult version, however, didn't sit with me quite as well as a Flake 99 would.

Katrina made a huffing sound by the door and started muttering something about wearing a dress whilst the weather was still good. I didn't reply. My attention was distracted by the tab I'd left open on my phone about the VIP meet and greet tickets for Joker's Ashes. I scrolled the page up and down a few times, reading and re-reading what it involved: free poster, autographs, selfies with the band – the usual. As tempted as I was, the only thing that stopped me was working out whether I'd make it on time after my shift on Saturday. In order to meet and greet you had to arrive an hour early, and that meant facing London's tubes during rush hour. Just the mere thought of being squashed between lots of sweaty people was a put-off. But still, it was nothing a bit of prep, body spray and breath-holding couldn't solve.

I bit my bottom lip as I thought about what Harry had said to me when he'd sent over the screenshot.

"Chance of a lifetime…"

My finger hovered over the 'Buy Now' button. The decision was just a press away. And with the devil on my shoulder repeating those words over and over into my ear, resisting temptation was no longer an option.

'Screw it. It's only £20.'

And just as the doorbell rang, my confirmation email came through.

***

Katrina was evidently right to be concerned between the importance of a dress or a skirt. Aside from everyone in our group wearing a mixture of floral patterns and flowy dresses, the other attendees weren't too dissimilar. No inch I scanned of the small room was free of chiffon or rainbow colours - except me, who sat at our table donning a pair of skinny jeans and a rather cosy black and white baseball top.

'Aren't you hot?' Tracey, who sat opposite me, commented.

I was boiling, but I didn't want to admit it. After the girls had arrived at our apartment, they'd tried to convince me to get changed into something "sunnier", and tugged at my sleeves, telling me that I was going to be too warm in what I was wearing. But I was defiant. To me, the night was nothing to get particularly glammed up for. It was a psychic switch, for goodness sake, not London Fashion Week. Plus, it wasn't *that* hot.

'Not really,' I lied, wiping away a giveaway sweat bead from underneath my fringe before it slipped its way down my face, 'you know how sensitive I am to the cold.'

Tracey's rogue eyebrow pinched into the air, most blatantly unconvinced. But, to my pleasure, it seemed to grind the unwanted conversation to a halt.

According to my phone, it was already 19.09pm. Nine minutes in and the psychics still hadn't arrived. Another ironic matter - if they were psychic, surely they would have seen that one coming? Katrina, Tracey and Cherise passed the time by taking selfies altogether, trying to choose the right picture to upload to Facebook. I, however, used the opportunity to check my confirmation email from earlier. My heart raced looking at it. It was done. I'd bought it. I was going to meet the Joker's Ashes – on my own. Maybe I should've thought that part through?

Suddenly, distracting me from my phone yet again, I felt Katrina put her arm around me, encouraging me to join in with the selfies. Despite how it seemed, I seldom used my phone. It just seemed that whenever I did, Katrina was always there trying to tear me away from it.

'Come on, Sims - smile. Can't not have your pretty face in the photo, can we?' she said, grinning at me hopefully.

'Sure,' I replied, placing my phone back in my jeans pocket and tilting my head towards hers, ready for the mandatory event tagging photo shot, hoping I wouldn't look too sweaty.

'Say, *Psychic Switch*, ladies.' commanded Cherise, who held the phone that floated above our table.

'*Psychic Switch!*'

We held our smiles for five seconds; using the camera's timer to its fullest worth to ensure that perfect snapshot was taken. After all, it was going to be uploaded to every social media platform the online universe could offer. Life in the modern era is odd like that. I don't know when it started, but it seems that we're now in an age where we have to document everything. I'm all about photographs and capturing special memories, but I don't understand why anyone else would care about what so-and-so ate for lunch or what TV programme they were watching that evening. Apparently though, I'm in the minority on that one.

Minutes later, the door to the room opened and four people made their way inside. According to the lady at the greeting desk, they were our psychics for the evening. Quarter past seven – only fifteen minutes late. Everyone else applauded and the girls all jittered excitedly, optimistic smiles pinned to their faces. However, my scepticism was on high alert. Despite the rave reviews of others who'd been there before, I wasn't going to hold my breath.

Each one made their way to a table. Apparently, they were drawn by "unique energies" that pulled them towards each space. There was no such thing as coincidence; of course, it was all to do with the unseen forces of the sixth sense. Again, I wasn't convinced.

It was almost as if we were on a competitive speed date, whereby a group of women all hoped the psychic's attention would hone in on them, and, as if by magic, those who wore the most hopeful appearances were usually the first to be spoken to. Notably, the same few women kept getting "chosen" and were offered morsels of whimsical information about potential grandparents who'd passed over (which seemed a given since these women must have been in their sixties) and what basic hobbies they enjoyed doing (usually what the majority of people did within the selected era – baking or sewing). And, after an hour of sitting through the regurgitated tripe, my patience fell short.

'This is stupid,' I whispered to Katrina, whose captivated expression only seemed to become deeper rooted.

'Shh,' she hushed, 'you've just got to be patient. Someone will come through for you.'

But, who? My grandparents were still very much alive and kicking (thankfully). My great-grandparents weren't (God, bless their souls) but, they didn't know me. Not personally. Maybe as a baby, they did, but that hardly counts. So, who on earth would come through for me? And if they did, what would they have to say, anyway?

'Hello, my dear. How are you?' our psychic asked soothingly. Her silvery Czech accent glided in our space so euphonically that I didn't even realise she was talking to me. I was too busy staring into space to notice, using her tuneful voice like a backing track to other thoughts that floated in my mind, until Katrina's abrupt nudge brought my attention back to the table.

'What?' I uttered whilst straightening up and pulling my chair in. 'Oh, hi. Yeah, I'm okay. You..?'

My response was a mix of embarrassed and confused. Usually, it was me who asked how people were. That was my day job. It was weird to be on the flip side of the coin for a change.

'The spirits have told me to speak with you,' she calmly said, pausing as if she was listening to an invisible entity standing to her right. 'Come to my table afterwards, my dear. There's something important you need to know.'

Within seconds, her face shifted from calm to grave. There was something in her eyes that emanated with worry. Then, and only then, was when I started to feel somewhat scared. *What could the underworld want with me?* This must have been part of a standard act, I assured myself. The usual way they lure the sceptic into belief; softening them up with warm words. No, it was rubbish. *Wasn't it..?*

All of the girls were staring at me, their eyes piercing my skin with wonder and awe. Attempting to remain as nonchalant as I did before, I tried not to show that any of this was affecting me by smiling back at them, subtly removing the nervous sweat bead that lurked beneath my fringe again. You couldn't get anything past them, though. They knew the attention of the psychic had caught me hook, line and sinker.

'Whoa,' Tracey mouthed. The others nodded in agreeable astonishment.

Our side of the table fell silent. The other half remained focused on the psychic, listening intently as she directed the flow of conversation to a middle-aged lady in a floral skater dress. All other sounds in the room fell into muffle. There was only one thing I could hear clearly - her words repeating over and over in my head.

"There's something important you need to know."

The Private Reading

Staring at the mirror above me made me dizzy. Or was it the thought that I was about to discover something dooming in my future? I wasn't sure. Cherise, Tracey and Katrina seemed to be in awe about it, chattering amongst themselves during the interval about how they wanted their own private readings afterwards, too. The more I thought about it, the more I didn't want to hear it. Half of me considered it as absolute tripe - some mystical sentiment simply aimed to elicit curiosity and fear. But, by the same token, the other half of me completely caved into the belief that there really was something important I needed to know and that, if I didn't hear it, I'd regret it forever.

I continued to stare at my pensive reflection in the adorning ceiling mirror before being abruptly distracted by Katrina's nudging again, her eyes bulbous with intrigue.

'Are you going to find out?' she asked, scanning my face with utter fascination. I released a stubborn outbreath. Coming to terms with my mind's state of confliction wasn't something I ever found easy to express.

'I don't know,' I paused, breaking away from her gaze briefly. 'Look, just because you guys have a predilection towards this psychical hooey doesn't mean that I do. Life delivers upchucks of whatever it feels like spilling, it's not like anyone can really *know* what's coming.'

Just as I'd finished, I looked back at her. She looked thoughtful as she held in her lip and tilted her head, raising her eyebrows as if conjuring a reply that would totally curveball my words.

'Maybe so,' she began, 'but hearing her out can't do any harm, can it? I mean, if it is a load of *hooey*, like you say, then you can walk away knowing the only thing she's taken from you is five minutes of your evening. And, if it's legit, well, then you can be ever thankful that you know what's coming, and maybe even have the potential to change it. It's a freebie, anyway. No one else has got that privilege, so I'd take it if I were you.'

She had a point - a point that swirled my mind for a good while after.

When the second half of the evening set in motion, I sought out the psychic as she entered the room, staring at her wonderingly as our eyes locked. *Does she really know what's coming?* And as she sat down at the opposite table, engaging in conversation with a new set of hopeful people, I listened, and I wondered…and I made up my mind.

***

In deep concentration, she rubbed her ball softly - making sure every pearlescent fragment was glimmering brightly. Positioned in a small corner of the room, I nervously jiggled my legs, the purple crushed velvet table cloth tickling my knees every time I moved and the smell of amber incense filling the air around me. Every sense of mine was entangled with this alien concept and made me fall into a nervous smile whenever she looked at me.

I didn't like it.

Whilst I waited for her to set up, I admired the rest of the table as a means of distraction. I saw that next to the crystal ball and incense sat a few trinkets - a dream-catcher, a Chinese Dragon, feathers, gem stones - the cliché standard for a psychic spread. It almost annoyed me that I was slightly drawn to it. The combination of textures and shapes were alluringly calling on my hands to reach out for them. As if touching them would somehow unveil a mysterious energy that lurked within their vibrant armour. I wondered if this was the same "energy" that was referred to earlier in the night – the one that drew each psychic to a particular table.

Listening to my mind concoct such thoughts suddenly sounded ridiculous. This serendipitous affiliation was just my imagination running away with itself, wanting to believe in something bigger than the physical. So I swiftly shook it out of my head and tried to think about anything else but the spiritual.

Noticing my apprehension, the psychic kindly smiled at me and finally introduced herself as Madame Lilith.

'Is this your first time?' she asked, moving her sweeping black hair behind her ear.

I looked up at her jerkily and nodded, still smiling timidly back at her.

For a moment, she watched me curiously. It was as if she could hear my every thought, listening to them as they bounced back and forth inside my mind like a ping-pong ball.

'You know, many sceptics I meet feel the same way you do. When they first receive message, it can be very overwhelming - more so than for believer, because believer wants to hear something. Whereas sceptic, well, they're not sure how to take it. They end up caught in web of confusion, of hope, cynicism and curiosity. It can be very scary for them, delving into the unknown. But, it can also be very enlightening.'

I remained silent whilst she attentively shuffled her colourful tarot deck, before gently placing them face down on the table.

'So,' she continued, 'are you ready to find out what the cards have to say?'

I folded my lips inwards, no longer able to hear the thoughts in my head. They'd gone. Everything was silent. I needed to know.

'Yes.'

Lilith passed me the deck to reshuffle and told me to focus on asking the cards for guidance on a problem I sought answers for. That was when the thoughts began again. *What do I need to know?* I thought about my parents, about how the last three years had left such a mark on the whole family, the new dynamics that had evolved as a consequence and the repercussions from it all. I thought about how their climactic divorce was only the beginning of the end and wondered if there was anything I could do to help, even though playing the go-between was wearing me down. My mind then wandered to my own love life, or lack thereof. It reminded me about how everyone around me seemed to be pushing me to find someone and how difficult I'd found that to be since Jake. Everyone else appeared to find it so easy.

Was there a reason I didn't? Somewhere deep inside, was I broken? Then there was my book - my soon-to-be finished manuscript I'd spent so long putting my heart and soul into. Initially, it was just escapism from a stressful reality, a way to set free my hopes and fears and let them loose on paper. But now, it meant so much more to me. Both writing and music were the two things that kept me sane and gave me faith in life again. If I didn't have those creative outlets, God knows where I'd be. I just wished I knew if they'd take me somewhere.

As my train of thought finished, so did my shuffling and I passed the pack back to Lilith. She took them gently from my grip and spread out the foretelling deck, face down, and asked me to pick the ten cards towards which I was most drawn to. Despite my earlier misgivings, I honed in on the room's energy and selected the cards that pulled me in the most. What it was that drew me to certain cards and not others, I couldn't tell you. But as my hand hovered over the down-facing deck, I followed the warm magnetism swelling beneath my fingers and gently slid out each card that lured my touch, silently asking the same questions to each one I chose.

Once I'd finished, I placed my hands back on my lap and stared up at Lilith, watching intently as she laid out my choices into the shape of The Celtic Cross, slowly revealing the identity of the first card.

'Three of Swords,' she began, 'a card of heartache and division. This is card that represents influence on your current emotional state. It is what has brought you to where you are today. You see these blades? They show betrayal, as if someone you once trusted stabbed you in the back. But there is more than just one. This has happened before. It may refer to people or moments, but each one is significant to why you fear moving forwards.'

Jake. It must have been about Jake. His fluctuating moods confused me, leaving irrevocable scars on my heart. I always wondered if it was somehow my fault, even though, logically, I knew it wasn't. He betrayed my trust - him, my Dad, men in general. And each unsolicited action I endured made it harder and harder for me to believe in others.

As I digested those thoughts, I exhaled and nodded, mutely ushering Lilith to carry on. She mirrored my nod and carefully unveiled the next card.

'The Hermit,' she said with an unsurprised tonality, 'not to be confused with loneliness. The Hermit is actually about inner-reflection. It suggests that you are on spiritual journey. Metaphorically speaking, you have retreated to lick your wounds post-battle and are now learning how to pick yourself up again. But, as shown by the swords, it has left you hurt. You're caught up in your own heartache. You need to take a step back from yourself and re-learn how to trust, because all this self-analysis is only holding you back.'

If this was about Jake, then she was right. Still, her proverbial expressions could be applied to so many people's situations. It's hardly unusual to have a scumbag ex these days. Nevertheless, I sat quietly and watched her pick up card three, awaiting the next message.

Lilith smiled as she turned the card to expose a woman rubbing the chin of a nestling Lion.

'This next card is more positive,' she stated, 'it reveals plans and intentions through choices you're making right now. I sense you are working on a project; possibly creative? The card in this position says that you must keep up with it, for it will be your fortune. Despite your mistrust in others, you believe in your creations. That is why you have chosen Strength card. Success will come to you, as long as you remain dedicated to your cause.'

By this point, my initial fears began to reside. Everything she was telling me so far - albeit applicable - felt so ambiguous. The mistrust, the pain, the fortitude – isn't that just a general pattern for everyone's past, present and future? To be told that I'd recover from life's hurdles because I was of strong disposition wasn't something unique to me. Not really. Not enough.

Turning over the next card, Lilith's face dropped, but only briefly. Exposed on the table was a man dressed in red, standing beside a wall of stilts wedged into the ground. He looked blocked in, staring longingly at the view in the distance - a beautiful verdant summit obscured by the dividing wooden spikes. I could tell already this probably wasn't the greatest of cards.

'Usually, Nine of Wands is unfortunate card,' Lilith explained, 'as you can see, the man, he is trapped. His desired view blocked by posts in ground. What he wants is so close and yet so far. In this position, though, based on rest of your spread, it is about gathering strength. There is still much needed to be dealt with inside of you - a lot of bad memories that have left their mark, current events that still demand so much from you. But, fear not, for they are not impossible to overcome. Once you have dealt with your heart, you will be able to tackle any obstacle that stands in your way. So, stay focused on your projects and take life as it comes. Everything else will make sense in time.'

I let out a little smile. Thinking about a life where I no longer felt trapped by my inner struggles would be a dream. Imagine that, a potential time in which I'd be free. It all seemed rather far away though, and having youth on my side didn't mean that I had any more patience in waiting for it.

All of a sudden, my mouth felt dry. I was only halfway into the reading, and although I still remained somewhat unconvinced, I felt anxious. I didn't like the idea that there was potentially someone, or something, watching my every move, my every step and listening to the inner-workings of my personal thoughts and fears. Taking in a quick breath before Lilith reached for the next card, I leaned over for my glass of water, hoping a quick drink would calm me down. But my motion was jerky, and my hands were shaking, inevitably knocking the table as I reached for my glass, jigging card number five onto the floor.

'I'm so sorry!' I apologised, completely flustered by my unexpected clumsiness. 'Do you want me to get it?' But Lilith had already stretched down to pick it up, her long jet-black hair curtaining her face as she did so.

'Interesting,' I heard her say excitedly. She placed the unidentified card onto the table for me to see, extending an ivory finger towards the image of a pile of coins mounded beside a forlorn-looking man. 'You know way you've been feeling for so long? Trapped by unexpected misfortune, waiting for things to change? Well, this is now. Seven of Coins here means that everything you've struggled with is about to end…A transition is coming.'

Eager to discuss this supposed transition, Lilith pushed card six towards me, still facing downwards.

'This card represents immediate future. Something that will, I think, change the way you view matters of the heart. You will like this card. I want you to turn it and see for yourself.'

I looked at the shiny blue card in front of me, wondering how on earth she could be so sure what lay beneath the surface. It could have been any card. What did she know that I didn't?

'How do you know I'll like it?' I questioned, shaking my head in disbelief at her certainty.

Self-assured, she softened her gaze and took hold of my cupped hands that rested by the mystery card, 'Because,' she began, 'you made decision today that made this shift possible. Outside influences have placed pathway for you to make this choice. The time for change is now.'

Releasing my hands, she bowed her head in the direction of card six, voicelessly asking me to turn it over. I looked at her and then fixed my gaze back to the card, carefully peeling its cobalt coat out of sight and revealing what prophetic image hid underneath.

'The Emperor?' I quizzed, not understanding the significance of what this regal man sat on a throne could mean to me.

Lilith leant forwards in her chair and rested her smiling face on the palm of her hand, 'There he is,' she affirmed, releasing her free hand to gesticulate her excitement, 'your Mr X.'

My eyes bulged and I felt my stomach collapse at the weight of my heart falling from its internal drop tower. Only in my daydreams did I refer to Mr X. Never had I ever spoken about him to anyone else or even inferred my yearnings for this fictional man in conversation to anybody. There was absolutely, irrefutably, no physical way she could have known about him, unless she'd stolen my notepad from the apartment. Not even a slither. To say I was spooked would have been the understatement of the century.

'This man, he is real. He is one you will meet very soon.' She continued, 'Finally, you can permit yourself to believe in love again, for he will show you what you have yearned for. The Emperor is a man of willpower and ambition. He can rule and be respected by others because he is true and fair. On the horizon, he waits for you.'

She paused, clutching both her hands and tilting her head, as if someone stood next to her was whispering in her ear, and as they spoke inaudible words, she agreeably nodded.

'He is foreign man,' she declared, 'not too far away in familiarity, but distant in miles. Water stands between you, but not language.'

Lilith smiled to herself, 'I sense him to be a keen traveller with passion for adventure. He is older than you, but not by much - maybe only couple of years? Take note that he is in position of power, at least to you. You will respect his role just like citizens do of the Emperor. This meeting will be significant to rest of your life. Remember to not let your head rule your heart for once. Despite your fears, he is true, and you must do whatever you can to believe that.'

Shivers surged through me, goose-pimpling my entire body and causing every hair to rise and brush against my sleeves. That one statement changed everything I thought I knew. In spite of all I believed, I couldn't help but be fascinated by what she was telling me. It was so detailed, so accurate to my internal feelings and thoughts, and the adamants carved on her face made it all the more difficult to deny. She knew things that couldn't be known. This was no longer your average reading.

The cards that followed seemed to reaffirm this notion, explaining that my attitude and environment would be the groundings for my future success in love and career, and that over the next few years I would see evidence of it all come to light. Everything seemed to be going well, until The Tower showed up.

Lilith closed her eyes and grimly furrowed her brow.

'This is what the spirits warned me about,' she announced, still clasping onto the edge of the unfortunate blue card. 'The Tower signifies calamity and ruin. What you think you know to be true will be taken. In this instance, it is represented by physical event that will take toll on your emotions. Everything you know to be safe, to be there, the threat of its destruction is set. Seeing it coming is not an option. It will be a shock, hence violent image. I cannot tell you what exactly it foretells or when it will be, but you *must* take care of ones you hold dear, for you may not get second chance.'

Urgency speared her words. The energetic shift seemed to be wearing on her and she started to breathe jaggedly.

A look of concern flooded her face as she began to tightly scrunch her violet blouse.

Worried, I leaned forwards and reached over for her. 'Are you okay? Do you need me to get someone?'

Lilith shook her head abruptly. 'No,' she uttered hoarsely, 'it's the spirit. They can't breathe. I can feel it in my chest.'

After a few seconds of struggle, her breathing settled once again. Helplessly, I watched on, staring as her reddened face slowly recovered from the experience.

'We don't have to do anymore if you don't want to. Honestly, I think most of my questions have been somewhat answered, anyway.'

She shook her head again. 'No,' she repeated, 'your last card is vital. I'm okay.'

Nodding, I waited for her to regain composure.

Determinedly, Lilith cleared her throat and reached out for the last card. The inevitable card that would, if all else was followed, signify the ultimate consequence from each predicted event.

All sign of metallic blue was gone, the table was now a psychedelic display of colour, and thankfully, my ending card's meaning was just as bright.

'Eight of Cups,' Lilith said, still rather croakily, 'do you recall transition I mentioned before? This is it. Your world is going to go through many changes in your immediate and long-term future. Some changes will be beautiful, others, they will carry great pain. This card represents how you will deal with those events. Life won't be easy, but your accomplishments will reinforce strength during these hard times. They will enable you to generate a more positive outlook, rather than fall back into sadness. As a character, you are strong. You will be able to put the past behind you. Trust me when I say that.'

I smiled, dubiously. After a rather overwhelming reading, that ending seemed almost formulaic. And disappointingly so, it reinstated my doubts.

'Thank you, Lilith.' I said, picking up my bag as I got up to leave the table. But just as I did, she took hold of my sleeve.

'One more thing - you see the water?' she said, pointing towards the tarot. 'That is sign. In order to put the past behind you, you must cross the water. What waits for you there is your new beginning. You'll know what I mean when time comes.'

I didn't know what she meant. Crossing the water could be symbolic? Or, if it was physical, then maybe I was meant to do something incredible, like swim the channel? No, that would be silly. I'd never do that. Covering myself in goose fat just to stay warm would go against my beliefs, anyway.

Nevertheless, I thanked Lilith again and began to walk back to the girls, who were cradled together at the round table in the adjacent room. The smell of sandalwood incense dispersed and the air around me suddenly felt weightless, it was as though I'd crossed over a dividing border, departing the pressures from an unseeable realm, and venturing back to reality. My skin tingled at the thought of it.

I continued to walk, nearly back into the room filled with chatter and heat which I'd grown so unaware of whilst I'd been sitting at Lilith's table. But just before I'd reached the splitting threshold, I heard Lilith speak once again. Unexpected words that sent chills down my spine.

'Be wise to what choices you make, Simone, before it's too late.'

I stopped in my tracks, frozen by an unknown force, tempted to turn around and ask her what she meant. But I was afraid. I didn't want to know. It was already too much to take in.

Katrina saw me and enthusiastically waved me over to the table. Shaking my head, I freed myself and strode over to her, ignoring the pressing words that now echoed the hollows of my mind.

'Well?' Katrina asked, her eyes as wide as a child's. 'How was it?'

I didn't want to tell her. I still didn't know what exactly to make of it all. Some of what Lilith shared could be applied to anyone, I was certain of that. And yet, other parts were so unique to me that I couldn't help but think that meant there was an undeniable truth in her foretelling. For a moment, I stood there quietly, contemplating these thoughts, before quickly fixing a smile to my face and resting a friendly hand on Katrina's shoulder.

'As I said earlier - a load of hooey.'

She looked upset, her big, hopeful eyes shrinking with disappointment.

'Really? That sucks. And she seemed so good at the table. Oh, well. C'mon then, Sims. I guess we need to get back home and sleep before *Trunchball* whinges about our dark circles at work tomorrow.'

We gathered our belongings and headed for the door. The girls walked in front, Katrina leading the way, and I held position at the back, my guilty conscience weighing me down. I looked back towards Lilith's table, hoping that through acknowledgement of her presence I could somehow atone for such denial, but as I steered my vision to the room's back corner, it was empty. The purple-clothed table abandoned. All trinkets cleared. Nothing but the wavering smoke of amber incense in the air remained. As if by magic, she was gone.

The Café Grilling

Another day down, another day without the D. Seb
wasn't sure what to rip me more for, the fact that I - the
biggest cynic on the planet - had attended a psychic
event, or the fact that everyone there was female.

'Have you ever considered using those snorkelling
skills you gained in the Caribbean for another kind of
diving? It seems obvious the world is trying to tell you
something,' he teased, cockily stirring his marshmallow-
laden hot chocolate like he'd just made the best joke
ever.

'And have you ever considered that your comedic
talents are utterly wasted at UCL?' I flatly retorted,
staring at the Belsize Bakery's front door every so often,
waiting for Dad to come through. 'Honestly, Seb. You
could give Michael McIntyre a run for his money…Not.'

As always, Dad's punctuality was as good as Katrina's
for work. She was late that morning, too. Both of us
were exhausted from the night before, or in her case, the
night before last night. Even her customary cappuccino
couldn't revive more than a shuffling walk from her on
the way there. Alexandra's crumpled face resembled a
smacked arse when she saw us saunter through the shop
doors. Only her smile wasn't even vertical, it was
completely absent - even more so when she saw Katrina
nearly falling asleep standing up. Suffice to say, she got
sent home pretty swiftly after that and told to make up
the time on Saturday. That was my lightbulb moment.
Offering her my shift on Saturday meant I could head to
the Joker's Ashes gig in leisure time. Kats was too tired

to quibble, so I merrily switched our days on the paper rota hooked to the wall, scribbling out my Saturday and writing *D/O* with accomplished glee. If anything really was cosmic that week, I guessed that was it.

Seb noticed my distracted glance.

'Stop eyeballing the poor door. It'll think you're giving it the come on.' He mocked. 'Dad will be here soon.'

I looked at my phone and noticed he was now running fifteen minutes late. Honestly, he was as bad at timekeeping as the so-called the psychics.

'Do you think he's gone to the right place, though? There are quite a few cafes around here...'

He rolled his eyes at me, 'Sims, it's double B's. All the other places here are chains. He'll find it.'

Suddenly, the bakery doorbell pinged and its resounding chime alerted both Seb and I from mindlessly sipping our drinks.

'Oh, finally.' I declared, getting up from my seat and walking towards my dishevelled Dad who stood sheepishly in the doorway. He was dressed in a thin loose jumper, hanging unflatteringly at the weight of its overstretched fibres. Nothing he wore looked clean. Even his khaki jeans looked like they would waltz their way to the nearest washing machine given half the chance.

Isn't it strange how, initially, when a couple break-up, it's the woman who flails about hopelessly and yearns for that person to come back to them, whereas the man embraces his freedom and lives out every rebellious dream he's ever had? Then, once the drama settles down and the emotions no longer run high, the roles are reversed. In front of me stood that representation - a man painted with regret and longing, unable to know how to go on now he'd lived out his mid-life crisis. It was sad to see, but simultaneously, it was his own doing, and I didn't want to be any more involved than I already was.

'Dad, what's happened to you?' I asked, semi-embracing him in a hug, with my fingers atop his manky jumper as though it were a product of quarantine. 'You look a mess.'

'Nice to see you too, Simone,' he replied sarcastically, a hint of tremble in his voice. 'I've come all this way on those sodding trains and that's how you greet your ol' Dad?'

It was the first time I'd seen him in months and my shock overtook any diplomacy. Seb, on the other hand, may not have been able to hide the fact he was thinking the same as me, but his kind-hearted flamboyance worked much more in his favour.

'It's good to see you, Dad,' he said, clutching him in a shiny hug, his sequinned white shirt and brace buckles reflecting in the above lighting with every squeeze. 'Simone is right, though, for once. You don't look as dapper as usual. But, it's okay. We can fix this. When you come to visit my halls, I'll sort you out with some of my new clothes and face creams. We'll get you back on your feet and batting the ladies off in no time.'

Dad smiled whimsically. He stared at Seb as though his words were the nicest thing anyone had told him in months, 'Thank you, Son. I'd like that very much.'

Anything to steer the conversation away from himself, Dad soon clocked Seb's gloriously sweet hot chocolate, and with no hesitation, went to order himself a mug before settling down around our table and catching up with us.

'Oh, wow,' he began, scooping at the whipped cream on top with his spoon, 'this is delicious! I'll definitely be paying for this at the gym later, though. So, kids, how's tricks? What have I missed in the land of my two little adventurers?'

Sometimes, I wondered if he remembered how old we were. He'd only conceived us and grown up with us, after all. Surely he knew we weren't six still? Saying that, if the bag of Haribo sweets he gave us every time we saw him were anything to go by, then I guessed not. Talking of sweet foods, like heck he'd even care about attending a gym. That was not my Dad. This man in front of me, virtually licking out a spoon of cream, was definitely not my Dad.

'Très bien, mon père,' enunciated Seb in a French accent as thick as his chocolate beverage. 'Things in my world are fantastique! Uni is really easy so far. Honestly, I don't know what everyone whines about – it's pips. Anyway, my hall roomies are top. They're mostly girls, but that's fine with me. We have a laugh. Oh, and I met a nice guy, too. His name's Tariq, he's ridiculously hot, and smart. We went out yesterday and he was telling me *all* about the most famous psychological experiments ever conducted. One was of this guy who tested Classical Conditioning on a baby to make it scared of a white rat by pranging a hammer on a metal bar every time they were present together. Of course, it was crazy unethical and left li'l Alby with a bunch of phobias. But I told Tariq, "*Look Mr, if you can save my waistline and get me aversive to sugar, then you can bang my pole anytime."* Oh, how we laughed!'

The phrase, "TMI" came to mind. Both mine and Dad's eyes widened at the thought of Seb's not-so-subtle innuendo. Being a fully-fledged adult wasn't something we'd ever look at him as. He was Dad's baby boy and my baby brother, and he'd stay that way until he was at least forty-five-years-old.

'Sounds like a catch!' Dad posed almost too-enthusiastically, obviously trying to ignore the connotations alluding to his son's sex-life. 'I'm pleased you've found someone to connect with. You deserve a nice…man, in your life.'

Two years later and you could see time had little effect on Dad getting used to the fact that Seb would never be taking home a lady-friend. Don't get me wrong, he wasn't homophobic or upset by his orientation in the slightest. But I think that so much time away from the family made him almost forget what the norm for us as a unit was. We weren't conventional – not that many families are these days – and he still needed time to adjust to our, shall we say, *"Unique qualities."*

'And what about you, blossom?' he posed, his interrogative eyes glancing over the hot chocolate cup and onto me. 'It's been a long while since you've had anyone special, isn't it?'

And just like that, I was cornered. I forgot how swiftly this question could rear its ugly head. But before I could even say anything, Seb kindly offered to fill in the blank.

'Haven't you heard, Dad? Sims is drinking from the furry cup now.'

Hot chocolate resurfaced the cup as Dad spat it out.

'What?' he yelped, obviously aghast with fear at the prospect he was never going to get any grandchildren.

'Shut up, Seb, you dickhead. For God's sake,' I yelled, banging my crass little brother hard across the shoulder. 'Dad, please ignore the human-sized cheese string sitting next to me. He's just trying to be funny, and *failing*.'

Dad patted his lip with the triangular napkin from the table, carefully wiping away any residue of hot chocolate that escaped in his fearful jump. This was turning out just as expected: an absolute embarrassment.

'Okay, good. Not, that if you were gay that it would be a bad thing, of course! It's just…' he stuttered, desperately trying to not dig himself into a hole. 'So, you're still single then?'

I rolled my eyes and inhaled vehemently. This question seemed to stalk me harder than Freddy Krueger did in people's nightmares.

'Yup, still single,' I stated, twiddling with my helix piercing in apprehension of the imminent conversation fast approaching.

'Oh, blossom. That just won't do.'

And so, it began.

For about five minutes I stayed quiet, listening to wise words about how I needed to move on from Jake and find somebody new. That time is of the essence and I'm only getting older, and that being a spinster with twenty-seven cats was not the future he wanted for me.

Already bored, I only actioned nods and laconic replies in the right places to help bring the conversation to a prompt end.

'Uh-huh. Yeah. Mmm. Right. Men hate pet hair, got it.'

Things only got worse when Seb stuck his ore in, echoing everything Dad was saying and smarmily bringing back his sardonic notion towards my sexuality.

'No matter what path you go down, Sims,' he opened, 'pussy is in your destiny.'

Buttons well and truly pushed, I rose from my seat and slammed my fists down on the table. 'For the last damn time, I'm not a bloody lesbian!' I shouted, blood boiling inside.

Aware of the potential scene, Dad gently placed his hand on my arm, ushering me to sit back down.

'We know that, Simone. Your brother was just teasing. Anyway, we won't say any more.' Dad fixed his gaze on Seb, who simply spooned whipped cream into his mouth. 'I have to show you a quick pic of my friend Gary's son, though. He's about your age and single too. I think you might like him.'

But before he could even unlock his phone to show me, my face reddened. Hot, angry veins bulged from my temples, and like Mount Etna, I blew.

'Seriously – are you guys for real? What's with this obsessive focus on my love-life? Like I've said a thousand times, I'm happy on my own, doing my own thing. I don't give a crap how long I've been alone for and blind-dating men is not top of my to-do list, Cilla Black. Especially when the only positive credential they have is their age and gender – *whoopdedingledoo*! Anyway, why should I take romantic advice from either of you? You're hardly idols on the matter. In fact, maybe if you guys stopped thinking with your dicks for a minute and started using your heads instead, then our family wouldn't be such a fucking broken mess.'

This wasn't how I'd planned my afternoon, but I couldn't stand to be around them a minute longer. Unable to control my anger, I pushed back the chair and picked up my bag, avoiding eye contact with both of them as I left my parting word slicing the atmosphere at our table.

'Later.'

No one chased after me as I stormed out of the quiet café and rattled the door's bell with my incensed departure. Men don't tend to do that when women are mad. Women always want them to, but that's not how they're wired to respond. That's why men get so annoyed when you follow them after an argument. They need space to cool off. They don't want to hear you trying to be nice or understanding or apologetic, it's too much. They just want space. And that's what I needed, too - somewhere to escape from the noise, away from everybody and everything. Yet, in this modern world full of buzzing phones and incessant badgering, that place is pretty hard to find. But, I did know one place. Somewhere so out of reach, only I knew how to get there.

***

Steep pitched guitar-shredding pierced the room, growling screams shot their way through the thundering string work and heavy drums beat hard into the walls. Music was my escapism - a place to go when the world became too tough. No emotional ties, just me and the speeding notes, each one taking me out of time itself and painting me into an abstract reality where everything was how I wanted it to be. I was who I wanted to be.

I opened my eyes from the bed, taking in my small beige bedroom. My poster of Iron Maiden was fraying at the edge. Putting it by the door was never a good idea; it always caught on the frame every time someone opened it. Memorable pictures hung on the corkboard adjacent to it. So many good times caught on camera all cherished the old fashioned way. None of this uploading to Facebook lark, just classic polaroid shots taken and placed with pride somewhere I could see them every day, without worrying about Wi-Fi or having any battery left. Across the A3 board were a plethora of scattered images, from my recent trips abroad, outings with the girls, to classic pictures of me as a kid building sandcastles with Seb and blowing out birthday candles with Mum and Dad smiling widely behind my chubby-cheeked face. They were good times. Eliminate the last few years and take me back there because that was when I was last truly, freely, happy.

Tears tried to burrow their way out of my eyes, so I sat up straight and used my hoodie sleeve to wipe them away. Staring at me from across the room was my white wardrobe, crookedly standing with the door ajar. It only had three wheels left to roll about on. God knows where it went when it was moved in here. I looked everywhere but to no avail. So, that's how it stayed – slightly wonky but functional, with its only odd tendency being that the left door opened every so often due to the lack of balance. As long as it worked, I could live with that kind of dysfunction.

Whipping myself out of bed, I walked over to it, pulling the creaky door open to look inside. Amongst the piles of folded jeans and hoodies hanging up were pretty dresses I never wore. They'd either all been bought for me as gifts (people trying to make me more feminine) or that I'd bought for a special occasion (someone's wedding, a party...a date?) none of which ever really happened. One day, I hoped they'd be worn. Never did I want to be one of those women who just pranced about in her best outfit for the sheer hell of it. There had to be a reason. Albeit my reasons were probably less likely to occur than an ice age in Dubai, I still held out hope.

On the top shelf of the wardrobe sat my band tops, all black, as you can imagine. I took them all out and laid them on the bed, trying to find my baseball-sleeved Joker's Ashes one. It may have been a few days away still, but being well-prepared was never frowned upon.

Unfolding each one to expose their distinguishable emblems, I finally came across it. With the band's name and album title embossed in white, resting against a grey background, the top's design was the least elaborate out of all the ones I owned, only its black sleeves separating it from its t-shirt counterparts.

I laid it out on the bed and smiled. Seeing the band live was what I was most looking forward to. In all the years I'd listened to them, never had I gone to one of their gigs - strange, really. Life is what it is though, and I just never found the opportunity to see them play when I was looking. At least now I had that chance.

Next to the top, I put their CD discography. Most of them were too dark for autographing, bar one. It wasn't one that matched the album title on the top, but it would do for a memento. They looked pretty cool next to each other, so I decided to take a picture. Alongside the others I planned to take that night, it would make a good part of a collage for my board.

Suddenly, an abrupt bang on the door distracted me from my thoughts.

'Simone Hartley,' came the booming voice, 'what on earth is this racket?'

Katrina stood in my doorway with her fingers lodged in her ears, face as askew as my wonky wardrobe and one eye squinting tightly. 'Turn it down, will you?

Zig-zagging the tiny space in my room to reach my iPod docking station, I quickly turned off the music.

'Sorry Kats, I thought you were out.'

'I was,' she said, walking into my room now it was safe for her eardrums, ' sleeping all day got boring, so I went to that nice wholefoods place and bought some fancy drinks and calorie-free pasta. They think of everything these days. Mind you, it'll probably taste like a bowl of McDonald's straws. But if it keeps me trim then who am I to make a fuss? Anyway, what's with the deafening music? I thought someone was being murdered in here.'

I mustered a little laugh to that. Katrina hated my music. She was more of a pop lover than metal-head, but that was fine. Everyone has their differences. As long as you can accept them and are on a similar wavelength in how you see the world, then you'll get along just fine. That's how we were – the flip sides of the same coin.

'Honestly, it's really not worth talking about,' I replied, moving my Joker's Ashes top and CDs off the bed so I could sit down. Katrina looked unconvinced.

'As much as I'd love to go and cook up my plastic pasta right now, I think this conversation is totally worth talking about. So, I'm going to stay here until you tell me. Comprender?'

Everyone using alternative languages instead of English today must have been a memo I had missed. Either way, I submitted to her raised eyebrows and folded arms, and told her the truth. I explained what had happened at the café, and how everyone seemed to be on at me about finding a boyfriend, the guilt I was carrying for not wanting to be a part of Mum and Dad's quarrels or hearing about their emotional shifts towards one another. As obvious as it must have already been by my raging music, I summed up my ramblings by saying that I was just feeling sick and tired of it all.

Katrina looked at me sympathetically. She knew what I was like and how easily things could get to me. To her, all of the things I mentioned would be water off a duck's back. But to me, I carried them. A bit like Agnes Parker, who, in 1592, struggled across a bridge with a bundle of hay on her head and milk in her hand. That was, until, a fateful gust of wind blew her off and sent her plummeting into the waters below. Emotionally, that's how I felt – like I was sinking to the bottom with no way out. All I wanted was some freedom and some peace. Nevertheless, that concept seemed out of reach.

'Oh, my dearest darling Sims, what are we going to do with you, eh?' She came over to sit beside me on the bed. 'Look, I know things are tough at the moment with your family and that the ever-changing dynamics is driving you a bit barmy, but you've gotta realise something…'

A finger popped up on her hand. 'One - they love the bones of you. Even Seb, for all his wisecracks, he totally adores you. That's just how he shows it. You of all people should know that.'

The next finger came up, 'and two - your folks are probably just as baffled about how to handle this sitch as much as you are. They're dealing with their own grievances too, remember? But, unlike you, they may not have anyone else to talk to about it. And, as much as you may not need help from your family right now, that doesn't change the fact that they still need it from you. This is why you guys are the first to bear the brunt of it. Because, even though they're adults, they're still human. They still make mistakes and need a little bit of guidance along the way.'

Her fingers now outstretched and placed on her chest, Katrina finally finished her moving speech, 'Hand on heart though, Sims, I'm sure they don't mean to deliberately upset you. That's the last thing they'd want.'

She was probably right, but it didn't make me feel any better. I think that must have been written all over my face because as she scanned my crinkled brow, she placed her expressive hand on my own and started to talk again.

'Did I ever tell you the story about when I nearly lost my Mum?' She asked me, of which, I quickly looked up from my woeful stare and shook my head at her, wondering how exactly this topic had never occurred until that very moment.

'Okay. Well, it was a few years ago now, before I moved into the city. Mum was at home, watering the front garden, merrily going about her afternoon like she always did - not worried that she was home alone because I'd be back from work soon and she'd have plenty to keep herself busy until then. But, unlike all the other days before that, on this day, I got a call whilst I was still at work. It was half four. I still remember it as clear as day. I was staring at the clock above the kitchenette's fridge when the lady on the other end of the phone told me that my Mum had suffered a heart attack.

'As you know, she's okay now. You've met my Mum; tough as old boots. But, seeing her in hospital that day, so vulnerable, so helpless, it was terrifying. I really didn't know what to do. I was so scared. My head played through so many selfish scenarios – *Why has this happened? Who's to blame? What if she doesn't make it? What if I never get to tell her I love her again?* Ultimately, it was the last scenario that broke me down.

'What I'm trying to say is that, we waste so much time being angry at others over such stupid things - shutting people out because we're sad, not saying how we feel because we're scared – and, inevitably, we miss chances. We hold ourselves back from experiencing so many incredible things because of our own stubbornness. It's like people are programmed to abstain from being happy or something. It's so weird. Not to say that what you're going through isn't a little shitty, of course. But you've gotta look at it this way - if you hold onto this feeling and something bad happens to someone you care about, will you, in five years' time, regret showing love to that person despite their flaws, or losing them having said nothing at all?'

A tear ran down my face. Not for one minute was I expecting to have such a rollercoaster epiphany.

Everything she said was true. I was being silly letting the little things bog me down, and, in spite of recent events, I did love my family. Being mad at everyone for picking on my flaws was fair enough, but I had handled it shoddily. Plus, the thought of something bad happening to my family and not making peace with them beforehand was just unbearable.

'You're right,' I agreed, nodding back at her, 'my family may be crazy and annoying but, they're still my family, and I love them.' Again, I wiped away the renegade tear from my face, looking at Katrina before embracing her in a big hug.

'I'm glad that you got another chance with your Mum,' I said to her. 'There's no part of me that can even imagine a world without Momma Kats.' I chuckled into her shoulder before breaking free.

'And thank you. This chat has really opened my eyes.'

She smiled sweetly at me, 'Anytime, honey. Now,' she said, hands tapping her lap, 'whilst you smooth out your forehead, how's about I go whip us up a bowl of plastic pasta and set up a cheeky film to watch? No more of this ROARRAWWR music.'

I laughed. Katrina's impression of a screaming vocalist was brilliant. Like, half lion, half demonic cheerleader. Bizarre as it was, it made me happy.

'That sounds amazing. But please, promise me you'll never do that noise again?'

'I thought I was rather good - ROARRAWWR!'

'Stop,' I cried, curling at the ribs, 'please, Kats, you sound like bloody Smeagol, for God's sake.'

'Okay, okay. I'll stop. But, I'm still choosing the film.'

Dramatically clasping my hands to prayer position, I beseeched to the ceiling above us, 'Oh Lord, please have mercy and don't let her choose another third-rate Netflix rom-com.'

'Hey,' she yelped, shoving a cushion at me, '*Sierra Burgess is a Loser* was really good.'

It was, I'll admit. But winding her up was always better.

The Gig (Part 1)

Nothing else around me seemed to sink in, except the words of the song playing in my ear.

Iris, by the Goo Goo Dolls, is an all-time favourite of mine, and since hearing it again whilst watching the City of Angels with Katrina a few nights before (thank God she chose that over a repeated viewing of The Duff – I don't think I could've coped with anymore teen chick flicks, even if Robbie Amell is a bit of a dish.) I couldn't get it out of my head.

They say that, to try and let go of a song that's constantly replaying in your mind, you must sing out the last lines. Apparently, your brain won't repeat something that's been finished. But, what the boffs who conducted that study obviously neglected to consider was the fact that some things are simply too good to stop reliving, which is why I didn't want to stop singing it. The song resonated so much with me and I just wanted to keep getting lost in it.

At its heart, it's a love song, yet, it is also so much more. It tells the tale of the protagonist's feelings towards themselves, describing an unattainable love with himself and another, as well as life in general. By this, he expresses that, whilst love exists, it's not always easily reachable. It's both ephemeral and it's endless. It's there and it's not. It's everything and it's nothing. When you watch the movie, you'll understand, and I highly recommend you do watch it. It had me and Kats in the best kinds of tears, and also gave us both a massive yearning to catch a wave together one day (I promise this has every relevance, but you need to watch the movie first.) Neither of us, however, could do that at the time. So she went out for a run instead – standard Katrina.

Now walking out of Mornington Crescent's terracotta bricked station and into the open air, I was greeted by a fresh evening breeze that tickled my smile. It was a beautiful night. Out of respect to it, I carefully tucked away my iPod wires and placed my train ticket into my pocket, bidding goodbye to the Goo Goo Dolls and my tide-riding daydreams, and saying hello to the picturesque surroundings in front of me.

Across the road stood the Koko in all its ivory columned glory, prettily illuminated by the towering streetlights beside it; the only divide being the set of traffic lights in-between. I walked across and approached the building eagerly. In less than an hour's time, I'd be meeting the Joker's Ashes in person and I still couldn't quite get my head around it. By contrast though, I was also rather calm about the whole notion.

In my eyes, they were still ordinary people who did ordinary things - I preferred to focus on that. Although, it would be impossible to ignore the fact that these so-called "*ordinary*" people also have the exceptional ability to create extraordinary music. In all its formats, music speaks to the soul. Anyone who can craft something so powerful that it touches the heart is without doubt incredibly special. But, that doesn't mean that they, as individuals, should be placed on a pedestal. Like everybody else, they still eat, drink, sleep, wash and play Sudoku on the loo (well, maybe not that last one. That's probably just my Dad, but, you catch my drift.) Therefore, with this thought in mind, my plan was to treat them in regard to that. I wasn't nervous; however, I did wish I'd spent more time listening to their albums that week. Dizzy up the Girl had spent most of its time on replay, but still, no one cares if you don't know the words off by heart at a rock gig. You just stand there approvingly and nod, or go crazy and head-bang so hard that your hair whips someone else's eye out. And, if that fails, start a mosh pit and pray you don't break anything.

As I walked inside the Koko, I noticed how gloriously decadent it was. Within the main arena, rows of red balconies spiralled with gold hovered above me. Romantic baroque-styled statues were carved into the walls alongside them, and a spherical light hung in the centre of it all, ready to shine multi-coloured prisms onto the scarlet room. It was an endless stretch of cinematic grandeur and contemporary vision, all cleverly intertwined in its design. Each intricate element echoed its early 20th Century history - hardly the first venue that would spring to mind for a metal gig. But, even so, never had I appreciated it as much as I did in that very instant. When I'd been there before, it usually felt so small. Saying that, though, it was usually crowded by the time I'd arrived there for previous events. Being a VIP certainly had more perks than it was given credit for. Just to experience the building in its virtually empty state was wondrous in itself.

At that moment, my expectations for the evening shifted and the thought of the night ahead suddenly made me feel nervous - a sensation I didn't plan on. Turning around searchingly, I located the velvet walled bar in the distance and walked towards it. As unusual for me as it was, I needed a drink.

A few other people were at the bar already, all of us VIPs. The rest of the crew, security, and photographers stood beside the main doors, chatting to one another about the organisation of the evening. They appeared rather frazzled in their communication. For a second, I wondered if it was even going to happen, that maybe the band would just not show up? You can never predict these things. I tried to bring my mind back to the drinks board in front of me and eyed up the bizarre list of cocktails available. It boasted a strange mix of dessert-like dishes as drinks, such as Mama's Crumble, made from mixing Apple Sourz with Spiced Rum. Suffice to say, I was intrigued, and also slightly overwhelmed. A drinks menu this complex would need time to take in.

'Belle's Rose is delish,' an unexpected voice pitched to me, 'you should try that one.'

Embarrassed by my obvious lack of cocktail connoisseur, I smiled awkwardly back at her, 'Thanks, but I think I'll just stick to water for now. Are you here for the meet and greet too?'

What a stupid question. This unknown girl was covered in tattoos, her hair was platinum blonde and streaked with flecks of green. She'd tied it dramatically into a side-ponytail which hung over her ripped Joker's Ashes tank top. It was pretty evident that she was a fan.

'Mmhmm,' she answered whilst sipping her iridescent ruby drink, 'I've met them before, though - spent *ages* talking to them. They're such a nice bunch. I can't wait to see them again. You'll definitely get your money's worth.'

I wanted to ask her what they were like and where she'd seen them before, but the loud approach of the security team and photographer stopped me in my tracks.

'Places, people! The band is on their way. Everybody form an orderly line.'

We were ushered like sheep into a field pen, carefully placed in a queue to await our meeting. I looked around at the others in the line and listened to their conversations with one another. Everyone was in pairs except for me, and all of them seemed to have met the band before. They would probably take their time to catch up with old faces more than engage with new ones, especially one who was on their own. I could envisage it already. Me, standing there meeting them one by one with a quick handshake, a pitying stare and a, *"Thanks for being a fan!"* But, what else should I expect from a meet and greet? That's literally what it is. You meet them, you greet them, then you get shooed off, and they go off back to their rock star tour bus to rid themselves of all the sycophantic germs we'd infested them with during our mandatory hugs.

All of a sudden, the chatter around me dispersed into snippets of incomplete sound. Unfinished sentences were left hanging in the air as the big red doors opened and unveiled four men walking through. The light from above hit them so brightly that, for an instant, they were merely silhouettes; unidentifiable outlines making their way towards us. But as they came into view, one by one, we realised who they were.

'Hey guys,' said the tallest one, animatedly saluting to us all with arms as wide as the stage, 'nice to meet you!'

Said tallest member (also known as the Joker's Ashes' frontman, Brody Baker) was the first to greet everyone with a massive smile and a tight squeeze. To say he was lively would have been a massive understatement. Brody had this vibrant energy only a confident singer-type could possess. He was constantly lifting people up and fist-bumping them all as he went along, completely at ease with the entire process. If it was a mechanical thing, it certainly didn't look like it. In fact, I would have said he relished in the whole situation. But then again, even if he didn't, looking like a sourpuss is hardly something you can get away with when there's a horde of press and adoring fans surrounding you.

Talking of fans, as expected, there were more of us than of them. From my position near the end of the line, I watched and absorbed the view, taking in everyone's movements and words, so that I'd know what to say when my turn came. It was in that moment I realised I didn't know all of their names (brilliant timing, right?) Brody I was sure of – no matter how much of a cave you live in, no one can escape finding out the name of a band's frontman - and I knew one of the others was called James (their screamer) But two of them looked so similar that I couldn't quite work out which one owned the name. Which meant that I was about to meet four people; one of which I knew for sure, two members I contemplated as potential candidates for the same name, and one I had absolutely no idea whatsoever. What kind of a fan does that make me, I hear you ask? One that listens to the music and doesn't watch the videos or buy posters to drool over, that's who. Or, maybe, just a useless one – I'll let you choose.

Before I could consider this thought any longer, I was met by a big smile and a hug of equal measure by one of the potential James', the shorter of the two, first to greet me in the line.

'Hey there. Aw man, it's cold in here,' he shivered as he embraced me, 'how do you Brits stay warm in this? It's mad, bro.'

Unless you hadn't otherwise guessed, they were American. This was one fact about them I did already know, luckily. So, I was quick to the mark to talk about all the quintessential British weather-related topics I had under my hat. Hardly the stuff of rock and roll dreams, but, it suited me. I felt relaxed. It was nice to have a meeting as chilled as that (no pun intended) and amazingly, the name business didn't even come up. I cleverly managed to skirt around the topic and discuss other things. Like, what part of the UK was their favourite to visit, how they had enjoyed the tour so far, and that they were pussies for moaning about the temperature here in September.

'Seriously, it's been pretty good for this time of year.' I stated. 'But I guess you guys can't handle a bit of nippy wind...'

'Nippy?' Interjected Brody, curiously tilting his head away from the fan he was signing an album for. 'Okay, now you've piqued my interest.'

For about ten minutes or so, I stood talking to both Brody and potential James. The conversation flowed so smoothly. If I'd been blindfolded, I would never have guessed I was talking to musicians from one of the biggest bands in the metal music scene. They were so normal - so down to earth. Well, apart from their crazy tour stories and security guards circling around them like a castle moat, that is.

'Have you tried the cocktails here? They're lethal,' Brody began, enthusiastically sharing another tale from his bag of tour memories. 'Our manager, Dave, got so drunk on them last time we came here. Oh, you should've seen it. He was on his hands and knees outside pretending to be a dog, barking and everything. I don't know what they put in that stuff, but man, it makes some pretty awesome video footage.'

I laughed at the sight of him re-enacting this moment. Poor Dave looked completely bewildered from his position in the room's back corner as Brody gestured towards him, woofing and fake licking his paw.

'Love you, man!' Brody added, pointing towards him, Dave now completely red in the face as he saluted back, slowly walking out of the room with a guitar and a tail between his legs. 'Anyway, you should try one of those drinks, they're awesome. In fact, I think some of us are staying after the show to relive the experience. Come join us if you want?'

Shocked, I stood there soundlessly for a moment, taking in what I'd just heard.

Did I just get asked to hang out with the band?

'Oh, I don't know,' I stuttered nervously. 'I'm not the biggest drinker.'

'That's no problem,' Brody reassured, 'you don't have to be. Just know the invite's there, 'kay?'

I nodded, too gobsmacked to know what else to say. Until suddenly remembering that, in all the time I'd been stood there chatting to them, I hadn't even taken photos or obtained any of their autographs yet. And so, digressing away from the topic of dogs and drinks, I whipped out my CD and asked them for their squiggles and a selfie before they had to go. The album I'd brought with me got passed around so fast that I didn't even see which member wrote which signature, which was a tad annoying as it ruined my ploy in figuring out whose name was whose. Nevertheless, Brody and potential James ushered me to the wall for a group photo, calling over the other two band members before passing my phone to their photographer to take a few pictures. That was when my heart burst through my chest.

Standing next to me was the most striking guy I had ever witnessed. Dark blonde hair escaped from his red beanie, silver-blue eyes shone brightly underneath his side-swept fringe, and, just like the ocean in the moonlight, his glistening smile mirrored back at me so beautifully that I nearly got lost in their inviting reflection. He was a perfect vision. Everything I'd ever looked for in a man and had never even known it until that very second. But, this was no occasion for idle fascination.

With time of the essence now, I had no choice but to quickly pull myself together and turn around to face the camera, exchanging nothing more than a brief, *'Hey,'* before smiling casually at the lens as though anything I was feeling inside couldn't be seen on the out. Then, after a few clicks, it was over. My phone was handed back to me and the band was called off for a press interview.

Beneath my insouciant exterior, I felt my stomach drop in a way I'd never experienced before. *Surely that can't be it - finished before it even began?* I hadn't even had a chance to have a proper conversation with him.

However, in that sombre moment, just as they were all walking out of the room, he unexpectedly turned back around and smiled at me; an innocent upturned grin that shot my heart straight into my throat. The zany emotion it delivered within me was so unfamiliar, so bizarre, and yet, it also made me feel strangely good. I didn't want it to be over. I had to know more – more about him. But…what was his name?

***

Throughout the gig I couldn't stop thinking about him. Even though the support acts were blinding and the atmosphere was electric, somehow, the thought of this blue-eyed-boy took over my entire mind.

This was so unlike me.

During the first interval, though, I inconspicuously googled the band (now I'd made the conscious decision to take up Brody's offer and meet them for drinks after the show; I had no choice but to learn their names. Because calling them *'you'* or *'potential James'* would hardly go down well, and I had to know *his* name) Once I'd got round the plethora of non-descript internet pages all pertaining to the band's discography and influences, I finally found what I was looking for. It didn't take long to work out who was who now their names and pictures were put together. Firstly, potential James was actually called Edward Linden, the band's drummer. Then, there was taller potential James, who was in fact, the real James Warner - their screamer and bassist. Of course, I was already certain about Brody, which meant that by common denomination (and a very reliable Wiki page source) there was one member left...

'Ethan Brenner – also known as 'Burner' on stage (because he shreds his guitar so fast that it makes the strings wave like smoke) – is the Joker's Ashes lead guitarist. He was born and bred in Minnesota, USA, and has been in the music industry ever since he was nineteen-years-old, with his first band, Killer Venom...'

Ethan Brenner. That was all I wanted to know. Seeing that he was 5'9 and that his birthday was in April was just pointless trivia. My curiosity could be my Achilles heel sometimes, so I quickly cut off my data and closed the Wiki tab before I learned too much more. Spoiling the element of surprise is such a buzzkill. I wanted to know about him from what I experienced in person, not through scrolling the world of the internet. Plus, seeing the emergence of weird online fan fiction within the search engine, featuring Ethan as the main character, was enough to creep me out. Not that he'd written it, of course. But just seeing that his level of fame was high enough to have followers that would incorporate him in imaginary Yaoi manga was a bit much.

The flurry of guests made their way back into the main venue for the start of the next support act. Drink of water in tow, I followed, swiftly glugging the icy cold beverage as quickly as I could before I'd have to carry it into a probable wall of death. Getting it dunked on me in the midst of all the bashing wasn't on my list. Metal gigs can be pretty sketchy at times, and going solo was never the wisest idea, especially when you're a tiny woman; like myself. And so, apprehensive of bruises and broken bones, I hid myself in the back corner, just to the side, so I could still see the stage. Obstructed as it was (mostly by infuriatingly tall and wide people) it didn't stop me appreciating the music. As long as I didn't have to watch the back of someone's head during the Joker's Ashes set, I'd be fine.

Out of the blue, emerging through a side door and standing themselves beside me, was Ethan. My insides were going crazy at the sight of him, but I did that very clever thing by acting really cool and carefree, only acknowledging him outwardly with a quick smile and a nod, and he did the same. For a while I even pretended to be on my phone, just to look like someone out there cared about my being here, but he didn't seem to notice. He was too busy watching the band on stage to worry about my inattentive nature. Then, after only a couple of minutes of having his presence next to me, he went back through the same doors that he came in from.

Oh, how I'd wasted those precious moments by acting so nonchalant. I could've kicked myself! I *should* have kicked myself - stupid woman. We're all guilty of it, though. To the ones we really like, we pretend not to care, in case things get awkward and we're subjected to rejection. No one likes to be rejected. But, if you "don't care" in the first place, then you can't suffer the embarrassing ramifications that follow. That appeared to be my body's game plan. My mind, however, was now shouting very angrily at me.

Determined to not let my involuntary state get the better of me, I tried to keep my cool and remind myself to just relax. '*Be normal. You've got this.*' All of the generic rubbish we girls need to say when we're face-to-face with a guy we like. Nevertheless, being normal seemed such a great mystery to me. I mean, what even was normal these days? What do guys like/dislike in a girl? What if my "normal" was his, *"WTF"?* The great wonders of the modern psyche would always baffle me, of that, I'm sure.

However, regardless of these conflicting thoughts, my only real mission that night was to simply not act like a plum.

Whilst watching the rest of Joker's Ashes set, that was what I intended to be – my version of normal, confident with it, and definitely not a tiny purple fleshy fruit. After all, confidence in your own skin is the most attractive quality in anyone. That was what I kept telling myself, anyway.

The Gig (Part 2)

Time seemed to stand still in the bar. From my little cornered seat, I drank water, jotted down thoughts in my notepad and clock-watched, every so often checking my phone to pretend it looked like I had some kind of purpose for sitting there. Rather than just hopelessly waiting to see when the band would arrive - *if*, they would.

Alongside my unreadable notepad scribbles, keeping me company were the three photographs taken from earlier in the night. Although the time frame they carried could have only been a matter of seconds, the wealth of emotion captured within them seemed unending. In every picture taken we were stood side-by-side; my place in the line-up remaining firmly central, cosily leaning into Ethan. Our body language mirrored an inextricable closeness that could easily be mistaken for a couple. Observing it was strange, we both had our heads tilted towards one another, a restful stance that perceptibly echoed comfort, and a pair of wide smiles which conveyed warmth as well as happiness. If a picture is worth a thousand words, I guessed this must be what they meant.

It had been thirty-five minutes since the show finished, and as much as I knew things took time to take down and load up in tour buses etc., my patience grew thin. There were only so many times I could stare at those images before it bordered obsessive, or wander off to the loos to redo my makeup and hair (albeit, I'd left my brush at home, so my asymmetric black bob now appeared of closer resemblance to that of a busby hat) before people started wondering if I had a bladder problem or - more embarrassingly - that I'd been stood up.

Maybe they weren't coming? Maybe they just felt sorry for me because I was at a gig on my own like a lame little Larry? Whatever the reality of the situation, I wasn't going to give it much longer. Even if this was a once in a lifetime opportunity, I refused to sit in a booth on my own like a Billy no-mates forever. An hour seemed reasonable enough. If they weren't there by 11pm then, as far as I was concerned, they weren't coming.

Frustrated, I glugged back my drink, slammed my notepad shut and picked up my jacket. It was now five to, and I'd finally given up. I felt stupid. The bartenders kept staring at me and so did the other punters, eyeing me up and down with pity. It was humiliating. I couldn't take it. And so, with hasty pace, I made my way to the exit door, marching angrily with every tread.

Why would you even sit and wait for someone like this, Simone? Just for a glimpse? This isn't you. What are you even hoping to gain from this situation, anyway?

Racing thoughts entered and exited my mind as quickly as I did the main room's doors, distracting me from my surroundings. I was unaware of the cups dropped on the floor or the sticky patches that attempted to glue my trainers, so I quickly turned around, pulled up my sticky shoe, grunted and picked up my gaze, before walking straight into Ethan.

'Whoa there,' he said, jerking back from our collision, 'I am so so—wait a sec…' he motioned, scanning my face intently, 'you were at the meet and greet, right?'

Embarrassed at my tousled state, I staggered between a smile and a frown, conscious of the fact that my heart was beating ten to the dozen.

'Indeed,' I said, semi-brusquely, brushing myself down with one hand, notepad still firmly gripped in the other. That was when I looked at him - the crystal threads in his searching eyes slowing down my every movement. I hated to admit it, but, he was utterly surreal.

Ridding myself of the stationary stalling that fixed me in place, I finally responded to his question.

'I mean, yes. That was me. I just nipped in the bar for a drink before I hit the road. Well, water. I wouldn't drink alcohol and drive because that'd be irresponsible. Not that I'm driving. I mean…I caught the train here.' Endless word vomit spouted from my mouth and I could feel myself cringing the more I spoke. I had to think of something sensible to say to round up my babbling.

'Who drives in London, right?'

Smiling merrily at me and obviously enjoying my embarrassing display of gawkiness, he answered, 'Very true.'

'So…are you catching the train home now?' He asked.

'*Nooo,*' I lied, the word tripping of my tongue before I could work out why I'd even said it, 'I was just, getting some fresh air - gathering my thoughts and such-like.' I started waving my little notepad in the air. 'No work tomorrow so may as well go all out and write.'

He laughed as I gestured a celebratory jiggle to the notion of a day off, cutely rolling up his black hoodie sleeve as he did so. Peeking from his elbow were the markings of a tattoo. I couldn't quite make out what it was, but the sight of his veins stretching further down his forearm distracted me in ways that shouldn't be experienced in public. My mind nearly ran away with itself, but I tethered it back to reality just in time. Bright lights weren't the best at concealing attraction.

'Awesome,' he chirruped, 'well, as much as I wouldn't want to tear you away from your thought gathering, a few of us are having a couple of drinks now. This place has some mean cocktails.'

'So I've heard,' I interjected, awkwardly trying to regain composure by looking at him coolly and undoing the nervous tension in my shoulders.

'Yeah, so erm,' he continued, 'do you wanna join us?'

Beneath the rock musician bravado, he actually seemed a bit nervous, too. Maybe I was wrong, but the way his voice softened when he asked me to stay, how he'd intently pulled down the back of his red beanie and adjusted the stray blonde hairs that poked out from underneath - carefully tucking them away - all the while smiling at me the entire time, made me think otherwise.

'Yeah,' I answered, grin bigger than ever, 'that'd be...awesome.'

*****

After waiting a couple of minutes for the rest of the band, we re-entered the bar area. The same ogling punters stared at me again, but this time, their rubbernecking was withdrawn at the sight of my company.

Not such a lonely loser now, eh?

At the bar, I made a couple of suggestive hints to Ethan that the Mama's Crumble cocktail sounded nice. I then went over to secure a cosy booth in the corner, patiently waiting for him and the others to bring back their drinks. As I sat there, my phone's buzz alerted me from thumb twiddling, and I quickly whipped it out of my bag to see who was messaging me.

Katrina.

'Are you coming back soon?'

Smiling to myself, I considered telling her that I was staying behind for drinks, that I was with the band, but more importantly, that one of the guys was ridiculously hot. The idea was flawed though – it wouldn't end there. Knowing Kats, she'd send through numerous excited emoji faces and my phone would buzz so unremittingly that it would sound as though I had a broken dildo in my bag. Plus, I'd only be inviting several full-on conversations about it over the next few weeks, concerning whether I was going to talk to him again, did I get his number, did I kiss him, blah, blah. Then Seb would somehow find out. He would retract his satirical comments regarding my sexuality and manage to turn the conversation X-rated by asking if I'd finally got some D.

No, it was best to just say nothing.

'Not yet. Don't wait up! X' was all I was brave enough to type. After being subjected to such an array of unpleasant thoughts, my response was narrowed down to the monosyllabic.

All of a sudden, the sound of drinks hitting the table brought my head up from my phone.

'There we are,' Ethan announced as he placed two vibrantly coloured concoctions down, 'one Mama's

Crumble and one Kermit's Juice. You can choose whichever one you like.'

'Thanks,' I chirruped, coyly smiling at him as he sat down beside me.

Positioned to my left, he sat with his back turned to the overhead light. Our spot was dimly lit, but I could still make out his prominent features. Shadows cast from the above light rested in the most striking of places on his face, crafting his sharp jawline with perfect definition, brushing smoothly against his streamlined nose and softly blurring his olive skin. Though, to me, light or dark, the most captivating thing about him was his celestial stare. Like stars in space, they twinkled brightly, taking me out of the room and transporting me straight to the heavens. I felt powerless to their gaze. With just one look, I was lost, unable to concentrate on anyone or anything else around me. My mind simply drifted elsewhere, filling itself with unrelenting thoughts that disconnected me from all conversation. I had to stop myself. Conversations only work when you paid attention to them.

Hours slipped by, but I didn't notice. All of my focus was on Ethan and his on me. Even with the rest of the band around us, we barely interacted outside our bubble. And when our conversations became deeper, more exciting, I couldn't afford to be distracted. I wanted to hear what he had to say. There was so much more to Ethan than just his boyish good-looks. He was smart, exuberant, savvy, brilliantly funny, and most importantly, absolutely fascinating.

During our time together, we discussed so many things. Anything from the light-hearted to the exceptionally profound and everything in-between – it was fantastic. And within this rather animated conversational narrative of ours, the topic soon voyaged to creativity. He told me about his passion for music and how it made him feel to be able to express himself through the sound of the strings, disclosing how - despite his music teacher's rotten judgement - it had been one of his most motivational outlets, and that even when times were tough, he never gave up.

'If you have a dream you should go for it,' he stressed, clutching his glass and looking towards me, discernibly devoted to his stand. 'Don't let anyone else's opinion stand in your way. If I'd listened to her then I'd never be where I am today.'

Something about that hit home with me. He was undeniably dedicated to his cause, and rightly so; his musical talent was irrefutable. But there was also sadness attached to such artistic commitment. With a demanding work schedule and a love for something that doesn't occur within a nine-to-five basis, Ethan admitted that finding balance in his life proved wholly problematic. And, almost too-excitedly, I confessed that I, too, shared a similar problem.

'People just aren't flexible when it comes to creativity and how it works,' I fervently declared, tapping my little shot glass on the table. 'It comes in spits and spurts, flurrying through your mind like a jungle stampede. There's no organisation to it. Whatever's in there has no mercy, no concept of time. It just comes when it comes. And no matter how much you try and silence it, you'll fail. The noise can't be stopped. You just have to go with it. That's why I bring my little notepad everywhere. Just in case, you know?' I paused, taking another sip before pensively stating, 'I fear there are few folks in this world that would truly be able to engage with that.'

That was when I saw his captivated expression. He was amazed. Every line in his skin was pinched with passion, begging for me to carry on. It was as if I'd just spoken his language. Maybe he wasn't used to that? Nevertheless, I had to go and ruin the moment by stating that, despite this issue, I was, *'happy to be single!'*

Idiot.

Something was salvaged the moment I mentioned my book, however. Explaining how, finding someone who'd work around that, also appeared implausible. Because, honestly, who else would cope with a partner who loaded up the laptop at 3am with late-night artistic flow that just needed spilling there and then? It really is quite a ridiculous notion.

'Really?' he enthusiastically replied, jaw well and truly dropped, 'I know you said you were writing down your thoughts, but, I didn't realise that you were writing an actual book. That's awesome.'

Then the sweetest smile arced on his face.

'You're like a modern-day Jane Austen.'

I smiled back playfully, utterly giddy at the fact that he'd just compared me to one of the greatest novelists in history. Also, he was positively crackers and I loved it. Who'd have thought that discovering a mutual zest for the creative could be so binding? Though, as crazy as it sounds, finally having someone to discuss this ineffable emotion with was the highlight of my night. No one else I knew even cared about books, let alone understood the meaning it carried to write one. But Ethan, he did, he knew exactly how it felt. The strength it gave you, the freedom to explore your inner-most thoughts, the burst of imagination flowing freely through your fingers and splashing out onto white pages, creating colour in a greyscale existence. Down to a tee, he knew it. And in a way, it's like he knew me too.

'I bet that you're gathering inspiration right now,' he jittered excitedly, motioning his fingers to our table, 'in this moment, this very place - you'll take something away from it. And, the best part is, you, as the creator, get to decide how it all ends.'

In all honesty, I wasn't aware that I was gathering any inspiration at that time. But, by the same token, I wasn't going to discount the potential for it either.

Then, he paused, for just a few thoughtful seconds, gathering his emotions into one heartfelt quote.

'When reality fails to write the perfect ending, your imagination can take you there.'

I couldn't have put it better myself.

Just the way he expressed his words made me fall for him more. He spoke with such conviction, such soulful intelligence. It was inspiring. *He* was inspiring. If only I'd known of the catalyst swirling in that moment between us, building the very foundations of a prospective new world. How far this unrivalled connection would one day take me, though, still remained a mystery.

Despite my conscious vow of abstinence from love weighing heavily on my mind, something primal within me was awakened. Everything about him was so inviting. Inside and out, he was exactly what I wanted. I couldn't help but find myself scanning every inch of his face, beginning with those glorious eyes of his and working my way down to his rather edible lips. *Man*, I wanted to kiss those lips. Why did he have to be so close to my face? Trying to resist the urge became so much harder when he was barely an edge away.

I'd probably had too many cocktails.

Aware of my inhibitions potential unleashing, I politely took myself off to the loo to freshen up, insisting that I needed to begin drinking water when I got back.

From inside the bathroom, my giddy but sozzled reflection stared back at me.

What is this feeling? How is this even real? He's just so...incredible.

After momentarily relishing in glee, nearly to the point of humming silly tunes like people do in the movies when they'd just had nookie for the first time in forever, I then overheard a beleaguering conversation coming from behind me. Two girls were within their cubicles talking to one another about a bloke who'd – as they put it – *totally* mugged them off. Apparently, he was coming across as into them both, but in actual fact was playing them off against one another. Thus, keeping his options open and making the other one feel stupid for even thinking she had a chance.

'That's these musician types for you, though. They're all egotistical wankers.'

Suddenly, it dawned on me.

What if I was being played?

This unchartered thought infiltrated my mind like a burglar, slowly creeping into my brain and robbing me of all innocent belief. I didn't want to think it, but I couldn't help but be aware of its potential truth. After all, it wasn't so long ago that I'd experienced that same confusion with Jake – not knowing where I stood. As harrowing as this concept was, it wasn't impossible. In that moment, my mood shifted. No longer did I feel a sense of elation. Instead, I was awash with disappointment, completely flooded by fear and drained of clarity. If this was all a joke, then I didn't want to be someone's punchline.

Upon my return from the bathroom, I saw a tall tumbler of water had been placed on the table. Annoyingly, it made me smile.

Surely, if he just wanted one thing, then he wouldn't respect my request to sober up? He can't be like the rest of them...

But, even so, now that the door of anxiety had been opened, the many unwelcome party guests soon made their way inside, each one casually reminding me of the sad reality outside the venue's walls.

'He's from America, how can you realistically maintain anything with someone so far away? What about his job? How can you trust someone you'll never see? No one's words can be taken at face value. Oh, and let's not forget the fact that he's in the limelight, for goodness sake. A man like him is only single because they get sex on tap. In fact, he's probably got another girl lined up at the next tour venue just like you – gullible, foolish and infatuated. You aren't special to him. Why would you be? What have you got to offer someone like him? He's established - a real go-getter. You work in a shop and write stories in your bedroom. Go figure.'

My mobile phone illuminated 2.30am in bright white letters. With the abundance of sad thoughts overwhelming my frame of mind, I told Ethan that I'd have to go.

'You can't go yet,' he yelped, his periwinkle eyes desperately pleading with me, 'I might not see you again for another year – maybe even two! No, you've gotta at least stay until the bar closes. Please?'

His eyes depicted such innocence. I didn't want to believe that they could disguise a lie. There was just no possible way that the man who sat before me could be anything but the truth. For all of the rebellious tattoos scattering his arms and calf, the small stretchers in his ears and the delicate nose piercing that graced his skin, many would care to disagree. But I knew that his look was not one to be feared, but one to be explored. Every inked artwork told a story, each little silver hoop expressing a personality that yearned for discovery. This man was far from narcissistic. Or, at least, that's what I wanted to think.

Persuaded by his imploring honeyed tones and the thought that we may not see each other again, I stayed. Nevertheless, even in my decision to remain with him, I couldn't shift the sentence that kept repeating itself in the back of my mind.

Whatever the reality, all you can do is accept the situation for what it is – one night with an amazing guy.

Because, no matter how much we delayed time's arms from ticking, the end was nigh. Soon, the sun would come up and we'd both have to go back to our daily lives. Me; living with my best friend, dealing with my imprudent family and selling aromatic skin care to the hipsters of London. And him; writing music, touring the world and, most possibly, meeting a whole host of remarkable people who he'd share this same bond for the creative with. Our lives were poles apart. How we'd even connected in the first place was beyond improbable. And yet, we had.

Strange as it all was, not once when we were together did I think about him as *'The guitarist from world-famous metalcore band, Joker's Ashes'* In fact, we didn't even discuss anything band-related. To me, he was just Ethan – a twenty-five--year-old guy who liked to watch Rick and Morty, bake pecan pies in his spare time and discover new places to travel. From the little to the big things he enjoyed, he was cool (even if watching TV wasn't looked upon favourably in most people's eyes, I loved Rick and Morty too, so excused its appearance in the line-up.) In a way, we were like two peas in a pod – both creative, both passionate about globetrotting, and music, and food, and politics and oh, just, so many things. Even he seemed shocked by our similarities and was totally convinced we must have met before.

'I just feel like I know you so well, Simone. It's crazy. Are you positively sure we've never met…?

I laughed as his fulsomeness. 'I'm *pretty* sure this is the first time.'

As if I was going to admit that I felt the same.

Come 4am, after an evening of laughter, musing discussions and occasional surreptitious glances at one another, we finally left the Koko. Together, we walked towards the tube; our steps guided by the amber streetlights. It was cold outside, the notorious "nippy wind" making its presence known. With only the thin covering of my black jacket for warmth, I shivered as I walked.

'Are you cold?' Ethan asked me.

'A bit,' I answered, crossing my arms in front of me for extra protection, 'I'm okay though.'

'Here,' he said, taking off his hoodie and wrapping it around me, gently placing a friendly arm around my shoulder, 'no need to freeze on my account.'

From beginning to end, he stayed on my left-hand side all through the night. It was strange how being in his vicinity made me feel such contrasting emotions. Half of me was so relaxed, as if being with him was like finding the missing piece to a puzzle, finally completing a jigsaw that previously seemed unfinishable. And yet, simultaneously, the contusion on such pristine feelings filled me with dread. Like exposing such vulnerability could make way for a stab in the back. As inconceivable as I wanted it to be, I couldn't erase its likelihood. And suddenly, it all felt ridiculous. *I* felt ridiculous.

Whichever way I looked at it, it was pointless. We would probably never see each other again, so why did he want to keep me with him for so long? What did he *really* want from me? These resurrecting ruminations bubbled up inside me and the feel of his arm holding me close only made them rise up further.

'No bother, I'm used to being cold. Alongside being forever alone, that's another reason I get called the Ice-Queen.'

As soon as the words rolled off my tongue, I hated myself for saying them. Wholly unyielding, my body no longer invited his touch, and instead, tightened itself into a rigid statue, turning away from him and facing the empty street-lit roads.

'I should really be heading home,' I said, still staring absently into the building fasciae.

By this point, I wanted to go. Maybe it was tiredness, or just the immense amount of unwarranted thoughts that ran amuck in my head, but I was done with dragging out our beautiful night into this tainted disaster. Out of everything I'd expected to take away from that evening, feeling this way was not on the list. And, in spite of how happy he'd made me feel, I was too scared to let him know. For this reason, rather than being honest, I delved into the proverbial masquerade drawer and donned a mask of indifference, voicelessly expressing that, *'It was nice to meet you, but don't let it polish your ego.'* It was an utter lie, but it was the safest option I had.

'Well, it's been lovely getting to know you, Simone,' he softly professed, clasping me in a farewell hug. 'And you've gotta let me know when your book is out – I'd love to read it.'

Into his warm skin I smiled. 'I'll let you know. I promise.'

Upon our separation, I passed him back his hoodie that had rested on my shoulders. Its sweet musk drifted with it as we said our final goodbyes.

As the night drew its curtain call, there was no encore, only Ethan walking one way and me in the other. Both of us slowly making our way back to the sides of the fence we belonged, unspoken thoughts carried in tow.

The Raging Torch

People-watching is something of a pastime for me. I suppose that, when you work in retail for as long as I have, it becomes a big part of the daily ritual. And more often than not, the experience is a pleasant one, leaving you happily intrigued and willing to engage with the interesting folk who stroll through your gaze. Heck, sometimes, you even make friends with the walk-ins. But, then there are other days in which you'd rather nick Harry Potter's invisibility cloak and just vamoose out of there ASAP, rather than speak to customers. And as much as it pains me to admit, today was one of those days.

'So, what is *Tulsi* good for? And, sesame oil – tell me, why on earth do I need something from my Friday night stir-fry in my skincare regime?'

This impertinent old woman was really starting to do my swede in. Bold as brass, she stood there, picking up every item in the shop and pulling it apart, questioning its validity, price, ethics, medicinal value – everything! Nothing I told her was insightful enough either. To her, I was just *"a bit of fluff trying to flog her empty promises in a jar."* Blood vessels nearly fit to burst, I'd all but nearly flipped my own lid before Katrina thankfully swooped in and saved the day.

'Ooh, Tulsi is magical,' she began, picking up our sample pot and dotting contents of the cream on her hand to demonstrate, 'it's packed with polyphenols: the powerhouse anti-oxidant that fights free radical damage. Our skin goes through a lot, thanks to the environment, so having this little wonder in your skincare regime is truly a holy grail. That's why in Sanskrit it's called "Tulsi", because it is simply incomparable to any other plant.'

The ill-tempered pensioner looked at her sullenly.

'Hmm,' she grumbled, furrowing her brow as she put down the product in question and picked up the other, 'well, what about the stir-fry one?'

'Sesame oil is also an amazing neutraliser of free radicals, but more notably, it's a fantastic anti-inflammatory,' she began again, reeling off her encyclopaedic knowledge of all that is Ayurvedic skincare. 'It absorbs quickly into the skin, making it look and feel youthful, as well as super soft and strong. Essentially, this is because of the remarkable way sesame oil molecules penetrate the skin; by gathering oil-soluble toxins and moving them straight to the bloodstream where they're eliminated as waste.'

'My face is not a landfill site,' the crinkled old bat cried out, her paisley red headscarf nearly dropping off in shock. 'Everything there is as it should be thank you very much. And, as for being super soft and strong,' she continued, inhaling as she prepped herself for her rant's grand finale, 'I was looking for a moisturiser, not a magic potion in which to be turned into Andrex toilet paper. What nonsense!'

Banging the bottle on the wooden stand, the incorrigible woman harrumphed and turned away from us, flapping her long beige coat as she made her way out.

'*Good day,*' she bid, arrogantly sashaying out of the door, holding down her headscarf when she was met by the fierce outside wind.

'What the fudge was that about?' I asked, still gawping at the door where the woman had not so long ago been stood.

'God knows,' Katrina said, staring at the same spot, 'old people can be crazy stubborn.'

'What does she think we are; crazed alchemists or something?' I stated, and in caricature eccentricity, I hunched my back and started dramatically flailing my arms about. '*Here, step inside my lair. Pass me your sacrificial offering to be placed on my transmutation circle of peril, and I will turn it into an enchanted remedy that will transform your face forever!*'

I then finished off my thespian display with a cackle worthy of an Oscar.

A clueless spell cast itself upon Katrina's face. She had no idea what I was talking about.

'You've been watching that anime stuff again, haven't you, Sims?'

'*Maybe*,' I replied, back in my usual manner again. 'But, I'd honestly have no qualms about turning that old bag into a chimera, if I could. Not that she's too far off a fire-breathing monster already.'

After that night at the Koko, going back to this kind of reality suddenly felt so empty. Excluding the sparkling company of my best friend, listening to other people in the shop whinge to me about their unkempt faces just annoyed me. Not to mention that the Christmas playlist was already on in the background. We hadn't even had Halloween yet, which I always felt was necessary to move past before the festive tunes were put on repeat, and yet, Cliff Richard was evidently here for the foreseeable. And those irks were just inside the world of my job.

Outside of it wasn't much better. I was either stuck with Seb, bulldozing into my apartment, disturbing me from editing my book, only to flounce on my bed and tell me all about the oh-so-handsome-and-clever-Tariq (how he ever got any of his uni work done, I will never know). Or my mum, ringing me on a daily basis with trivial chit-chat about the garden or the neighbour, only to slowly integrate the unwanted conversation of Dad – again, which, by coincidence, was another person outside the shop who was annoying me. Sure, my blow-up with him in the café was uncalled for. I'd taken it too far. But, even after explaining to him my reasons behind it, he still wouldn't let up. Continuously, he harped on at me about Gary's son, Ryan, and how much we had in common, and how fantastically funny and good-looking he was. But I didn't want to get to know bloody *Ryan*. I didn't care if he was a "*strapping young lad*" or the fact that we both shared a penchant for DC trainers. It simply wasn't enough for me to form any solid affection for the bloke. Which brings me to my last annoyance; the irrepressible and incessant infatuation that now riddled my entire mind – Ethan Brenner.

Desperately, I tried to think of anything and everything else but him, or that night, or how it made me feel, or how much I wanted to experience it all over again. Even the city streets seemed to play an active role in keeping these thoughts alive. Since meeting Ethan, I'd never even noticed how many nearby places featured his name – Ethan's Bar, Brenner Walk and Ethan's Place were just a few. It was crazy. No matter where I went, I couldn't escape it, and maybe a part of me was glad of that.

For so long, I'd been without emotion, completely closed off from the prospect of love, and living my life without a significant other was no issue. But now, I'd met someone – someone who set my heart ablaze with passion and liberated my soul from the darkness. My eyes finally opening to the possibility that my imagined Mr X may not be so far out of reach after all. He was simply like no other; incomparable, a bit like the Tulsi. And damn it, I wish I hadn't messed everything up.

Regret walked beside me everywhere I went, casting shadows of sadness everywhere I looked. *Why did I have to let doubts feast on my hopes? Why couldn't I just be normal, like every other girl on this planet, instead of this stupid worrywart? Surely there was no real fear to be had?* But it was too late. He was gone, and so was that night. Fate pushed us together only for me to pull it all apart.

Wait. *Fate* pushed us together…

My mind raced back to Lilith's pale finger pointing towards the Emperor Tarot card from my psychic reading a few weeks' prior.

'There he is…your Mr X.'

Saturated by the anchor that plummeted its way down inside me, this great sinking feeling weighed heavier and heavier in my chest the more I remembered.

'This man, he is real. He is one you will meet very soon…This meeting will be significant to rest of your life. Remember to not let your head rule your heart for once.'

No, I thought, *it can't be him* - there was just no way. I shook my head of the reminiscence. This was neurotic. Thinking this way was ridiculous. The circumstance was purely coincidental, nothing mysterious about it. It was imperative I rid these nonsense thoughts. Life was already hard enough to concentrate on without that fantastical rubbish ambushing my head as well.

At that moment, something Seb told me came rushing into my mind:

'Tariq says that trying to stop yourself from thinking about something that's already on your mind is pointless. Like, imagine if I told you to not think about a skateboarding penguin. But it's already in your head, isn't it? And the more you try to not think about this super fly penguin, who could give Tony Hawk a run for his money, the more he skates back in your head.'

The point of his statement was about denial. Denying yourself of something you want when it's already on your mind won't make it go away. In fact, it'll probably just get stronger. This thought, however, was a part of Seb's new "get fit" regime. Even though Tariq was apparently all up for Seb's pole banging suggestion, he also thought he'd share a few other alternative psychological tips to help, hence this little nugget. So, whilst Seb was out trying to sublimate his doughnut cravings into crunching on apples and almonds; I was using it to remind myself that my brain's infernal repetition of my time with Ethan was merely because I couldn't channel that emotion into anyone or anything else. That, and as transient as it was, it held a lot of value to me. More value than I'd ever realised it could have.

I felt like Asae and Riri from the 80s manga, The Days of Rose and Rose. Although, my story was slightly different to theirs, the sentiment was similar. In their tale, the two sisters had fallen for the same boy. Neither of them knew this, however, and when Christmas came and they'd both planned to give a special present as a confession of their love for him, they were both shocked to discover that he already had a girlfriend. Ultimately, neither of them receives any affirmation from the boy as to whether he likes them or not. But they do find something else of much higher value - becoming aware of oneself through the existence of others.

So, whether the love was unrequited or reciprocated, their words affirmed growth achieved through romantic experience. This story made me wonder if maybe, even without answers to my burning questions, I had somehow grown as a person inside, too. At least now I knew that I wasn't completely robotic. I mean, for a good while, I thought that there was more activity going on inside Mount Fuji than inside me, and that volcano hasn't erupted in over three hundred years. However, as liberating as it was to know that I wasn't dead inside, I dared not share these thoughts with anyone else. As surprising as it might be to some people, I didn't want to shout from the rooftops about what had happened. Most people would, I'm sure, but I'd already had enough of my mind playing my idiocy on loop. No one else need join in.

***

As days turned into weeks, and weeks turned into months, still, thoughts of Ethan remained firmly in the back of my mind. In the most stupid of moments, it would remind me of him; generating memories of how he'd smiled at me, his comical mannerisms from our cosy booth, or things he'd said during our time together. Sometimes, my mind would even wander to a place of dissection and break up his words, trying to work out if there was anything else beneath their artistic orthography. *Could there possibly have been any link to an underlying emotion when he'd asked me to stay? What about when we'd discussed our likes and dislikes, and he became so aflame with wondrous surprise when he discovered our mutual adoration for things? And what about that final farewell, where he held me just that extra bit tighter and for that extra bit longer - did that mean anything? Did any of it?* I guessed I'd never know.

On this cold winter's afternoon, I stayed at home with a sore throat and these pestering thoughts. Alexandra would rather have a rat infestation than a sickly employee lurking in her store.

'Oh, good grief, stay where you are, girl,' she'd snapped to me on the phone. 'Selling medicinal skin care is already challenging enough, let alone when the person trying to sell it is ill. No, you keep your germs at home.'

So, that's what I did. My scratchy throat and I hung out alone in the apartment, drinking many cups of lemon and honey rooibos tea to nurse the pain (as per the commands of the many notes left by Katrina on our kitchen cupboards) whilst simultaneously attempting to distract myself from the sore subject of Ethan.

My distraction rested upon editing the final touches of my manuscript. It was near enough done, but I wanted to go through it with a fine toothcomb. Forking out for an editor was not an option on my wages, so I was left with no other choice than to check it all over myself. I endeavoured to be as unbiased as possible when it came to killing my children, which - before you become terrified thinking I'm a mass murderer - is writer's slang for, *"eliminating unnecessary wording from your work."* And although I'd killed a few paragraphs off already, I'd also added a lot in their place. As much as I hated my brain for replaying that night at the Koko like a broken record, it gave for some creative insight the piece was severely lacking before. Prior to that experience, my knowledge on how it would feel to be truly comfortable with somebody was limited. After all, Jake was hardly a great reference point, so I guess that the endless mental looping did have its upsides.

The rain beat hard against the window in my bedroom and my wonky wardrobe creaked from the cold, both of which zoned me out from my writing. Suddenly, I became all too aware of my throat. It ached every time I swallowed and no amount of water seemed to make it any easier. Nothing felt easy these days, but that was hardly a surprise.

As things stood, family, work and friend-wise, my life was like an endless re-run of *Groundhog Day* - tirelessly repeating the same pattern every day, still trying to avoid that *doozy* of a puddle. To say I was depressed would be taking it a little far. I was just…sad. I wanted to put it down to the short, dark British winter days. A lot of people experience the same feeling at this time of year.

But as I stared listlessly out of my bedroom window, like a prisoner peeking through the bars, I stared at the people wandering below me – with their brollies blowing uncontrollably and their disgruntled fists waving at the cursed grey sky above – and I knew that I wasn't feeling the same doom and gloom as other people. I couldn't know for sure, obviously. But I continued to watch anyway, as if these ant-sized strangers played an active role in reassuring me that I was no different. And I planned on watching for as long as it took to believe that notion, or until the city skyline faded into a foggy blackness again; as it did every day.

Alerting my attention back to the room was the sound of my phone buzzing. I sighed as I walked over to it, imagining the usual rubbish that filled up the small screen's face, constantly begging me to be interested in a new YouTube video or something on the news. Only sometimes would I submit to such demands. Today was not that day.

Harry's face popped up in a little circle, asking me whether I was considering going to Download Festival next year, and if I'd be coming up to Nottingham for Christmas.

Crumbs, I thought, *has it really been that long already?* Time sure flies when your life is stuck on repeat.

I told him I didn't know. Although I was a sucker for gigs, this was a bit different. Half of the acts hadn't even been released yet and I didn't want to fork out for something I was unsure of. Plus, I'd made no plans to go home in the summer. Or winter, for that matter. December came around so fast that I didn't even see it coming. How typical of me – never seeing things coming. Even if that psychic reading was right, I'd had a heads up and was still no good at putting pieces together. My brain simply pushed it all aside so I could focus on the here and now. If only I could forget other things just as easily.

Blasting open the front door, a grumbly and bedraggled Katrina ambled through, shaking her long wet hair, crimped from the cold like a shaggy dog.

'I feel so gross,' she cried, 'tell me why I even bothered going to work in this?'

'Because you need the money?' I croaked, sauntering in from my room and into the main lounge area wrapped in a dressing down. I was grateful for the distraction of her presence, even if it wasn't the most cheerful.

'No, nothing is worth this,' she declared, shaking her hands, 'it's practically a monsoon out there.'

I plonked myself down on the sofa and watched as she shed her coat and then went to squeeze excess water out of her hair over the kitchen sink. She was unusually grumpy. Normally, a bit of rain wouldn't bother her. It'd be me that would whine and groan about it and she would tell me that *"a shower from the clouds"* was somehow good for me. I'd never believe her, of course. As far as I was concerned, anything that invited ugly kinks into my hair and splodged my eyeliner into unsightly inkblots, was certainly no friend of mine.

'I'm surprised you didn't use it as an opportunity to unleash your inner-Mo-Farah.'

I could imagine her whipping the murky streets in her famous pink and white trainers.

'No way,' she echoed from the sink, 'have you seen the roads? They're more slippery than an ice rink. I don't want to fall over and die, Sims.'

Fashioning a languished expression, she walked through the lounge still twisting her hair between her hands. Her green eyes furrowed with disdain towards the unwanted wet weight on her head.

'How are you, anyway?' she asked, her voice softening now she'd sat down beside me. 'Did you see the notes I left for you on the doors?'

Raspingly, I laughed. 'Yes, I could hardly miss them.' I replied, looking at our paper-ridden kitchen, 'it looks like a cop's whiteboard in here.'

'Well,' she said, sitting proudly, 'I like to be thorough. Plus, I may as well make good use of my Ayurvedic knowledge somehow. Although, it doesn't *sound* as if you've been as obedient as I'd like...'

And just like the police, she was totally onto me.

'Do I really sound *that* bad?'

Her confirming nod told me that: yes, yes I did.

'Sweetheart, don't take this the wrong way but...you could give Rod Stewart a run for his money with that gravelly throat.'

I sat back in animated horror. 'I'm surprised you even know who Rod Stewart is,' I hoarsely announced, 'aren't you more R'n'b than OAP?'

'Oh. My dearest, Simone,' she said, shaking her head, 'you, of all people, should know not to judge a book by its cover.'

Her face fixed itself with sincerity upon said earnest declaration, but it didn't take long to falter.

'Okay, truce. I only know of him because Julian keeps playing his album on ruddy loop. Over Christmas, the bar is thinking of doing some kind of themed *love-in*. You know, like a singles night type of thing? But anyway, the whole event has kind of taken over and he now won't stop going on about it. For instance, last night, we were snuggled on the sofa, watching romantic movies - my choice, of course - and suddenly, he gets up. Like, shoots up, knocking my rested head onto the sofa's arm. *Bang*! And he starts shouting, "*EUREKA!*", like he's discovered the meaning of life or something. Turns out he'd worked out the perfect songs for the singles night playlist. Well, *he* thinks they're perfect. I'm indifferent. Like, who in their right mind is going to feel remotely sexy listening to 70's crooning and 80's synths, for God's sake?'

Nestled inside my dressing gown, a supine state overwhelmed me. Anything to do with music and romance, and I knew where the conversation was potentially headed.

'I can only imagine the quixotic lust that will overwhelm the attendees,' I said, attempting to bring the conversation to a conclusion, rather than on repeat.

'Exactly,' she jumped, getting more excited about my remark than I initially anticipated. 'It's going to be such a nightmare if he doesn't change it, and he will be whining about it for weeks after, too. That's totally going to ruin future movie nights. Oh, Sims. I just wish I could make him understand.'

I didn't know what to say to her. I'd been off the dating scene for so long now that knowing how she was feeling was becoming a near impossible venture for me.

'Tell him that, if he doesn't listen, all bedroom activities are off-limits. That's what I'd do,' I said, hoping that my nugget of wisdom would be helpful somehow.

Katrina turned back to face me. 'Not *quite* the advice I was looking for, Sims. But, then again, it might work.'

I shrugged my shoulders, before eloquently summarising my reason.

'Men like sex. Restrict it and he'll be like putty in your hands. Submitting to your ways of thinking will be far easier once he has blue balls.'

Maybe it was my statement or possibly the fact that everything I said sounded like Marge Simpson, but it made Katrina laugh heartily. Nevertheless, it didn't stop her from bringing my emotions crashing down.

'Spoken like a true expert,' she began; smile wide on her face, 'not that I could do it, mind you. I would be so cranky without sex. But, I guess being single for so long takes that need away, eh?'

I bowed my head at that. If only she knew the amount of feelings I'd been harbouring ever since that night at the Koko.

A part of me wanted to tell her, just to prove that I wasn't completely dead inside. Single or otherwise, I wanted to tell her that those feelings still existed within me. It was irksome, though. No matter who I spoke to, they all seemed to think the same thing – that I was being stubborn, and that, if I wanted to be with someone, then I should stop being so fussy and simply find someone. It was as if falling for a person was as easy as choosing the weekly groceries. Plus, they neglected to account for the fact that I'm the girl who is every guy's friend. I'm the one they feel comfortable around because I like the same things as them. Heck, even Harry had said it to me once before.

'To me, you're like a dude.'

Isn't it amazing how one sentence can completely eradicate all sex appeal? I'll not forget how those words did just that to me, and I often wondered if, instead of seeing a girl, he saw me with stubble and a baseball cap on. I hadn't thought about that for a good while, but in that moment, it came flooding back.

Maybe I've been looking at this all wrong? Is it possible that the person I finally liked saw me the same way others do – like a boy?

What did it matter now, anyway? Delusions of grandeur were all that these persistent thoughts amounted to. I was just a pensive fool who wore my heart on my sleeve, secretly tilting it out of focus in hope that one day I'd forget it was there, too.

Contrasting emotions left me diffident to reply. For a second, I stared at her, pitifully cloaking myself inside the inviting dressing gown, trying to work out what best to say without it somehow backfiring on me.

'Being single has its perks, I guess.' I finally stated, digressively telling her about how the famous inventor, Richard Browning, flew around London in his homemade jet suit. I lived in hope that such a jaw-dropping story about alternative ways people fill their time would steal her away from prying on my matters of the heart and in a way, it worked. She may not have been interested much in the story, but, it did manage to stop her poking her nose into my love life.

'That's weird.' She responded, 'people do crazy things when they're bored. *Anyway…*'

She then pushed herself up from the sofa and made steps towards the sticky-note filled kitchen. 'Save your throat. I'll make you a Manuka honey drink. I brought you some back from Holland and Barrett on my sopping wet trip home. Yes, I'm amazing, I know. No need to thank me. Just don't tell Alexandra. If she hears I've been fraternising with the enemy she'll probably have a fit.'

Conversations now drawn to a close, she and I spent the rest of the evening huddled together on the sofa. The blinds were drawn to shut away the damp darkness that filled the outside world, and we talked, drank tea (I swear, if you'd tipped me upside down, I'd leak out enough to hydrate at least ten people) and watched several terrible girly films.

Sometimes, I liked it that way. Just me and my best friend, living for the now in our little apartment bubble where nothing and no one else mattered – we just, were. It's funny, but, when you think about it, often our favourite memories are the simplest ones. No frills and fancies required; just ones that make you smile whenever you look back on that special time. The kind you don't even know you're making until you reminisce. And mine, as corny as it may sound, were times like these.

***

Note to self: *no more editing until after Christmas.* Working until late at the shop and then coming home to finalise my seemingly endless manuscript was incredibly wearing. As dedicated as I was, there was only so much juice in my human battery. I needed sleep, time to wrap presents, finish doing up the apartment's decorations – did I mention sleep?

Mum and Dad hadn't helped matters either. Once again, they'd decided to try and be "civil" and see if they could arrange something special for the family to do at Christmas – you know, let bygones be bygones and get everyone together for the occasion type of thing. Ultimately though, it just ended in chaos. Even Madame Lilith wouldn't have needed her tarot cards for that one. Tensions became high the moment they started reminiscing about us kids, exchanging shared memories of niceties until they slowly slipped to the *shiteties*. And there was just no going back once that point was reached. Incredibly, Christmas was cancelled before it had even begun. Luckily though – or, unluckily perhaps – I already had other plans.

I could hear Tracey, Cherise, Julian and Katrina in the room next door, chortling away and drinking bottles of bubbly; the seasonal spirit filling the air as much as it did their glasses. They couldn't wait to finally celebrate the festive period best way they knew how.

'I'm going to find myself a fitty tonight!' Cherise blurted superciliously, clinking her glass with Tracey's. Out of all the girls, she and I were the only single ones left. However, in contrast to her status, mine had been going strong for almost two years now. Hers had barely scraped two months. Plus, in all that time, I hadn't even been on a date. And, unlike her, I hadn't even flirted with the idea of those crappy online love apps. To be fair, though, I hadn't flirted with anything or anyone at all in about, oh...two months and fourteen days? Not that I was counting or anything...And as irksome as it was to admit, nothing and no one could compete with the events of that night. It was everything I'd ever wanted. How could I even imagine connecting with someone like that again? Surely, it just wasn't possible? Despite the prospect of the night ahead and the many awesome people I'm sure would be there, in all honesty, I still didn't want to think it conceivable.

'Honest to God, if I don't find someone tonight I think I'll cry.' I heard Cherise forlornly continue. 'The thought of going another day without some loving and I might just close up.'

My eyes bulged. That image depicted far too viscerally in my head.

Shaking it off, I continued pulling on my skinny-fit black trousers and royal blue peplum top. For the first time in a while, I looked, dare I say...pretty. But, what was even more surprising was the fact that I actually liked it. I chose the look specifically because it complemented my hair's midnight blue hue and it wasn't too dressy. Pink was never going to happen; I'd leave that courtesy to the other girls. But blue, I liked blue. It was grown-up and sassy, pretty but not girly. Besides, if I had to go to this darn singles night then I wanted to feel as comfortable as humanly possible.

Ever since mine and Katrina's little chat about Julian and his terrible taste in music, she hadn't stopped banging on about the event. She was concerned it would be a total flop, despite all of Julian's devotion to the project.

As things stood then, hardly anybody was coming (which was no surprise with the promise of a Rod Stewart playlist). So I did what all good friends do and – through gritted teeth - offered moral support by proposing to rally the troops together to attend the event. On reflection, this was probably a bad idea. It made me realise that I'd have no other choice than to put out the flame that burned in my heart. Of course, I couldn't tell anyone this. It was my pain that I had to deal with on my own. No one else need know. Nevertheless, as much as I knew it was my burden to bear and that it was time to relinquish my attachment to it, something inside me still struggled to let it go.

Moments before we left for the singles night, I quickly checked myself out in the mirror. My hair was behaving, makeup was good - everything looked perfect. All that was left to do now was work on what was happening beneath the surface.

Distracting me from my last-minute spruce up was my photo scattered corkboard hanging next to my reflection. As always, everything I captured went up there. All of the good times I wanted to remember when my mind could no longer envisage the recollections so clearly. Yet, despite the innumerable images, only one caught my gaze and locked it tight – the shot taken from when I'd met the Joker's Ashes.

Even after such a surreal experience, I wanted to try and look at it with normal eyes, like it was no big deal. Any other meet and greet and I'd have done the same. So I tried to treat it as so, by taking my usual trip to get the reel printed out, ready to hang up on the cherished panel of memories. I thought that by handling it in the same way as all of the others would somehow turn my mind away from such conflicted feelings. That, one day, I'd forget how it felt to be there and just see the smiles instead - simply remembering a night from a distant past. As it turned out though, I was wrong.

'Sorry, guys,' I said as I pinched the picture from its pinned position on the wall, staring hopelessly at the handsome beaming face of Ethan stood so closely by my photo-self's side. 'No hard feelings.'

And with that, I placed the chord-striking picture inside the bottom of my wardrobe, buried beneath a pile of clothes, hoping that, once out of sight, it would finally be out of mind.

'Sims, c'mon,' Katrina yelled, her voice penetrating through the crappy music playing in our lounge. 'We're going to be late.'

I closed my eyes, 'Coming,'

Shutting the wardrobe's creaky door, I walked over and took one last look in the mirror.

You can do this.

Then, without looking back, I grabbed my bag and walked out. Fantasies are for fiction. Reality is all we really have. I guessed I'd have to finally learn to accept that now.

PART 2

The New Guy

From the way he wolfed down pasta quicker than a sinkhole gobbled a car, right to his ridiculous obsession with coloured trousers, everything he did pissed me off. Matt was nothing like Ethan, and to this day, I'm still not sure why I'd even made the decision to give him a chance. Sure, he was a nice guy. Tall, dark and handsome – just what every girl wants from a dream man – but I wasn't every girl. And, as lovely to look at as he was, Matt was far separated from any man featured in my dreams.

We'd been dating for three months now. Initially, when we'd first met at that darned singles night, I was reluctant to even speak to him. I remember how he'd first approached me at that table in the bar.

I was happily slurping my banana daiquiri, just casually minding my own business whilst Cherise cracked on with every guy in the room and the others danced to 00's pop music I hated. He was wearing a white shirt and red tie with matching red jeans, and in my head a little voice echoed how much he resembled a used tampon - hardly the most arousing of thoughts. But, despite my judgemental eyes and obvious disinterest in discourse, he sat next to me and smiled.

'I'm Matt,' he'd shouted over the music, which continued to beat twitchingly in the club as I nodded back to him, unwilling to respond with my own name. 'Can I buy you a drink?'

Again, I glared at him.

Is this guy stupid? Can't he see I'm already sipping a daiquiri?

'Thanks, but I'm not thirsty.' I'd said, continuing to suck on my straw and watch everyone boogie merrily on the dancefloor.

For a minute, neither of us spoke. Only, I could sense his eyes pressing against me, drawing up potential conversations in his head with every absorbing glance.

'Not much of a pop music fan?' He'd asked, ever-persistent with his attempts at this conservational engagement business. 'Me neither. Pop music is for teenagers and people looking for hook-ups. I'm more of a classical man, myself.'

Now, I was interested.

'Not sure how well Mozart would fair at a singles night.' I flatly remarked, not wanting to sound too keen, just in case his chat faltered into Boringsville.

'Oh, contraire,' Matt gaily enthused, 'have you never listened to the wonders of *Leck Mich im Arsch*? Mozart's bawdy language in that song perfectly describes what a lot of these attendees are going to get up to post-partying, I'm sure.'

Apparently, flattery will get you everywhere, but in my world, intelligence far outweighs the obsequious. This is how Matt broke my silence. His fashion sense may have been whack, but, in a way, I quite liked his non-conformist attitude. He had smarts and I respected that. And, once we'd started talking properly, he made me laugh, too. Mostly because his laugh could've given Jimmy Carr a run for his money; it was so awkward. However, like food is the way to a man's heart, laughter is the way to a woman's, and Matt could deliver that tenfold.

'You're a funny guy.' I tittered, eyeing him up and down, and contemplating whether I really should ask the question. 'Did you want to dance?'

Delighted, he took hold of my hand and pulled me up to the dancefloor. Convention wasn't something that suited either of us, so we gestured silly hand jives and exhibited daft boogie moves to the music neither of us liked. His dancing was coined with far more hilarity than mine though, thanks to his towering height. The bloke wasn't far off a city skyscraper. Nevertheless, any kind of movement at 6'5 wearing a Butlin's type get-up is guaranteed comedy gold.

From her position at the bar with Julian, Katrina clocked us, showcasing an excitable grin so wide it could've been cartoon. Trust her to put 2+2 together and come up with 3,056. Matt made me laugh, yes, and he was good-looking in a quirky type of way, yes. But, he wasn't my type. Or at least, I didn't think he was…

That was when I started to feel awkward. Something inside me was saying, '*you're so mean giving this guy false hope. If you don't like him in that way then why are you doing this?*'

I didn't know. Why was I doing this? Maybe this was just reality trying to tell me to stop dreaming about the blue-eyed boy I'd shrined in my heart for so long and remind me that, '*Simone, Ethan was a hot rock star. The way you felt about him was nothing more than a dopamine rush induced by thrill. It was all hormonal – pure fantasy. This guy, however, is 100% real. It may not be love at first sight, but that sentiment's all urban myth, anyway.'*

Arguing on my shoulders, the Devil and Angel tossed their points back and forth so hard and fast that I felt like my head was in a Wimbledon match. It was driving me crazy. I had to get out of the noise.

'I'm just going to nip to the ladies,' I'd mouthed to Matt, pointing towards the toilet sign to the left of us. 'I'll be back after.'

'Okay,' He'd loudly pronounced in return, giving me the thumbs up before continuing to bop gawkily to the sound of the *"hey, hey, hey"* in Robin Thicke's famous song playing in the background.

Trailing slowly behind me, Katrina meandered her way from her seat at the bar to follow me into the bathroom. Of course, I should've known better than to think the Spanish Inquisition could be avoided.

'Hey Sims,' she'd called to me. 'Wait up.'

I stopped to turn around and face her, rolling my eyes at the prospect of the upcoming interrogation.

'Kats, I know you mean well, but despite common belief, I am fully potty-trained.'

She laughed, gently clasping my shoulders and nudging me forward into the loos.

'Oh, c'mon, satisfy my curiosity and tell me about Stretch over there. As part of strict girl code, it is mandatory to spill the beans whilst I accompany you to the bathroom. That's the law and we must abide it.'

Tilting my head back, I grumbled. 'I'm getting far too old for this kind of stuff, Katrina.'

'Hush now. Don't make this difficult,' she'd said, softly commandeering me towards the door. 'Now c'mon, tell me *everything*.'

Staring at our reflections inside the loos whilst lipstick was reapplied and hair was ruffled, we exchanged conversation on the enigma that was my beanstalk companion. As expected, the probing was heavy. Every detail about Matt had to be divulged to her, and since I'd only met the guy half an hour ago, that was pretty limiting.

'Is that it? You don't even know his last name, but you've already discussed arse licking?'

A jolt from one of the cubicles sounded behind us, its occupant clacking against the toilet roll holder and coughing unobtrusively.

'No, that was what the Mozart song was about,' I'd corrected, critically staring at her green-eyed reflection. 'As if I'd invite sexual deviance into my life within the first thirty minutes of meeting somebody, come on.'

'Oh, I don't know,' she'd paused, sliding her peony gloss across her lips. 'They say the quiet ones are always the ones to look out for. I can only imagine what kind of dark horse you are, my lovely Simone.'

Her cheeky wink irked me. I was not a dark horse and for the last time, I did not fancy Matt.

'You know what, Kats. You're totally right. What gave it away – the latex body suit in my bedroom, the whip hanging by my door? Or, was it the bullet vibrating madly in my purse? Oh wait, no. It can't be any of those things because I'm not a bloody nymphomaniac.'

Pumping her gloss back in the tube, she threw it back in her bag and looked at me.

'Simone, I'm joking with you. You do know that, right?' Her eyes drew a picture of concern and I suddenly felt bad for my satirical comeback, making me wince into a state of ruefulness as she took hold of me and carried on.

'Look, I just want you to be happy. For ages you have sat moping about our flat like a lost soul. It makes me sad to see you like that. If a guy can make you smile as widely as Matt has done tonight, well, then maybe you should just go with it? After all this time alone, you deserve someone nice.'

Absorbedly, I'd looked at her, thinking about her words whilst reflecting on my recent state of mind. She had a point. Seldom did anyone make me laugh these days, and with all the stuff going on with my family, maybe it would be nice to have some positive release – someone new to hang out with and enjoy the company of? I didn't have to *be with* him romantically for that. Though, even if I did, would that be so bad? Evidently, he was no Ethan Brenner. But, did he have to be? Such fixation on a reality that could never be mine was weighing me down, and I'd already decided that I needed to let go of it. So, maybe this was my chance? I just needed to give him a chance, in order to give myself one.

'Okay,' I replied solemnly. 'Thank you, Kats.'

Still holding me, she smiled.

'You're welcome, sweets.'

As all girl best friends do after a heart-to-heart in a club bathroom, we hugged one another tightly and swayed excitedly, exuberant from the epiphany achieved through our chat.

'Now hop to it, missy. I want to see some grinding.'

119

Scowling comically, I replied, 'I love you, Kats, but that is never going to happen.'

'Hashtag dark horse…'

'And no more, *dark horse,* already. Jeez…'

'Okay, okay, *sorry.*'

So, that was it. The reality of my world today evolved from a chat in a club toilet. Not the most profound of beginnings, but life has a funny way of turning out sometimes. However, if I could give relationship advice to anyone, it would be to not make any rash decisions whilst tipsy in a public loo with your overzealous best friend. Because sometimes, your gut knows things you haven't yet consciously realised. For example: the fact that liking somebody and *liking* somebody are two very different things.

Perhaps I'd have been wise to listen to those rumbles back then. In some ways, I wish I had. Instead of having release from a problem, I was only about to add to the pile. With a new one in the shape of a spaghetti-guzzling, piano-playing, redcoat lookalike who loved nothing more than to convince me to watch endless episodes of Dr Who and that metal music was bad for me.

'I just worry,' he cooed, emerging into conversation 15,091 about how my frame of mind was being negatively impacted by rock music. 'I read that people who like metal are really angry. And you know what happens to angry people? They get depressed. Depression is anger turned inwards, after all. Oh, it just breaks my heart to think of you as sad, Simone.'

Hugging me like a boa constrictor binding its prey, he squeezed my withdrawn body and nuzzled me on the sofa; his thick, dark hair swishing softly against my neck.

In return, I patted him with my free arm bent underneath his clasp.

'I'm not depressed, I promise.' I reassured, awkwardly continuing to tap him like a mother consoling her woebegone child. 'Guitars are just cool. I've always liked the sound of them. But there are plenty of other things I like, too, you know.'

Emerging from his burrowed position on my neck, he slowly looked up at me, his brown eyes glistening from the apartment's overhead light.

'I know you do. You're a cool cat. And such a pretty kitty as well,' his fingers started to twiddle with my hair, achingly trying to romance me with his touch.

It was awful.

'Haha, well, you know me - free as a bird, curious as a cat, Simone,' I announced, retreating from my spot on the sofa to go and boil the kettle. 'Anyway, haven't you got to go to work soon?'

On the sofa, he flopped down; his long legs stretching out and dangling over the arm.

'Yeah, but I wish I could stay with you instead,' he whined, pouting at me upside down from his place on my couch.

'Me too,' I lied, walking back over and kneeling beside him. 'But we'll see each other tomorrow sometime.'

'Whoop, whoop.' Excitedly, he pushed his face up into mine and gave me a kiss Spiderman and Mary-Jane would be proud of. 'I'll call you tomorrow then.'

Still slightly startled from the kiss, I smiled. 'Yep…tomorrow.'

Leaping up, he made his way over to the front door, grabbing his zip-up sweatshirt from the counter and blowing me a kiss as he left. 'Bye beautiful. I can't wait to see you again.'

I crinkled my hand into a jerky wave farewell. 'Bye…you.'

With the door's bolting close, my hand fell, and my body sagged. There was no way I could keep this up anymore. Three months was long enough to work out whether I was feeling it or not, and I most certainly was not. Matt was a lovely guy, but he was just too much. Like a dribbling dog that kept dry-humping my leg, he was sweet, but I wanted him off. In my head, I'd already made my decision.

Sorry Matt, but I just can't do this any longer. Tomorrow, I'm breaking up with you.

All of a sudden, the door re-opened and Matt came flying back in, picking me up from my position on the floor and swinging me into another kiss.

'Man, you are just too good to leave,' he said, gazing longingly into my terrified eyes. 'I…' he paused, stumbling as he stared, '…I think I'm in love with you, Simone.'

My face dropped.

…Shit.

The Guilt-Trip

'You said what?' Katrina angrily spouted, nearly spilling the delivery box's contents on the hallway floor.

'I said...I loved him too.' I meekly responded, knowing I deserved every bit of back-lashing coming my way.

Shaking her head, she stared judiciously at my statuesque pose leaning against the doorframe and cuddling a tea cup. We both knew that I didn't want to be with Matt, so it was of no surprise that Katrina was judging me for my recent declaration.

'For God's sake, Simone. Talk about duplicity,' she cried, placing the box down in the stock room ready to be emptied onto the shelves, 'I may not be the biggest fan of the guy, but you can't go messing with his head like that. Plus, now how are you going to leave him? You've well and truly shot yourself in the foot now.'

'I know,' I whimpered, furrowing my brow and curling my lip. 'But how could I say anything else? *Oh, well thanks for pouring your heart and soul out to me, Matt. Only I don't feel the same and would rather stick pins in my eyes than experience another one of your sloppy, wet kisses.*'

'*Eww*, is he a washing machine, too?' She asked; a look of disgust smeared on her face.

'Yes, but that's beside the point,' I exclaimed, plopping my cup in the sink and quickly rinsing it out before I had to retreat to the shop floor. 'He's just so happy. It must be me. Everyone knows I'm a fusspot. I just figured that maybe if I said it back, then I'd feel the same way, y'know?'

'And did you?'

I hesitated. 'I didn't *not* feel it…'

Katrina's green eyes glowered at me. 'What does that even mean, Simone?'

'It means…' I paused again, also trying to work out what I meant, '…that maybe one day I'll grow to love him the way he loves me?'

'You're talking out of your arse, Simone, and you know it.'

Agitatedly massaging my temples, I knew she was right. Stupidly convincing myself otherwise was only going to delay the inevitable break up, and now I'd said the words, I'd ball and chained myself to a situation I didn't want. Tied to Mr Safe-Bet was not where I wanted to be. And yet, I was the one who put myself there. *Stupid, STUPID Simone.*

'Oh, Katrina. I'm a horrible person,' I moaned, hitting my head against the wall, 'what am I going to do?'

'Beats me.' She stated, nonchalantly picking up another box to empty in the stock room. 'But, my love, you'd better work out what you want one way or another, because this mess is bigger than just you now.'

Like everything else in my little world, I tried to work out how to deal with it. But just like the rest, I didn't know the answer.

Breaking someone's heart seemed like an unavoidable option, and I really didn't want to hurt anyone. This wasn't meant to happen. I wasn't meant to feel like this. But I did. And in the pit of my stomach, I knew it would be wrong to stay with him, for it churned at every guilt-ridden submission. Yet, accepting my lonely alternative seemed so uninviting. No one's imagination is wild enough to keep them company for life, so surely it was better to have a real, living, breathing, touchable, in-the-vicinity boyfriend than no one at all? Couldn't that be enough? Oh, how I hoped it could be.

***

With each month seemingly stitching itself to one another like a seasonal tapestry, summer came around in the blink of an eye. Our cold dark days soon turned warm and bright - so close to one another that I sometimes lost track of time completely. April began with a fierce snowfall that barricaded Brits inside their homes. Then, only a fortnight later, the worst heatwave in seventy years came to laud over the scenery, melting everyone and everything within its path. The only way I could keep up with the ever-changing weather was with Matt's trousers. Just like a traffic light, a red pair was worn over winter, green during spring, and now, with the emergence of summer, yellow was left to reign.

I stared at him as he exited my bathroom wearing these vibrant denim wonders and smiled. Somehow, the more time went by, the more I'd managed to appreciate his funny little ways - some of them, anyway.

'You look like a giant daisy,' I said as he walked around my bedroom, tousling his wet hair in a towel.

'You think?' he asked, looking down at his white t-shirt and yellow jeaned combo. 'Well, flowers make people happy, so maybe I'll brighten somebody's day with my look.'

I chortled. He was blatantly oblivious to the fact I'd just delivered him a back-handed compliment.

'Quite possibly,'

Hair now considerably shaggy, Matt looked back at me as I lay on the bed, tap, tap, tapping away at my laptop.

'What are you doing, anyway?' he asked, moseying over to take a peek. 'You're not talking to that Harry, are you?'

'No, I'm just checking on the sales of my book.' I answered, blankly gazing at the screen whilst trying to navigate my way around the labyrinth website. Technology was never my forte.

Talking to Harry wasn't something I'd do so conspicuously anymore. Unfortunately for me, Matt wasn't a big fan of his and felt particular umbrage whenever he caught me video-calling him over a cuppa. So now, any interaction had to be kept hush-hush. It was yet another thing that I had to sacrifice. But, as much as it was a problem, I'd convinced myself that since Harry and I lived so far apart, it wasn't necessarily the biggest issue. Plus, in spite of this insecurity, Matt was also very supportive, especially of my writing. And, at this moment in time, the book I'd finally felt confident enough to self-publish was my main priority.

'Oh?' he answered, flopping down next to me and noticeably jogging my bed. 'How's it doing?'

That was the sixty-four million dollar question.

'Honestly?' I pitched, working out a way to say, *'absolutely shite'* in the most diplomatic way possible. 'The three people who've read it so far *really* enjoyed it. Five stars all the way. Woohoo...'

Of course, when relaying that information, I forewent telling him about the review from ScienceGuy1879, whose opening line next to the lowly one star was, '*It was like trying to get an old banger started...*'

Prick. Like *you* could do a better job? Stick your nose back in a chemistry book where it belongs; you total *MC Square*.

Derision and girlish huff aside, though, the truth was, I was utterly distraught. Heart and soul, blood, sweat and tears, they were all poured into that manuscript, only to receive barely any recognition whatsoever (or worse, a scathing one). No, I didn't expect to suddenly become as big as Jojo Moyes or Marian Keyes overnight, but *damn it*, I wished I could have been so lucky. Investing so much time in that story gave me a purpose outside the shop walls. It made me feel bigger than just a customer assistant. As if, potentially, a dream could somehow be forged from my bedroom and create a life so much greater than this. But having less than ten sales, over half of which were most likely dutiful family members feeling obliged to show their support and one mardy little keyboard warrior, didn't fill me with the greatest of hopes.

'Give it time, beautiful,' Matt said, softly stroking my shoulders, 'it's still early days yet.'

'Yep,' I nodded, internally wallowing in self-pity, 'indeed it is.'

Kissing my cheek, Matt upped and left my room to dry his hair, leaving me with nothing more than my distracted thoughts for company. Annoyance ever-growing, I slammed down the laptop's lid and buried my head in-between my folded arms. Life seemed to be changing for everybody else except me. Whilst things on the surface did seem different; ultimately, in my heart, everything still felt the same. I was getting nowhere fast. My dreams crashed and burned before the race had even started, and trying to convince myself I was happy with things moving in alternative directions to my wants and desires only frustrated me further. For example: Matt, my lovely - but *oh so vanilla* - boyfriend.

Nothing he did was wrong. Yet, it just wasn't right, either. As talented a soul as he was, his apathy towards life tore me up inside. He wasted his gifts because he'd rather watch TV than try and get a real job outside playing the piano at local bars. Any enthusiasm he had left was displayed in his penchant for outrageous clothes or silly YouTube videos. A mass of guilt would consume me whenever I thought how odd that approach to life was, especially when it was hardly a sin to be a fan of something. But I couldn't stop the agitation for it from growing. And then there was his judgemental attitude to things that made me happy.

Whether it was about my love for horror movies or heavy metal, there was no escaping his furrowed brow. In fact, I became so paranoid about triggering waterworks that I stopped listening to my favourite music altogether. Instead, I indulged in Bach and Chopin, hoping that if I listened to Fantasie Impromptu enough times then it would eventually override my desire for the fierce plucking of an electric string. It didn't, FYI. Like a sexually frustrated teenager confined to a life of abstinence, I only wanted it more. Vexation grew in every element of my core, and I was struggling to stop the explosion from bubbling over. Understood was something I never felt. And yet, there I was, nearly six months into a relationship I kept complaining under my breath about.

So as much as a part of me was growing to appreciate him over time, the other part of me was dwindling away as a sacrifice. The phrase, '*half a dozen of one and six of the other,*' sprung to mind.

On the one hand, Matt was incredible. He was supportive, kind, funny, smart and reliable – all the things a girl looks for in a boyfriend. On the other, though, he was obtuse, insubordinate, lazy, judgemental and about as sexy as a novelty Christmas jumper. If this was love, then I found it unfathomable. Love isn't half-perfect. To say that is paradoxical. Perfect is complete, whole is unabridged, everything is all. If you subtract from that, then it is no longer perfect. Nor is it half-perfect. It is imperfect - broken, nothing. By not admitting the full truth to him, I was lying. Like there is no such thing as half-perfect, there are no such things as half-truths, either.

It was possible, that seeing Katrina and Julian plodding on so happily together worked to stir up envy inside me. Unlike me and Matt, they fit together perfectly. They were equally eccentric, lively and fun, always eager to try new things and explore them together. Their support for one another taught them new things about themselves, and they enjoyed growing as individuals as well as a couple.

Recently, I'd watched them at the apartment, looking up lightweight sneakers online and searching for exercise regimes to prepare themselves for the upcoming marathon. They were so intensely focused and excited; it was as if a glorious firefly glow shone around them.

Together, they were the epitome of an ideal couple. If you could've hash-tagged their relationship, it would've been '#goals'.

Closer to home, Seb wasn't so far off this idyllic notion either. With him and Terrific-Tariq still going strong after nearly a year, there was a lot to be admired. Not one to settle down lightly, Seb took their uniting very seriously and dedicated his whole heart to their connection. Even I didn't think they'd last as long as they had, and again, unlike me and Matt, their rapport showed no signs of wearing.

Talking of a love that never grows old, my Dad reignited his own flame in the form of petrol-head lust. From what I could tell, once men who've been tied down for a long time get the taste of freedom, they appear to indulge in everything they'd been suppressed to engage with during their previous relationship. This, in my Dad's case, came in the shape of a sweet little black MX-5, with a personalised plate to match. Mayzie (that was what he'd decided to call the road-skimming cabriolet) was his pride and joy, always arriving super buffed and polished wherever they went together. Even on the extensive road trips, she seemed to stay clean. Well, the pictures online made it look that way. Mayzie gleamed as brightly as Dad's triumphant grin whenever he posed next to her. Oh, he'd found love alright. I should've guessed it'd be mechanical.

As for Mum, she'd travelled a more physical movement, which I'm half glad and half not-so-glad about. Andrew, her colleague at the bank, finally reduced her to submission, and they ended up going on a date. As strange as it was for her to finally jump back on the horse, per se, by the sounds of things, she was really enjoying it. Apparently, Andrew was *"splendid company"* and was far more *"in touch with his emotions"* than Dad ever was. To be fair, as much as I thought that ginger-headed, skinny-as-a-rake, Andrew was a bit of a dickhead, if Mum liked him, then I guess I did, too.

However, upon reflection of all the happiness floating about in everybody's lives, jealousy began to riddle me like a parasite, ugly and only burrowing deeper. I knew I shouldn't feel this way, but I couldn't help it. Whether it be in man or machine, everyone else around me seemed to be complete; adorning smiles and planning out perfect futures with their prospective partners. Yet, no matter how hard I tried to feel the same, it just wasn't there. Don't get me wrong, I liked Matt, and in my own way, I loved him, too. But, more like the way a child loves a blanket – finding comfort in the threadbare cotton you've known so long. And it pains me to say it, but, that love plateaued a long time ago.

I could hear the hairdryer switch off and *kerplunk* to the floor, in the next room. The sound jumped my bones to my skin. I then heard the squishy sound of him slipping on the infamous fish flops his mum had bought him as a joke for Christmas. For some reason, he was infatuated with the ugly green trout slippers, and he took every opportunity to wear them whenever he could, which, of course, included around my flat. Just the mere sound of them slapping against the floorboards made me twitch.

All of a sudden, I felt angry. Angry at everything and everyone in my life - my pointless novel, my beige love-life, my best friend's and family's contentment, and my fear of a future doomed to mediocrity. These thoughts flooded my mind and washed away any sense of peace.

Where was the destiny I longed for? Was this really it? I'd put so much hard work into creating a positive life, and yet, all I felt was overwhelmingly bummed out.

My blood boiled with each clunking step Matt took around the apartment. If there was ever a tipping point, that was mine.

Leaping off the bed, I thudded towards my wonky wardrobe and pulled out a jacket. I couldn't breathe. I needed to get out.

'Just going to get some milk,' I fibbed in a pitch three octaves higher than my natural voice, speeding out of my room and staring past Matt in the lounge, my concentration focused on the exit door, 'won't be long.'

Out of my peripheral vision, I saw his raised finger, as if to say, '*hold up, I'll come with you,*' but I didn't give him a chance to speak. By the time I'd finished my sentence, I'd already shut the door.

***

From one angle, it was a hauntingly dark blanket of ink, buildings casting charcoal grey shadows on the river. Yet, another, and it would shift to rippling cobalt. But by the time I'd found my space on the bench, warmly illuminated by the sun's rays, bejewelled turquoise waters were all that reflected back at me. Zephyr fingers gently swept my hair from my face. Surrounding voices blended with the breeze's soft whisper. Shizukesa: that's what they call tranquillity in Japanese. In that moment, I guessed this must be how it felt to be at peace with oneself - no one and nothing else mattering, just me and my heartbeat echoing in the wind.

Being by the water always calmed me. If anything was ever on my mind, I would head straight to the nearest natural pool. There was something about the stillness of it that provided me with clarity - a sense of serenity bringing a new way to see the world. Somehow, even with all of its beauty charging my beating heart to a racing pound, I could still realise everything I needed to finally understand.

Walking past my view, pulling to a stop just in front of the Thames, was a Mum and son. Hand in hand, together they stared at the vast watery space dividing the path they stood on and London's notorious Tower. For some reason, the view of them took me away from my state of reverie, and instead, I homed in on their conversation, unknowingly keen to hear what they had to say.

'Did you know, Edward, give or take several hundred years or so, a Polar bear used to swim in this very river?' the mother intoned, kindly smiling down at her little blonde-haired boy.

Really?' he enthused, looking up at her excitedly.

'Why, yes,' she continued, brushing her hand on the back of his head, 'animals used to come in abundance to the Tower of London in olden times. They were considered royal gifts for the Monarchy. No day would go without the sounds of elephants and monkeys, all displaying their unique tunes for everyone to hear.'

'Wow,' he expressed, eyes wide like saucers, 'that's so cool.'

It was cool. And it made me think.

There's a life bigger than me out there - a life with a past, a present and a future. As far as the fabric of time goes, my life is a mere pinprick in its colourful patchwork. And, realistically, my frustrated visions were rather insignificant. Yet, somehow, consumed by all of my selfish woes, I'd lost sight of that. The person I used to be would never have stooped to such desperate lows – running out of her apartment without so much as a goodbye, envying her family and friends' happiness, and feeling belligerent towards a project that was never intended to be anything more than just for pleasure. What happened to me? Somewhere along the lines, I'd become distracted and heartless.

'...you must take care of ones you hold dear, because you may not get second chance.'

Madame Lilith's fateful words entered my mind as quickly as the passers-by came and went. Precious time was being lost, and I was the one wasting it, all for the sake of keeping up appearances.

How foolish I was. To have let things get this far already was too high a price to pay. But, not everything was too late for me. There was still one way to contrite the parts of my identity I'd forsaken to tunnel-vision, and I had just the idea.

The Old Life

'Are you sure you've got everything?' Mum echoed to me from the fuzzy Facetime image on my phone screen.

'Yes, yes. You don't need to worry, Mum,' I glibly replied, tilting my head. 'I have looked after myself for a good while now.'

'She's even potty-trained, Fiona, don't you know?' Katrina interjected from the kitchenette, grinning at our typical mother-daughter chat.

'Oi!' I said, turning back to face my smirking best friend as she washed her trainers over the sink. 'Cheeky woman.'

My mum laughed melodically from the screen. 'Okay, just as long as you're all set. I'm looking forward to having you over, sweetheart. Andrew's excited to finally meet you properly, too.'

'Oh goodie, Andrew…' I muttered under my breath.

'What was that?' Mum asked, tapping the phone as if somehow that would fix it. 'The connection on this thing is dreadful.'

'I said I'm looking forward to seeing you as well,' I monotonously replied, in the same way an idiot Brit does to a foreigner who speaks broken English. 'Anyway, I best go, Mum. I'll see you tomorrow.'

'Okay darling. All my love.'

'Ciao, Fiona,' Katrina sang in the background.

Bing-bong dial tone finished, and Mum's face back to a static circle; I felt it now safe to throw a sofa cushion at Katrina.

'Hey,' she cried, dropping soapy suds mid-block, 'what was that for?'

'Just because,' I blithely stated, grinning at her like a Cheshire Cat. Not often was I like this, but today was a good day, and my upbeat mood had taken a turn for the Devilish. Truth be told though, I also rather enjoyed being a wind-up merchant sometimes.

After my recent epiphany, my mind had transcended to a more positive place. I was making better decisions and feeling happier for letting go of inconsequential niggles that previously ate away at me. Surprisingly though, this was how said release manifested itself – by becoming a twenty-first century Dennis the Menace and using my best friend as a slingshot target for my mischievous conduct.

'Your shoes smell like poo,' I deadpanned, slowly blinking at her from the sofa as if the trainers' fumes were inducing me into a state of comatose.

'You smell like poo!'

Soapy suds splattered their way onto my head, Katrina's culprit fingers aiding their glide. Out of everyone I knew she was the only one I could do this sort of thing with. She was just so easy going. We both knew each other's humour, and it made everything that was ordinary into something so much more. I loved that about our friendship – the way we could go from shallow to deep in the blink of an eye and it be understood. We didn't have to be mirror images to be the same inside. That's how I knew we'd be friends for life.

Laughing, she chucked her shoes down in the sink. 'I give up with these. They'll just have to do.'

She cursorily dried off her hands and trundled over towards the sofa, plonking herself down next to me, jiggling the cushions in her abrupt landing. I looked at her, giggling as she shut her eyes and lolloped her legs on the coffee table.

'I don't know why you're so anal about them, anyway.' I remarked, 'they're just trainers. They're meant to get dirty. Plus, no matter how shiny you make them, it won't change the fact that you've virtually eroded half of the heel away.'

One eye open, she looked at me. 'Meh,' was all she retorted before closing her eyes once again.

'Weirdo,' I said, as I ejected myself and patted her on her propped up legs' 'Cuppa?' I asked. Looking back, I saw her nod, and I went over to boil the kettle.

If anyone had watched our daily lives – working together, living together, drinking tea, and watching movies together – they'd think of us like an old married couple, I'm sure. Maybe that's why I didn't want that kind of lifestyle replicated with a man? I already had all of those things in my best friend. If anything, I think I'd have rather been in a relationship with Katrina over Matt. Excusing the daily hair extension removal from the bathroom plughole and the fact that she was female, she was perfect.

Talking of Matt, he didn't take my departure plan to Nottingham for the week as well as Katrina had. Tears seeped down his face like raindrops sliding down a window. He couldn't bear the thought of me being away for even one second. It was exasperating. Even through my newly enlightened viewpoint, there was simply no way on this earth I'd ever be able to see past being suffocated. For someone so smart and witty, it surprised me how unashamedly clingy he could be. Insecurity wasn't an attractive quality in anybody – especially in your significant other – but I did my best to make him feel better about it.

'It's only for a week,' I reassured, tossing my fingers through his thick brown hair, 'I'll be back before you know it.'

He'd nodded back, a sorrowful protruding lip making its awkward presence known. I felt like his mother. It was awful. Sometimes, he could be so exciting and fun, and it would make me feel like I could remain somewhat content in our little unit. But then, there were times like these, where I think he was trying to be cute, but all it did was turn my stomach. His pitiful wrinkled brow didn't change my mind either. Sympathy wasn't an emotion easily drawn from me, but especially not for such a sorry display as that.

And yet, as soon as I'd brought back two cups of strong black tea to the apartment table, shuffling myself back onto the sofa, words that escaped Katrina's lips were the first to make me think twice.

'I hope you've stacked my cup with sugar, Sims,' she began, 'God knows I need it after yesterday's fainting episode.'

Fainting episode?

I quavered, just for a second, before pulling myself together and facing her with eyes aghast. 'What? Did you just say that you *fainted* yesterday?'

Nonchalantly, she reached for her cup, as if her statement was nothing more than a jovial quip. 'Yeah, crazy huh?' she replied, blowing down on her cup, 'when they say everything goes black, they're not lying.'

She slurped her tea, absolutely oblivious to the horror that filled my stare – how could she not realise this was serious? Fainting isn't an everyday occurrence. And yet, in spite of the fears that etched inside me, she seemed utterly blank about the entire thing.

'Julian said I need to keep my sugars up, that's all. I guess with all the running we're doing; I kind of forgot that I needed more energy. Just like that *Flush* guy you watch on TV.'

'*The Flash*,' I corrected, unthinkingly, still distracted by the cornucopia of other thoughts spinning my head.

'Are you sure it's just the sugars? Tell me you at least spoke to a doctor about it, Kats?'

'A doctor,' she scoffed, placing the mug on her lap, 'Sims, you and I both know that's a pointless venture. They'd only tell me the same thing and send me with my marching orders. No, I don't need a professional opinion to tell me I need to invest in some electrolyte drinks and more snack bars.'

A part of me wanted to be as relaxed about it as she was. I only wished I could be.

Back in school, I saw someone faint during choir. It came so suddenly. One minute, we were all singing '*All Things Bright and Beautiful*', and the next, the chorus of voices fell singular as the group turned around to see a white-faced girl who'd fallen like a domino to the floor. It scared me. Sure enough, she came to relatively swiftly, but as soon as that happened, she was taken to the nurse's room. We never saw her in the choir again after that.

'Maybe I should stay to keep an eye on you?' I asked, trying to keep my voice stable.

'What? No.' Katrina gasped, sitting up and placing her cup down so she could reach for my hand. 'Don't be daft, Simone. I'm fine. It's lovely that you care and all, but honestly, I'm okay. You don't need to be so worried. Especially if it leaves you with two unsightly lines between your eyebrows – I'd hate to be the reason for the formation of a number eleven on your pretty face.'

Recent memories had a tendency to zip into my mind like train-hoppers in rush-hour - in and out quicker than you could control - and the one that entered was one I wish I'd forgotten. At the time of hearing the story about Katrina's Mum having a heart attack, it served a purpose to make me realise the importance of letting go of silly gripes. But this time, it only riddled me with terror.

Is it relevant? Can a family history of sudden heart attacks be linked to fainting?

In all honesty, I didn't know for sure, and I didn't want to remind her of something so painful if it was unnecessary to. My gut churned at the thought of saying nothing, though. As if it was telling me to voice my worries anyway. But I couldn't. Not only for the fact that it was sensitive and my knowledge on the subject was limited, but because as soon as the words slipped out, then it'd be a reality we'd have to face. You can't take them back once they're out. In my mind, I believed it wouldn't be fair of me to do that. Plus, Katrina wasn't concerned and reassured me that Julian was looking after her. He was a bit of a fitness freak anyway and knew all about the right measurements for necessary nutrients and such. Thus, I felt like she was in safe hands. So, as much as there was a merciless thumping inside of me, pushing me to say something, I submitted myself to dutiful silence.

'Come on,' she said, tapping the sofa, 'let's watch a movie. I hear that *When We First Met* is really good. Plus, it's got Robbie Amell in it - my favourite. Just don't tell Julian, will you? His green-eyed monster isn't one I've learned to tame yet.'

'Sounds good,' I said, nodding my head in automatic agreement.

To this day, I still don't remember much of the film. It was more like a hum playing in the background to the thoughts echoing in my head. Round and round, they'd spin, dizzying me to a weary-eyed statue, staring vacantly at the screen.

***

The next morning, I awoke bright and early to an empty apartment. Traffic was barely sounding and Katrina had already hit the pavement. Evidently, the recent blackout she'd experienced hadn't fazed her one bit. Knowing this further quelled my concerns. She was obviously right - she just needed to eat more. And a tub of protein powder on the kitchen worktop gave away that she'd at least heeded the advice on the matter.

I smiled, examining the giant pot claiming its strawberry-flavoured contents were the *'perfect way to start your day!'* Katrina was such a marketer's dream.

Out of the corner of my eye, I noticed a little note beside the kettle. Picking it up, I saw it was from Katrina, wishing me a safe journey and to let her know when I'd arrived in Nott's. I loved that she stuck to old school note-writing. Too much time is wasted leaving people messages online, using the same blue box with its non-descript font. It was nice to see her handwriting – elegantly cursive with her favoured loop at the bottom of the letters Y and G. Plus, something about it felt extra personal. Even though the message itself was a standard one, I cherished it like a diamond, tucking it inside my phone's fabric cover for safe-keeping. That way, as soon as I arrived at Mum's, texting her would be the first thing I'd do.

***

On the train, my iPod was being a prick. It kept playing songs that reminded me of a certain somebody I thought I'd long erased from my memory. Emotions resurfaced that wound me up inside. They were so good it hurt. To think of them only filled me with a weird agitation. And now, annoyingly so, every time I heard the Joker's Ashes music, all I could do was think of him – Ethan bloody Brenner. This is exactly why I'd taken down the picture on my corkboard and why I'd shoved it and all of their CDs and merchandise into the back of my wardrobe – so that I could forget it ever happened and finally move on from the futile pull that plagued me. Only, I'd neglected to remember the sweepstake chance of my iPod playing them non-stop whilst shuffling through over ten-thousand songs.

Ultimately giving up on being entertained by music, I turned off the wretched device and chose to stare out of the window of the train instead, witnessing the passing scenery change from grey concrete to lush-green countryside. It was beautiful to see again. For so long, my views had been asphalt – not just in the physical, but in spirit, too. Seeing the colours made me happy. There's something magical about nature that does that to a person. One look at the vibrant landscapes, one smell of the fresh air and one gust of wind softly brushing your skin, and it's as though you've been set free. When I was in the city, the closest I could ever get to replicating that feeling was when I was beside the water. But nothing quite compared to the real deal. Being at one with nature truly was the richest experience money couldn't buy.

For the rest of the journey, I slept. Witnessing the pretty views sent me to a place of calm slumber and the warmth of the summer sun that irradiated the reel of fields heated the train carriage comfortably. Clutching my bag, I rested, dreaming of the week ahead. Peace was what I hoped for, the reality, however, would soon burst my bubble.

**

'Simone, sweetheart,' Mum welcomed me with open arms at the railway station, 'welcome home.'

I dropped my bags on the ground and reached out to her, embracing her tiny frame in a grateful hug.

'Mum,' I said, burying my head into her soft brown curls, 'so good to see you again.'

People probably think that Nottingham smells like berries and woodland, but contrary to common belief, Robin Hood County actually smells more like cider and a good night out. In the heart of the city, you couldn't escape the liveliness. The buzz of trams and cars takes you far away from the illusions of fresh forest fruits and historical bows and arrows, with the only things shooting past by contrast being the traffic and the flurry of students making their way to the shops.

'Gosh, it's so busy here,' Mum stated, looking around at the large clusters of people bustling past. 'Let's go home. I've parked the car on a double yellow around the corner. Granddad Jack's disabled pass comes in great handy sometimes.'

My eyes widened at the thought of my mum – a law-abiding citizen – so carelessly breaking the rules.

'Mum, you can't do that,' I cried, 'what if you get caught?'

'Nonsense,' she retorted, shaking her head, 'I've only been here five minutes. Now, come on. Any more dawdling or we just might.'

Now in a state of shock, I swiftly picked up my belongings by my feet and started making my way out of the classically constructed station towards the car. Mum, who helped me by taking the smallest of my bags, lead the way.

It had been so long since I'd been in a car. Life in the city rendered driving somewhat of a nightmare. So, it was rather pleasant to be able to chuck my bags in the boot of a spacious coupe and strap myself into a luxurious leather seat. Albeit the heat it attracted from the summer sun wasn't the nicest feeling on my exposed legs.

'All belted up?' Mum asked me, as if I was a two-year-old in a booster chair.

'Yep,' I replied, smiling at her and grabbing the blue badge off the top of the dashboard, 'best put this back before we go, though.

'Oh yes,' she flustered, ushering me to put it out of sight, 'put it in the side of my handbag, would you?'

I did as she asked, and once all was back in its rightful spot, we made our way to the place I once called home.

***

As we pulled into the long driveway, I heard the familiar yapping of Lizzie, who sat waiting patiently behind our white-framed lounge window. For a little cocker spaniel, she didn't half have a pair of lungs on her.

'Lizzie,' I called as I got out of the car and walked towards her at the window, her long maroon ears flapping in excitement with every bounding jump she made on the back of the sofa. 'I've missed you, girly.'

'She's missed you, too,' said Mum, who'd opened the boot and begun to take out my belongings. 'You can't imagine the amount of furniture I've had to sticky-roller in your room after I'd told her you'd be coming home.'

Home.

To Mum, this would always be my true home - the big Brunswick-styled brickwork house that towered in front of me. With its hanging pot plants and cosy encasement between rows of pine trees, many people would be pleased to call it their home. I, however, felt uncertain of this. So much of it was something I remembered. Memories of a life gone by playing like a film in my mind. But that's all I felt when I looked at it. As if, although I knew it so well, it was no longer mine.

Suddenly, I felt a tinge of sadness. It was like meeting up with an old friend, only to realise you no longer had anything in common. That the friendship you developed was strung up by yesterdays, and that what sat in front of you now was something you couldn't recognise.

I sighed, trying to push the feeling to one side - convincing myself this was purely because I was overwhelmed and that I'd feel better once I'd settled down inside.

'Come on then, Simone, darling,' Mum said, now standing next to me, 'you can't feel wet noses through a window. Let's get your bits in the house and have a nice drink. It's too hot to be standing outside all day.'

Silently, I nodded and smiled, patting the window with one last yearning finger before getting the rest of my bags from the car to take upstairs.

**

My room was just how I'd left it - completely absent of personality. Like every other inch of the house, the design of my room was firmly controlled by my mother. Her inflexible nature and adoration for the ornate meant that my expressive love of rock music and manga were kept to an absolute minimum. Most of the things that were indicative of my personality were shielded by cupboard doors or confined to a lowly drawer, only good enough to collect dust. Mum was meticulous, though - she'd never let it get dirty, even if I wasn't there to use it. The house was a showroom house, and it would remain that way for as long as my Mum had working arms and legs. Up at six religiously every morning, she would do all the household chores before she went to work so that everything looked tip-top all the time. Personally, I never saw the point in that - all of that hard work and no one to appreciate it except the dog. For example, in my room in London, I would only ever make the bed if anyone was going to see it. Any other day and it would be left crumpled enough to make Tracey Emin proud. Call it what you will, as welcoming as my old room was - with all its potpourri bowls and scattered sconces - I still felt as out of place as I ever did.

'Isn't it nice and cosy?' Mum sounded, entering my room with a warm cup of tea. 'I bought some bits from Next to make it pretty for you. Do you like it?'

'Yeah,' I said, taking the cup from her before it scolded her little pink fingers, 'it's lovely. Thank you, Mum. And, cheers for the tea. How'd you guess?'

Lizzie's wagging tail pounded against the door as she walked in beside Mum's feet, making her way over to jump on my perfectly tidied bed.

'You're my daughter, Simone, and if I know my daughter, I know how much she loves her tea.'

She was half-right, I do love my tea, but looking at the white-washed walls of the room I stood in, monochrome patterns mirroring each other like synchronised swimmers on each panel, I also realised how little she knew me at all.

Never one to judge, Mum knew of the quirks that set me apart from other females my age. When most girls went to wild parties and got trashed, I had my head in a book or my ears covered by headphones instead. I never was one to follow the crowd. But still, even with that knowledge, Mum suppressed what wild side I did

147

possess. When she and Dad were together, all they ever wanted was for me to settle down, gushing about how lovely it would be to bring back home a nice boy. Nothing like Jake, as I've said before, they weren't fans. Undoubtedly, this was because he was not only a knob but also because he was slightly rebellious-looking. That was my type, though – a bit of a bad boy. However, since then, I'd grown up a bit. Even with my heels dug into the ground like an ostrich burying its head in the sand, I had wizened to the notion of a more sensible relationship, like with Matt. He was the absolute epitome of what she'd wanted for me - perfectly refined and coordinated, just like this house. Oh, how happy she was to hear I'd found myself someone nice for once. If only I could share such emotion for my own predicament.

Thinking of Matt, I quickly decided to check my phone again after connecting to our Wi-Fi. He'd left me a few messages - some private, some public. I sighed, utterly vehement with embarrassment as I saw the sickly post he'd left on my Facebook wall.

'Wishing my girl an amazing trip up in Nottingham! Have a lovely time, beautiful xXx'

Urgh. How cringe-worthy.

As I ruffled Lizzie's floppy ears between my fingers, that disparaging thought crossed my mind, and a surge of guilt passed through me as I chucked my phone back in my bag. Feeling this way wasn't right. No matter my change of heart, I couldn't ignore it. But whilst I was away, that was exactly what I'd planned to do.

'I do love my tea,' I eventually replied to Mum, who still hovered by my bedroom door, 'I shall enjoy sipping it whilst I unpack. I won't be long.'

'Okay, sweetheart,' she said, backing herself slowly out into the hallway, 'I'll see you downstairs in a bit.'

***

When I came downstairs a bit later on, I was greeted by a room that sounded more like an airport than a lounge – what with all the fans oscillating round like Daleks – and my Mum, who'd told me she'd seen the post. Her comment was that she thought it was incredibly sweet, and that she wished Dad had been more like that with her. Maybe, most women liked slush? I guessed it made them feel appreciated. However, I, for one, found it to be nothing more than one finger away from vomit-inducing. To me, it just wasn't cool.

Wrapped in my fluffy dressing gown, I lay down on the big curved sofa and made myself comfy, Mum's eyes pressing on me judgingly.

'I hope you're going to get a bit more dressed up later,' she remarked, propping her glasses down onto the magazine she'd placed on our shiny coffee-table. I chortled internally when the nearby fan turned just in time to blow her curly hair as she leaned over. Her corkscrew locks gave away the wind's direction in such an amusing way.

Once she'd sat back in place, the light sneaking in from the window behind her scratched my weary eyes, causing me to squint as I replied, 'Why? What's going on later?'

Mum rolled her eyes as if I'd just asked a totally idiotic question.

'Andrew and your Grandparents' are coming over for dinner,' she declared, 'I thought I'd already told you?'

Alerted upright, I gawked at her with surprise.

'What? No. Mum, I thought it was tomorrow?' My eyes pleaded with her to move the date. 'I feel so dead from travelling. Can't we postpone?'

She shuffled, shaking her head at me. 'No, honey. I've already sorted out the food. Besides, Andrew is so keen to meet you. It'll be nice for us all to be together.'

Nice - a word I oh so detested.

'Fine,' I said - my imploring tone now wholly sequestered, 'then I best start now.'

Grumbling, I traipsed my way back upstairs to begin the extensive process of refreshing my tired face with black eyeliner flicks and powder. Looking presentable was no quick fix. And as I hobbled around my bedroom, rooting through my makeup bag, I could only imagine what thrills awaited me in a few hours' time.

The Awkward Dinner

Flat. That's what Andrew was - nice as pie but dull as dishwater. Sure, he'd done some interesting stuff in his life, like when he'd discussed his Kibbutz journey, I was beginning to feel interested in the man. But as soon as he played it down and said he'd spent the majority of the time washing up and that he *'didn't mind it'*, I began to feel hopeless. The man embodied everything potentially remarkable except for the fact that he, as a person, was devastatingly staid.

To be honest, as I sat there agitatedly rocking in my white dining chair, trying to show willing by eating a tasteless potato latke he'd cooked, I really couldn't for the life of me figure out what it was my Mum saw in Andrew. From his flame-red hair to his thick, black-rimmed glasses, he was seriously unexceptional – inside and out. It shouldn't have, but it kind of irked me. I wondered if Mum was rebounding and just didn't realise it yet. Dad may have been a cheating bastard with an addiction to cars and weird socks, but damn it, at least he was fun. If he were here, he'd put on some Led Zeppelin to break the tension in the air and inject some life back into this pitifully quiet room. Saying that, that was one of the things Mum didn't like about him. His vivacity could be too much for her sometimes. Maybe this is why she was with someone who was the polar opposite? Even so, I hated it. A few guitars to headbang to were in so much need right now. The silence was deafening.

'*Out of ten?*' Andrew's monotonous tone took an inflective turn. He was curious about something. I should've known it'd be to rate his comparably bland cooking.

'Err, a seven?' I replied, adding an extra seven generous digits to the truth, hoping he'd crack a smile. But instead, his face crumpled like a cloth.

'Ohh...' was all he said.

You're lucky I didn't tell you the truth, Andrew. Your latke was as flat and as flavourless as you - nil points.

Seated opposite from me were my Grandparents, who mirrored my evasion of the charred potato pancake. Granny Dawn placed her knife and fork down to the side of her plate and began to pour Granddad Jack and herself more wine before deciding to re-enact the Spanish Inquisition.

'So, Simone,' she began, whilst carefully glugging out the burgundy liquid, 'are you still enjoying living in London?'

Usually a devout hater for such conversation, for the first time in history, I revelled in a discussion that would soon potentially lead to a subject regarding my social pitfalls. Anything was better than force-feeding myself any more of that vile dinner.

'Yeah, London is fantastic,' I said enthusiastically, 'work is good, my friends are amazing, and there's always a good gig on when you're bored. Seldom does that happen, though. The city's too lively for anyone to ever get bored.'

Granddad Jack remained as mute as ever. It's not that he couldn't speak. It's that - unless he had a strong opinion on something - he'd leave most of the talking to Granny Dawn. After all, she was the matriarchal figure of the family. She always knew best - *supposedly*. So, in this instance, he wisely chose to let her take the lead.

'Oh,' she dejectedly uttered, swirling her drink around the glass, 'I would have thought you'd have grown out of this so-called, '*gig*' business by now, dear.'

If anyone could call a spade a spade, it was Grandma. Unlike Mum, who may not have understood my quirkiness but accepted it nevertheless, Granny was not the same. She grew up in a Victorian-era which placed heavy emphasis on etiquette and elegance. To my Gran, fingerless gloves and screaming vocalists were a far cry from anything ladylike. In fact, they were probably closer associated with the works of the Devil. So in her eyes, the thought of me engaging in such *heathen* activities rendered her utterly confounded.

'One does not simply *grow out* of gigs, Grandma,' I asserted, using my best Boromir impression, still trying to remain colloquially upbeat, 'they're great fun. Plus, I see plenty of old rockers there, too. It's not exclusively reserved for the young and the reckless, y'know.'

Tutting, she began to tackle eating her food again as a means of distraction, only to remember it was revolting.

'I don't think I'll ever understand it,' she continued, a look of contempt strewn across her face, 'people breaking their necks to all that noise is such a strange practice. And don't get me started on their tattoos and piercings. Ghastly things. You're such a pretty girl, Simone. I hope that this fascination with loud music and concerts doesn't take you to ruin yourself like those louts. It's bad enough that you pierced the top of your ear and coloured your hair to match the nebula. Don't you agree, Jack?'

Exercising zero patience in waiting for a natural response, she abruptly nudged Granddad in the ribs, indicating the cue to blindly concur with her statement.

'Eh?' he uttered, a bit of tasteless potato *flatke* falling onto his lap as he did so.

'Oh, for goodness sake,' she agitatedly sputtered, 'Wake up, England.'

The table fell quiet. An awkward silence held each guest's mouth tightly shut, bar my Gran and me, who continued to shoot verbal ammo in defence of our cause.

'Bad?' I huffily sputtered, rising in my chair, 'well, I quite like it, actually. And, I also don't think that there's anything wrong with tattoos, piercings or heavy music, either. In fact, some of the most creative and intelligent people are the ones behind such *'noise'*, as you call it. But if you're too narrow-minded to appreciate diversity in culture, then more fool you.'

Her eyes speared me. Absolutely no one ever defied my Gran's opinion. However, I did not take kindly to being told that my identity was flawed by anyone. Family or otherwise, they'd get a piece of my mind.

Andrew, who'd been solidly captivated by our performance for the last two minutes, suddenly began to make noises of discomfort. He raised his hand and pulled in our attention with his floating fingers.

'If I may say,' he calmly interjected, attempting to diffuse the friction, 'I think you both have valid points.'

I rolled my eyes. This guy was such a wet fart.

'Yes,' my Mum instantaneously agreed, 'all's fair in love and war. Now,' she rapped the table. 'Who wants dessert?'

Granddad Jack was the only one who smiled at the suggestion of pudding. Everyone else only wore an expression of petulance or fret. But Mum, who'd blatantly had enough of drama over the years, decidedly began to gather up everyone's unfinished plates and shoo the unease out of the room in unison.

'You can help me with the trifle, Simone,' she commanded, jerking her head in the direction of the kitchen.

'Whatever,' I replied, reverting to a state of teenage angst as I crumpled up my napkin and tossed it over my barely-touched plate of food.

Silence filled the room again as we ejected ourselves from our seats. Only sounds of lip-dabbing and irritated wine-swirling filled the air.

'Mmm, *Pooh-ding*,' was the last thing I heard, as I made my exit. Without fail, Granddad Jack's timing was always hilariously perfect. Mum executed a demonstrative stillness whilst I chuckled to myself. Of course, she was trying to hold back the urge to reprimand me for standing my ground. But she was caught between a rock and a hard place. I was only staying for a week, so what would be the point in starting an argument when all I'd do is leave? I wasn't exactly a child anymore, and I could be rather obstinate at times, and Mum knew that. So, rather than sending me to the naughty step like she used to when I was younger, she compromised by wearing a twitchy smile and using an inflected pitch, hoping it'd aid her tongue-biting.

'There,' she began as she passed me plate one with the garish yellow and red concoction dribbling all over it, 'isn't that a nice looking trifle? A little sweet treat never went amiss at a dinner party.'

I stared with scrutiny as the splodged offerings kept on coming, confused at Mum's version of *"nice-looking"*.

'Are we looking at the same dessert?' I questioned, raising an eyebrow, 'it looks like someone just ran over the Teletubbies and dumped their corpses on a plate.'

Obviously, this wasn't a time for mocking jokes. Mum didn't take too kindly to my sarcasm, and suddenly, as if an invisible switch had been flicked, her stitched-on-smile withered and her expression turned into frenzied outrage.

'Oh, for Heaven's sake, Simone,' she warbled, trying to stop herself from either crying or screaming, 'all I wanted was to have a nice dinner party and for you to enjoy being back at home. Yet, from the moment you arrived this afternoon, you've been nothing but a sulk.'

Her lip quivered as she began to spill out the contents of her true emotions, 'At any mention of Andrew, you fall into a mood. You've done nothing but pass judgement on him, don't think I haven't noticed. It's quite plain to see that you don't like the company I keep. And as for your poor Grandmother, you know what she's like. Why couldn't you just let it go? Would it have hurt you to keep your opinions to yourself, just for once?'

Completely staggered at the fact my entire family seemed to be ganging up on me, I too, could no longer control my festering rage.

'Really? You as well?' I said, shaking my head in disbelief. 'First, there was Seb constantly ridiculing me for being single, then Dad kept trying to hook me up with every guy he knew in a ten-mile radius, and now, even though I've pretty much done everything I can to appease you all by finding a *"nice normal guy"* and be independent, I've got Granny and you on my back acting as if I need to be moulded into some kind of submissive, remote-controlled Stepford Wife type. I mean, what the actual hell, Mum? Have you ever come to think that maybe I'm like this because of the family environment I've grown up in? Spending years amongst a marital battlefield is hardly the greatest of places to make someone believe in love, is it? It's hardly a surprise that I'm pretty fixed in my opinions. Believing in myself is all I have. Yet, you guys treat me as if my identity is inherently flawed, like I'm a project in need of fixing or something. If anyone's wrong here, it's people like you, living life with your eyes half-shut. Oh,' I continued, my staggered breath choking my words, 'and just for the record, yeah, Andrew's boring as hell. But hey, what else should I expect you to go for but a man that says, *"how high?"* whenever you tell him to jump?'

I finally paused, quickly ridding myself of the unwanted cutlery and serviettes weighing down my freedom.

'You know what?' I said, glaring at her with disdain, 'Forget it. I'm done with this charade. I'm out.'

God knows what Mum was yelling at me by then. I was too consumed by rage to care - rage and confusion. *What had just happened?* It all escalated quicker than I could comprehend. But by that point, I didn't even want to work it out. All I wanted was to be alone.

The Moral Compass

Never had I known two people to talk as much drivel as Mum and Andrew did. All I could hear from my room was constant pinging and *aww* sounds. He'd only gone home a couple of hours before, and yet they were already on Messenger exchanging pointless conversation that would make even the soppiest of Care Bears sick to its stomach. It was no wonder Mum thought that Matt's little comment on my Facebook wall earlier was so adorable - she was practically infested with the Love Bug. To this day, it still absolutely baffles me how we are related.

Later that evening, once Mum had finally finished gabbling to *Blandrew* and gone to bed, I ventured out of my room with a plan to sneak up a cup of tea and some titbits from the kitchen. Despite my brutally stubborn nature, even I couldn't deny the hungry rumbles of my unsatisfied stomach. Dreg offerings of the insipid latke I'd eaten earlier were not enough to keep the groaning sounds at bay. So I went down, as quiet as a mouse, to retrieve any food I could forage. To my disappointment, I noticed that Mum's habit of only ever buying in crappy chocolate biscuits and cakes hadn't yet waned. My poor psyche had a good old battle weighing up the pros and cons of that dilemma. Oh, how I wished I could at least find some dates and cashews to balance it out. However, as fussy as I was, starvation was far less healthy than a couple of McVities Digestives. And so, taking a leap of faith that my colon wouldn't hate me for what I was about to do, I stealthily took up two biscuits by my teeth and a cup of sweet milky tea in my hands. The house was silent. Only one creak of the stairs gave away my presence. I was surprised Lizzie hadn't woken up to see what I was doing. Usually, any sound or movement and she'd be off, barking like mad. But tonight, she slept soundly on my bed. Her only effort made was the soft blinking of her weary eyes as I came back in and slowly closed my bedroom door. Though, she soon fell back asleep.

Aware I had to be quiet in order to avoid any attention from Mum, I kept the lights off and ate my biscuits by the window, using my hands as a plate to catch any wayward crumbs.

Looking at all the surrounding houses in the night somehow calmed me. Maybe it was because I could appreciate all aspects of the neighbourhood now it wasn't decorated with distraction. No car alarms, no people walking about, no screaming children being forced to go to school, just the simple view of the streets and all the little lives that dwelled within them. As I stared out, I wondered what everyone else's lives held. What jobs did they have or problems did they take home? Did they ever wish for something else? What about dreams – what do the people at house no.65 dream about? Are they married with two point four children and have a traditional family holiday booked every year to the same place whilst secretly trying to hide the fact that they're both cheating on each other and that their kids are selling pot to their mates at school? Or, unlike me, are they actually happy? I guessed I'd never know.

Wiping the crumbs from my lips and pouring the rest in the bin, I went over to retrieve my phone from its position on my bedside cabinet. As usual, the screen was clogged up with white notification boxes, most of them crap. But, I did spot something interesting from Harry. *Ah*, Harry. We hadn't seen each other in so long he almost felt like a stranger; nothing more than a memory. And whilst memories keep people alive, maintenance is needed to make sure they don't fade. So seeing his message at that moment felt like a godsend.

Sorry, Matt. But I am going to talk to Harry. I may even have...a laugh with him. Oh, the horror.

For what felt like the first time in ages, we had a proper catch-up. It wasn't often that I'd sit down and erode my fingers to nubs over the internet, but when I did, I made sure the conversation was a good one, and Harry's humour without fail would always ensure that notion. However, today, his chat was more surprising than amusing. Of course, the element of surprise was also something he was notorious for, so I shouldn't have expected anything less.

"FD3@HY%78&CG!!" was suddenly displayed in his conversation box – utter gibberish that usually inferred something exciting was about to be announced.

"What, what, what?!" I quickly typed back, my fingers moving fast with excitement.

"You'll NEVER guess who's going to meet Ozzy Osborne..."

This boy was mad.

"Who...?" I paused before typing the obvious answer he was giddy for, "You? How?!"

A monkey emoji with its hands covering its mouth was quickly sent back, and then the dramatic ellipsis...

"C'mon Hugh - spill!" Hugh was a piss-take name I called him after the barista in Starbucks wrote his name down incorrectly on his take-out cup. Ever since his mocha came back with that adorable title on, the nickname just stuck, especially when he was being a facetious little tit.

"One clue,' he finally replied, "Donnington."

'*Oh my God,*' I whispered, '*he's going to bloody Download Festival.*'

"Nice!" I enthusiastically replied. "You finally booked it then?" But as I sat there, watching the speech bubble waver as he wrote his reply, I suddenly wondered, *how would mere attendance link him to meeting Ozzy?*

"Not quite…" he responded.

It soon became increasingly obvious as the cryptic conversation went on that Harry had applied for a voluntary role at this year's festival. He only worked in the Co-Op, so splashing the cash wasn't something he would do lightly. This, of course, made far more sense.

"Cheapskate," I wrote back with a winky face, "I joke. That's really cool. I'm uber jealous."

"You don't have to be…" Again, the ambiguous chat continued.

What is up with this boy tonight?

"How so?" I asked.

"Because…" cue dramatic pause which was causing my heart to not only race but my blood pressure to skyrocket, "…I have free tickets!"

My eyes bulged. I finally realised what he was trying to say.

"You mean," I wrote, trying to think of a reply that didn't sound like a jittery teenage girl who'd just received a love note from her crush, "I'm invited…?"

A nodding dog gif came back to me, and my body jumped with excitement.

"OMG, HUGH!' I typed with shaky hands, "YOU'RE A LEGEND!"

If it weren't for the fact that Mum was asleep in the other room and that I still wanted her to think I was making my insubordinate stand in misery, I would have leapt about that room just like Buckaroo after the last piece of luggage was loaded on his back. Seriously, I was ecstatic!

But, wait…

"What date is it again?" I tentatively queried, hawk eyes staring firmly at the white screen.

"14th June," he answered. "Surprised you don't already know. And you call yourself a rock fan…"

I did know. I was just checking.

It was on the same day as Katrina's marathon run.

Bugger.

***

Garden centres have always bored me. I don't know whether it's because it's full of odds and sods that make no sense in combo, or the fact that it's somewhere you only find appealing as you get older. The same goes for catalogues. Unless you're a teenage boy getting giddy over the lingerie section, they're only exciting reads when you hit forty. And right now, I was far from forty, and most certainly, far from excited.

'Ooh, look at this,' Mum stated cheerily, picking up the ugliest gnome I've ever seen in my entire life, 'it looks just like your father, but with better dress sense.'

I rolled my eyes. The jokes to cover up her feelings of denial were wearing thin now. Nevertheless, I suppose I should've been glad we were on talking terms again after the events of the night before.

'Uh-huh,' I uttered, glancing around to see if there was anything of interest that could potentially change the subject. There wasn't. So, I resorted to the only other conversation I knew Mothers relished: giving advice.

'Mum,' I inflected, 'what do you do when you make a promise to someone, but then something else crops up and pulls you in a different direction - like, a once in a lifetime opportunity type of thing? Do you break that promise, hoping the other person will understand? Or, do you say no to this unmissable chance, even though you really, *really* want to go?'

Mum stared at me as if I'd already answered my own question.

'Well,' she began, putting the gnome back down and clearing her throat, "it all depends on how big of a deal this promise is versus this unmissable chance. If it's something small like; you promised to pick up some dry-cleaning, then I'd go with option two. But, if it's something important, then you need to weigh up whether this unmissable chance overwhelms it or not.'

Words spoken like a true Mum.

'I thought you might say that,' I replied, thoughts still nowhere near making a solid decision, 'I guess I have to leave it to my moral compass to point me in the right direction, eh?'

She nodded. 'Indeed. Things might be clearer if you talk to the people involved, too. See if that can help guide you.'

I nodded back. 'Thanks Mum. That makes a lot of sense.' We both smiled for a minute, leaving a weird delay hanging in the air between us. In a way, it was kind of sweet - especially since our previous squabble - it felt good to reconnect. However, as cute as it was, I never have been one for indulging in silence for too long.

'Say,' I began, motioning my head towards the nearby café, 'do you want to grab a drink? They have some tempting teas by the looks of their menu.'

Smiling, she replied, 'Sure. Make mine a coffee, though.'

***

Family emergencies are always a good excuse when you want to get out of doing something. No one ever judges you for a family crisis. The same goes for cancelled trains. If a train journey goes pear-shaped, no one even thinks to question it. Delays and cancellations are just standard for the British rail system. However, evidence of my whereabouts plastered across social media was going to make both of those excuses impossible. I could be as careful as I liked; someone, somewhere (most likely Harry), would tag me in a photo or a status and reveal my treachery. *Be sure your sins will find you out.* And even if he didn't, I was a crap liar.

The fact that millions of crazy get-out-of-watching-Katrina-run reasons were running through my head already made me aware that I was doing the wrong thing. My moral compass was virtually spinning on its axis and my conscience was telling me rather incessantly that I was being an arsehole. And yet, all I could think about was how much I really would regret not going to Download.

Maybe I should just be honest? I thought, as I stared at my dormant mobile. *After all, honesty is the best policy, according to wise ol' Abe Lincoln.*

After a few more seconds of staring and tapping my finger repeatedly on the desk in my room, I eventually grew some balls and made the call, inhaling deeply as I did.

'You got this.'

The ringing stopped.

'Hello, sweets,' came the buoyant reply from my best friend whose world I was about to shatter, 'how are you?'

I paused, not knowing where to start - *do I just dive straight in there and get it out in the open, or do I do the little sparky chit-chat rubbish first?* All I could do was leave it to my unscripted ramblings to find out.

'All good,' I began, with a slight hesitation in my speech, 'well, apart from the quarrelling with my family last night, eating rubbish potato *things* that Andrew made, and going to a garden centre this morning. So yes, apart from all of that, it's good. What about you?'

There was a brief pause. I think I stunned her into silence. My gibbering had that effect on people sometimes.

'Sounds...eventful,' she finally responded, flummoxed tone accompanying her words, 'why did you quarrel? It's only been one day, Sims.'

I didn't really want to go into it again. Raking over my family squabbles just made me feel uncomfortable. It was like acknowledging the billboard-sized banner advertising what a ridiculous setup we were. I could already see it in my mind's eye – *Every Thursday night on Channel 4, The Hartley Family - the most bogus family in Britain!* Nevertheless, Kats couldn't see in my head, and if I couldn't tell my best friend what a mess my life was then, who could I tell? Plus, I'd rather hoped that hearing my embarrassing story might also soften the blow when it came to later telling her about Download.

'Long story short, no one likes my music and my Gran is a stuffy old prude. But we're okay now. *S'all good,*' I stated, allowing the words to make a speedy escape in order to desperately move on the conversation. '*So...* anyway,' I continued, 'how's your running going? No more fainting, I hope?'

Surely even Kats could tell by now that something was wrong with me? I never gabbled like this without reason.

'Err, yeah, it's fine,' she stammered, confusion blending with her words, 'Sims, are you okay? You sound kind of stressed.'

Finally, she was onto me. Not that that was a good thing, of course. Ultimately, it meant that the dreaded let-down conversation was about to become an imminent one.

'Trina," I began, before she interrupted me.

'Whoa, now I definitely know something's up,' she stated, her tone rising, 'you never call me Trina! What's going on?"

I took a deep breath and bit my tongue. Telling the truth always did hurt.

'Harry's invited me to Download, and I really want to go, but it lands on the same day as your run, and I feel like a jerk because I want to be there and support you, but I also *really* want to do this, and it's just so annoying, and I hate time and dates and everything else right now.'

And breathe…

A weighty silence rode the airwaves between us like a fat guy surfing the sea, filling the entire space.

'You should go,' her voice suddenly splashed through.

'What?' I remarked, shocked.

'You should go to Download,' she repeated, clarifying that what I thought I'd just heard her say was, in fact, exactly what she'd just said.

'Look,' she continued, 'I know how much these events mean to you and how much you've missed Harry etc. Waiting for me at a finish line for God knows how long just to shoot me a wave for two seconds really bears no comparison. So, I think that if you can, you should go.'

A state of disbelief overwhelmed me, causing my eyes to blink rapidly. Was she actually serious? Like, deadly serious? *No way*, there must be a catch. I was sure of it.

'And you're okay with that?' I questioned, utterly perplexed. 'Won't you be disappointed if I'm not there?'

Although I couldn't see her, I could sense her shrug her shoulders.

'Nah, it's fine,' she said, as casually as they come, 'I'll have Julian there anyway, and oodles of randomers to wave at. Plus, I'll see you the day after to tell you all about it. It's all good.'

She sounded as cool as a cucumber. Maybe she really wasn't bothered? Either way, with my emotions on a high, I wasn't going to bite the hand that feeds whilst it was offering me a buffet dinner. I'd made my decision.

'Well,' I said, 'as long as you're sure?'

'Yes, yes,' she stated, the sound of a protein tub being opened accompanying her confirmation, 'go have fun, sweets. You've earned it.'

I wasn't sure how I'd earned it exactly, but I wasn't going to question her notions.

'Thanks for being so understanding, Kats. You're amazing.' My happy pitch was hard to submerge.

A genteel laugh escaped her. 'It's fine, chickadee. Anyway, look, I best dash. Julian will be here in five for a jog and a jiggle.'

A *jiggle?*

'Errr,' I stuttered, 'dare I ask…?'

'Oh, Sims,' she laughed, 'you totally know.'

A tiny bit of sick came up and spoilt my happy place.

'Nice…Well, I best let you go then. Thanks again, Kats. I promise I'll make it up to you.'

'You'd better,' she chuckled, 'love you, my darlin'. Catch up *lateeer.*'

'Love you, too,' I parted. '*Byeee.*'

Excitable exchanges now over with, I brought my throat back to its standard resonance. But not before doing a little dance of celebration.

'*I'M GOING TO DOWNLOAD*!' I sang, cavorting about my room like I was auditioning for a role in Step-Up. No matter how old you get, dancing like there's nobody watching isn't bound by time, and I was taking full advantage of that. This was me happy, and I liked it. Not only had I told the truth and got my best mate's approval, therefore able to attend with a guilt-free conscience, but I was finally going to be able to let loose and immerse myself in the one thing I loved: music. Nothing could bring me down from the bouncy edges of cloud nine I was jumping on, nothing except the crash-bang back to earth upon sight of Matt ringing me.

At that second, I wondered if he'd somehow heard my plan and was about to admonish me for it. But that was crazy talk. There's no way that would be true. Nevertheless, as a consequence of that thought, I guessed that whilst I was walking the path of honesty, I may as well do the whole trek. Well, maybe not the *whole* trek. Some parts in the shape of Harry needed to be cleverly omitted.

God, have mercy on my soul (and eardrums)

The Music Festival

After a week of ear-bashing, I bore no guilt for attending the festival. In fact, hearing Matt whinge about not being able to hack another day without me and that he didn't understand why I'd rather go to this *"noisy"* event rather than come home spurred me on, if anything. The guy was unbelievable. But, even so, I wasn't entirely heartless. It was still early days for us and I still wanted to try and make this work. So I decided that - in spite of my previous emotional seesawing and current annoyance that he just didn't "get" my taste in music - when I got home, I'd plan something special for us to do. I wasn't entirely sure what that was yet because my head was filled with bands, music and epic theme park activities. But I'd work something out.

Maybe my euphoric mood was to blame for my sudden change of heart and upbeat approach to our rather stagnant relationship? In my head, I'd somehow figured that having a few days apart and living a life that made me feel like Simone again might enable me to look at him with fresh eyes and appreciate him as the same guy I once fell for. Although my affections never really went much further than a close bond of friendship, and even, admittedly at times, were a little empty, I wanted to believe that a bit of space was all I needed to get back on track. Right now, however, my main focus was getting into Donnington, and good grief, it was proving a nightmare.

Most of the cars were parked up a good few miles away from the field, and those were considered the lucky ones.

I, stupidly, left late that morning thinking I'd get some kind of VIP spot for being invited by a crew member, only to be sadly mistaken. With Harry's abrupt text message to, "Get a frickin' move on, woman!" because that special space most certainly did not have my name on it, I bolted out of my bed like lightning and got myself out of the door, only to be stuck in the queue of the century. Waiting to get parked in the giant meadow by the venue didn't last too long, though, thankfully, and Mum's car seats were pretty inviting during the delay. However, walking up to the ticket admittance once a space was found was another story altogether.

The Great Wall of China is shorter than this walk was, I'm sure. From a field of cars to a field of…grass, it just never seemed to end. The only way I knew I was going in the right direction was by following the flow of people and the manky waft from the porta-loos nearby. Day one, and already they'd been obliterated by dirty campers who'd gone too hard on fast-food and beer the night before. *RIP toilets*. Finally, though, after what seemed comparable to accomplishing a trek around Middle-Earth, I made it. Gandalf would be proud. Nevertheless, in addition to the invisible elderly wizard who stiffly proclaimed, *"You shall not pass,"* all that stood between me and the music was a ridiculously long queue…Sigh.

Whilst I waited - my trainers steadily glueing themselves to the muddy terrain - I decided to fill the time by squeezing in a few owed messages, namely to Kats, who was first to receive my eagerly typed out, "Good luck!" text. A part of me still felt bad that I couldn't be there with her. And I did keep thinking that being at a rock show over supporting your best friend play Mo Farah for the day was a little morally skewed, but she kept telling me otherwise. Plus, like she'd said, I'd be home tomorrow evening. We'd catch up then, and all balance would be restored. That was what I kept telling myself, anyway. But despite my constant reassuring thoughts aiming to keep my face the picture of happiness, Karma had other ideas.

'Oh, great,' I groaned, pulling up my stripy red and black hoodie to protect myself from the sudden downpour, 'just what I needed, stupid British weather.'

No matter when Download Festival was scheduled for, somehow, the rain always made sure it gate-crashed. One year, its presence was so torrential that the festival was even renamed, *"Drownload."* It could actually be considered rather funny if it wasn't so annoying. I wasn't laughing, though. I was far too busy being cold, late and pissed off.

'Screw you, clouds,' I cursed to the nubilous skies above, 'you suck.'

Onlookers must've thought I was rather batty, but then that was hardly unusual at a place absolutely rife with people spinning their hair like windmills to the sound of electric guitars. I was pretty boring, in comparison. And anyway, who else wouldn't be a bit miffed after they'd spent all of fifteen minutes straightening their hair into the perfect sleek style, only for it to be frizzed by rain in a matter of milliseconds? Being grumpy was allowed.

Then, finally, after what felt like I'd been standing in the same spot for millennia, the queue suddenly ushered into movement. *Hurrah!* I should have guessed though, that despite my new-found grin, my happiness would be short-lived.

Within moments, the smile that had previously etched itself on my face was redrawn into a frown. Not only was the rain spitting down hard as it fell from the heavens, but the ground beneath my feet was proving just as undesirable, if not more so. Holding back a frustrated scream, I lifted my foot out of the mud, ready to witness the evidence of whatever resulted in such a toe-curling squelchy sound, and it was just as I'd expected.

Poop: actual, nasty, smelly, brown poop.

Am I at a zoo or a festival right now? Urgh.

I bit the corner of my cheeks to keep my annoyance inside. There were too many people around me to have a tantrum, and I'd already made enough of a show of myself yelling at the sky earlier on. No matter how annoyed I was, things couldn't get worse. All I had to do was wipe my foot on some grass, keep my frizzy hair hidden underneath my hoodie until I could brush it in the loo, and just make my way inside. Then I'd be able to enjoy myself. Surely that wasn't such a hard thing to achieve?

'Excuse me, miss,' the security man by the ticket entry table said, 'this bag is too big to enter.'

This was just not my day.

***

'What is it with women and oversized bags?' Harry stated, staring at me judgingly as we walked through the field. 'You're lucky I was here, or you'd have been as stuffed as a Portobello mushroom.'

Knowing people in high places really did have its perks. He was right. If it weren't for him, that miserable security man would've just sent me packing. But we women do need our necessities on us at all times. Because you never know when you'll need hankies, a lipstick top-up or hand gel. And to be honest, in a place like this, hand gel was an absolute must.

'I know. I'm sorry,' I replied, feeling a little forlorn from my previous agitation, 'but it's not like you'd told me the exact dimensions of a bag I was allowed to bring.'

'Well,' he scoffed, adjusting his Hi-Vis jacket, 'I hardly expected you to replicate Mary Poppins and bring everything but the kitchen sink to a frickin' gig now, did I?'

It was only 12.30 in the afternoon, and I was already completely exasperated by it all. First the traffic, then the rain, then the poop and then the grumpy festival dictator, and now I was being reprimanded by my mate who looked like something you'd wave at a Bon Jovi concert. And, as if things couldn't get any worse, my fluorescent friend was about to abandon me.

'Anyway,' he said before I could even think of a reply, 'I've got to head back to my post. You'll be alright now, won't you? I can trust you to not get into any more trouble?'

I glared at him, wanting to remind him with my eyes that I was more than capable of navigating myself around a field on my own.

'Yes, Hugh,' I replied monotonously, 'I'll be fine.'

'Good,' he said as he looked from left to right, trying to find his bearings, 'I'll see you later then. Have a good time and don't forget to tell your face to crack a smile!'

As he ran off, I smirked at him sarcastically, rolling my knuckle as I pretended to wind up my other hand's middle finger. He just laughed. That's the nice thing about having guy friends. You could be as mocking as you liked, and they'd still find it funny. Try doing that with a girlfriend. Trust me; the outcome is far more unpredictable. Talking of which, Katrina would have been running by now, and I hadn't heard a dickybird from her. Then again, I supposed she was in-the-zone. When she had her head in the game, there was no taking her away from it. No wonder she wasn't worried if I was at the marathon or not. Knowing her, she'd have just blankly zoomed past me whilst I waved in her direction, anyway. Still, though, I was starting to regret not being there. This day wasn't turning out as well as I'd expected it to be.

Aware that I had no other choice than to amuse myself, I decided to explore the gigantic field on my own. There was certainly plenty to see; food stalls, fashion outlets with cool trinkets and accessories influenced by popular bands, game areas and even tattoo booths. Honestly, if you could dream it, Download had made it. And it was pretty awesome to see everything in action.

For a while, the only views I'd seen had been the repeated ones from work, in my apartment or on the tube, so it was refreshing to be in an environment with so much buzz. Plus, even if I didn't come home with anything more than a memory of seeing some cool stands and hearing some good music, the vibe was inspirational. I even thought it could become the foundation for a new story one day.

You never know.

With my head in dreamland, I'd forgotten all about my crappy hair. That was until I touched it and felt how the mixture of spitty rain and hairspray had given birth to a crispy love child. It must've looked like I'd head-butted a bird's nest. So, with a quick turnaround, I made my way to the porta-loo section in the middle of the field. It was right next to the main-stage, so if I could find a sanitary loo and brush my hair in good time, I wouldn't miss the first show. Until then, though, I didn't want anybody else seeing my hair as it was.

As I walked, I quickly took my phone out of my bag to check if my reflection was as unsightly as the image in my head, and that's when it happened.

Within a split-second, my heart jolted in fear. But not because of what I saw in my reflection, because of what I heard from behind me - an unexpected ghost from a not-so-distant past calling my name.

The Reverie (Part 1)

Time has this funny ability to stretch out life like dough; continuously pulling away from your past only to know that – no matter how far away it is – it's a part of you, and that, one day, should fate see it fit to roll it back, everything you once thought was a distant memory comes back into the present day. And all those things you previously believed were no longer binding are moulded back into your life, as if they'd never even left. That was how my heart felt whilst it played a symphonic beat at the sight of him, leaping and sinking all at once. It was like having Bach stuck in my chest. I didn't know what to do or say. So I just stood there, jaw-dropped, completely frozen, waiting for life to make the next serendipitous move.

'Well if it isn't Jane Austen,' he remarked. 'Long-time no see.'

Approaching me, wearing a familiar red beanie, a bicep-hugging black t-shirt and a smile that would make any woman go weak at the knees, was Ethan bloody Brenner.

'How are you?' he asked, clasping me into a welcoming hug.

I wanted to say something cool, something impressive. But he'd caught me off-guard, and the unforgiving rain had tossed half of my hair on my face, so I felt anything but composed. Time wasn't going to pause for me to fix it, though. Nor would it give me a moment to work out what to say. I had to think on my feet. I had to say something charismatic and charming. Something that would make him think I was an endearingly special individual - something like...

'How the hell did you spot me in the middle of this feckin' field? It's bloody massive!'

Nice one, Brain. That was a triumph, even for you...

Still holding my arm, he smiled at me. He probably thought I was special, but not in a good way.

'I'd know that midnight blue hair a mile-off,' he answered, studying my nonplussed expression, 'look, I've got to go help the band set up for our stage now but, did you want to hang out later? It's been so long.'

My heart leapt a million beats - *Yes – a thousand times, YES!* My face remained as idle as a fat guy on his couch.

'What time would that be? Only, I have a few acts on my list to see first.'

You, Simone Hartley, are tallying up these blunders at an enviable rate. Just wait. The Guinness Book of World Records will be asking for your picture to place next to the phrase, 'Most Faux Pas' Delivered in Under Thirty Seconds.'

'Err,' he stuttered, releasing his hand from my arm and using it to rub the back of his neck, 'around three?'

There was no way I could turn this opportunity down. This was fate – it had to be, and there was no way I was going to slap its hand away once again.

'Sorry,' I apologised, shaking my obtuse front away, 'I don't know why I even said that! Three would be great.'

He smiled. 'Great!'

We both grinned awkwardly, like a pair of twitchy teens in a school hallway, neither of us quite knowing what to do after accepting the proposal to hang out at Pizza Hut on Friday night – *do you say something else?*

Do you tell them you can't wait? No, that's just so uncool. Oh, it's just too confusing.

'Ethan!' A voice suddenly called over.

Phew. Saved by the band.

'C'mon, man! We need to get set up.'

Ethan and I both nervously laughed.

'Sorry, that's my cue,' he said, pointing in the direction of his bandmates, 'see you…later?'

'Sure,' I nodded, ushering him to go, 'See you…around three.'

Our cheesy grins remained intact as we said goodbye, and I continued to wave at him until my body zoned itself back into reality.

It's true what they say. The brain does become more stupid when you find someone attractive. This is another little nugget I recall Tariq sharing. I remember it clearly because I took the mick out of Seb mercilessly as a result. Apparently, parts of the pre-frontal cortex actually switch off when we like someone, rendering most of us about as useful as a chocolate teapot. It was probably why, during that moment with Ethan, it felt as though the entire world had disappeared. All trace of noise and flurry became unobserved. It'd definitely been a long time since I'd last experienced that kind of occurrence. I think the last time was…

…the night we first met.

Oh, jeez.

And the worst part of it all was that Matt didn't come into my head once. Not one time did it occur to me that maybe what I was embarking upon might be wrong. In essence, it should have been completely normal to catch up with someone I hadn't seen in a while. But nothing about this situation was normal. The people involved, the setting, the excitement - they were all dynamics that shifted the context of this from snowflake to avalanche.

And I didn't give a damn.

***

In the midst of my wandering, I suddenly realised I was an idiot. How on earth did I not know he'd be here?

When I'd looked at the schedule earlier, I briefly skimmed it for big names I followed; I didn't see the Joker's Ashes anywhere. To be fair on me, though, the people he was with definitely weren't members of the band either. I was perplexed. If he was setting up, then he must be playing a set. This realisation made me do the one thing I hated - Google him.

Yes, I felt like a stalker. Yes, I really should've been replying to my texts from my actual boyfriend. But while I was in this frenzy, I needed to know the answer to my burning question. I needed to know the name of this other band he happened to be in and see him play. There was no way I could be this much of a nincompoop not to know that he was in another bloody band. And I call myself a metal-head.

Silly, *silly* Simone.

Turning on my data was probably the worst thing I could do. The abundance of messages that came through was mortifying, and the fact that at least ninety percent of them were from Matt was the worst part of it all.

Actually, scrap that. In hindsight, the worst part of it was probably the fact that I swiped every single notification away in one triumphant flick of the finger.

He was just so suffocating! Even all the way up in Nott's, he was getting in the way. Eventually, though, once my screen stopped filling up like a sink with a busted tap, I could finally concentrate and look for the information I sought, without accidentally tapping on a message and feeling obliged to interact with it.

According to the wonders of the World Wide Web, Ethan also played with another band called, *Perception of Heart*. I must admit, even with all my knowledge of the rock world, I'd never heard of them before. But still, that didn't necessarily mean that they sucked. Plus, it seemed like a good opportunity to hear some new music. So, before I got roped into reading any more about him on his Wiki page, I headed straight for my Download App and looked for when and what stage the band would be playing.

Once minute later, I was on my way there.

***

Standing in the tent was like playing the starring role of a sardine in a tin. There was absolutely no room to move - a typical rock show. If you weren't lucky enough to bag a spot in the front row, you were undoubtedly going to suffocate under some sweaty guy's armpit for the foreseeable. Nevertheless, as I stood there, attempting to contort myself in a fashion that would avoid being prodded by spikey hair or covered in booze, I wondered if this immense crowd was a good thing. After all, such a big turnout is usually a sign of talent. In which case, I also wondered why on earth, such talent would therefore be shoved into a gazebo tighter than a duck's backside.

A few of the people around me were coupled off. It was kind of bizarre to see such a love-in. Most other gigs I'd been to, people kept themselves to themselves. But here, nearly everyone seemed ready to whip out a glow stick and get their sway on. I started to wonder what on earth to expect.

As the lighting transitioned to speckled darkness, I stood there on my lonesome and watched as the show began. The band's presence soon greeted the empty stage and its isolated musical instruments, and the imminent arrival of Ethan walking towards the microphone made me smile. If I could've moved my arms, I'd have waved.

'What a turnout,' he said, pulling back on the acoustic guitar strapped across his shoulders, 'thank you so much for coming to our show.'

The crowd elicited a mixture of whoops and raised cups as he spoke. I continued to watch in awe.

'Okay, so, to anyone who's watched us play before – welcome back. It's so good to see you all. Are you guys having fun so far?'

I looked around as the obedient audience cheered back at him, synchronically crying out in agreement and whistling.

'Epic, that's what we like to hear,' he continued, taking a strong hand and moving his floppy fringe off of his face, almost successfully distracting me entirely from listening to what he had to say. 'So we're going to start with a song close to our hearts. We wrote it on our tour bus on the way back from Germany around four years ago. For that, you could probably call it one of our classics. I remember it taking us only an hour to create, which is a bit insane. But who can stop inspiration when it strikes?' he asked rhetorically whilst softly smiling.

'If you know how it goes, sing it back.'

The drummer began to beat a rhythm that got the crowd going even more. People's whooping turned to screams of excitement as Ethan then swung the guitar around his front and started strumming a few bars alongside. It was at that moment I realised this wasn't going to be like any rock show I'd ever been to.

Echoes of the cymbals rippled throughout the tent until everyone fell silent. Not even a whisper could be heard. And then he began to play notes that sent shivers down my spine. It was an ineffable sensation. I'd never experienced anything like it before. Even though my view was obscured, I watched on, captivated, as Ethan started to sing.

A voice of velvet wrapped itself around me. Warm and soft, it blanketed the air. It was as if, suddenly, I was the only one in the room. Everything that I'd previously noticed disappeared. Every sense I'd been aware of gone - all I could feel and all I could hear was his delicate voice as it stroked my skin in surround sound. His voice was beautiful, and so was the song.

Unlike what I'd initially expected, lyrically, it was quite profound. None of the usual power-riffs and crazy trills filled the room. It was something so much bigger, something so much more meaningful. Everything about it had the ability to take you far away - to escape reality, to reflect upon the past, to see the future. It was transcendent. In sound, it may have been soft, but in its soul, it was momentous.

For the entire time he sang and led the guitar into its crescendo, everyone stood absolutely still. The only thing moving was the rapid beat of my heart.

A gentle breath was the last note he played before opening his eyes once more to view the awe-struck crowd.

'Thank you.'

And oh, how they cheered. What started as a tiny room filled with awkward elbows and zero personal-space suddenly became united. Not one person could deny the emotion that filled the air. Every single soul was touched. And so the applause kept on coming, and it kept on growing until there was no stopping the triumphant chorus from singing the band's praises.

It was magical. And that was only the beginning.

***

After the set was over, I needed to take five. Experiencing all of those tingling sensations was definitely a tiring revelation (as well as dodging the many spiky hairdos). So I felt like getting some air would probably be wise.

Just outside the tent, I shook my head, trying to rid the thought that this wonderful emotion was something that should make me feel guilty. My moral compass had a handy knack of ruining things that made me happy. More often than not, it steered me to places I didn't want to go. Why did the *right* thing always have to feel so damn wrong - or in this case, vice versa?

The pang of guilt directed me to my phone, telling me to answer my boyfriend's messages, demanding I check in again on Katrina. But I couldn't. I didn't want to. For once in my life, I wanted to live in the moment. I wanted to throw caution to the wind and just enjoy myself: no technology, no stupid nonsense chats, just me and the moment. Surely there was nothing wrong with that?

'I'm pretty sure you guys can live without me for one night.' I said, before holding down on the button that switched off my phone.

It was almost cathartic, like taking back control of my life. I was unbound – free.

Anyway, having one night away from reality isn't a crime. It's not like turning your phone off makes you a bad person. In any case, if it somehow did, I'd make up for it when I got home. But, until then, I wanted to enjoy myself, and I could only do that if I reminded myself that I wasn't doing anything wrong.

Tap, tap!

I turned around suddenly.

'Ethan,' I yelped, stupidly, 'I didn't see you there.'

This guy gave me the jitters like nobody's business.

'My apologies,' he laughed, animatedly shrugging his shoulders. 'To be fair, though, unless you have eyes lurking under that midnight blue hair of yours, I'm not really surprised.'

To this day, I'm still not sure why I did it, but I prodded the back of my head comically to demonstrate that I definitely did not have anything but hair lurking back there.

'Nope – most definitely, eye-free,' I blurted.

That awkward teenager moment began again. Why couldn't the ground swallow me up as well as I did my tongue?

'Good to know,' he began, trying to pull back the cool into our space, 'so…thanks again for coming to the show. I appreciate your support. Mind you; it's not usually as cramped as that. I hope you didn't get too squashed?'

I'd be lying if I said I didn't. The imprint from my handbag would be marked on my stomach for days.

'Me? Squashed? *Nooo*,' I said, swishing a defiant hand through the air. 'I'm fine.'

I paused, trying to steer the conversation elsewhere.

'Anyway, you were great! It definitely took my mind off turning into a human mashed potato…' I mumbled before carrying on, 'I never knew you could sing?'

Nervously, he laughed whilst adjusting his beanie. I really should've stopped staring everywhere his hands were going. It must have looked very weird – like a frog scouting for flies - except I wasn't planning on catching him with my tongue.

Or was I?

'Well, I don't think I'm the best singer in the world,' he stated, 'but sometimes you just want to try out something new. All the hard-core metal stuff is awesome, don't get me wrong. I love it. But, it's just…fun to explore a different side of yourself sometimes.'

'Oh, I totally get that,' I agreed, feeling a sudden deep wave overwhelm me and take over my entire body's movements. 'We're all made up of different sides, and each one needs expressing. There's no *one size fits all* personality. Every heart is multi-dimensional.'

Smiling, he nodded back as if he wasn't thinking I was some crazy motivational speaker from a preachy talk show.

'Exactly...' he assented.

This staring business was not good. It felt good, but it also felt like I'd forgotten that he could see me back. God only knows what my face was doing, because my eyes were far too distracted.

'Talking of sides,' Ethan added, breaking the interminable silence, 'do you fancy grabbing some food? I'm starving.'

Again, I nodded, but more profusely this time, hoping that regaining my standard animation would somehow help me gather composure.

'Sure,' I agreed, turning around to point at a nearby stand, 'I saw a veggie stall earlier that looked pretty good. That is...if you're into that kind of food?'

'Are you kidding me?' he said, eyes smiling nearly as widely as he was, 'I *love* that food!'

Then, before I knew it, he'd grabbed hold of my hand and begun to dart towards the stall like Bullseye.

'Come on, let's go!'

As we ran along, hand-in-hand with the breeze whistling over our mile-wide smiles, I supposed that he must have been famished. Unsurprising really; all that bouncing around on stage must have been pretty tiring.

Or, just a wild stab in the dark here but, maybe he was actually...happy?

Whatever the case may be, and despite the angel on my right shoulder pecking at my ear, I wasn't going to let go.

The Reverie (Part 2)

'No way,' he sputtered, 'I can't tell you that one. It's not one for a lady's ear.'

'Oh, go on,' I pleaded, trying to hold back the laughter, 'I promise I won't judge.'

I shook my head at him profusely, determined for him to share every terrible dirty joke he could remember. He was a hard nut to crack, but after a lengthy dose of my puppy dog eyes, I managed to get him to cave in the end.

The night began to cloak our circle of laughter, and songs playing from the distant stage made the perfect backing track. It made a welcome change to be in the company of someone who enjoyed the same music. It was a pastime I'd long missed sharing with a likeminded other. And, as we sat, giggling like children, talking to each other about anything and everything, I couldn't help but feel completely and utterly at peace.

From our spot on the edge of the world, I sat back happily, watching as the stars made their appearance over the hillside - scattering the navy sky with glowing crystal sheen - before feeling a soft wind glide through the air and sweep up my chin to stare at them.

What a perfect sight it was.

'Isn't it wondrous?' Ethan peacefully observed. Our mood very much shifted from hysterical to awestruck. 'The night sky,'

Continuing to admire the view above, I nodded approvingly and smiled. 'It really is.'

For a while after, we just sat, both inaudibly appreciating the scene and drinking hot tea out of paperboard cups. It was the most beautiful thing. But, despite being in each other's company for hours already - stuffing our faces with vegan food, riding the festival Ferris wheel, nearly throwing up said vegan food on said Ferris wheel and then looping the field several times over until the feeling passed - there was still one thing I couldn't get out of my head. A burning question only he had the answer to.

'Ethan,' I softly broached, turning to face him, 'can I ask you something?'

Thoughtfully, he turned his gaze away from the stars and onto me. 'As long as it's not, *"do you want another falafel?"* Because as delicious as those balls of chickpea goodness are, I don't think I want to eat another one for a very long time. At least, not immediately before a fairground ride.'

'No, it's not,' I chuckled, before engaging back to my question, 'it's about that song, the first one from your set. It was rather...melancholy. Much more melancholy than anything I could've expected from someone so young...' I paused, trying to work out the right words to say, '...I guess. I just wanted to know. What it was that inspired you to write it?'

In anticipation, I sat with my head tilted, anxiously awaiting his reply, hoping I hadn't asked something too out of line.

At first, he didn't say anything. Ethan's eyes had turned down, and his lips straightened out, his intent focus drawn to the ground beneath us. In that instance, it was clear that his mind was doing all the talking, slowly working out what to say. And so, I patiently watched on until that moment came.

'Well, *Miss Austen*,' he chirped, a humble smile cracking through his solemn gaze, 'despite being *oh so* charismatic now, it may surprise you to discover that, growing up, I was actually a pretty lonely kid.'

He began flicking a blade of grass between his fingers, maybe as a means of transferring the emotions into something else. I wasn't sure. But I could tell this wasn't a story he particularly wanted to tell. For some reason, though, he shared it, and he did so with absolute grit.

'Life wasn't easy being the only boy from a broken home,' he continued, 'I was treated like an outcast – bullied for something out of my control. The kids used to tease me so hard about it. To the point, I either hit out or cried. Crying happened less often, though. Guys like me grew up realising that tears don't get you very far. My dad instilled that mindset in me rather early on. *"Men don't cry, boy! Pull yourself together!"* he'd say. That kind of upbringing made it near impossible to express my emotions. But that doesn't mean I didn't feel things. In all honesty, I felt plenty - maybe too much. I just didn't know what to do with it. It probably sounds stupid now but, without the ability to know how to express myself healthily, I just didn't feel like life was worth living sometimes.'

My brow furrowed, imagining the hardships Ethan had to experience growing up. I thought about how my parents' divorce was hard, but at least I got on with them. They drove me nuts sometimes, sure, but I was never in fear of them like he was. Ethan had no idea, but hearing his story made me re-evaluate my own feelings

towards my parents. Maybe I'd been too harsh at times?
They may have been pushy and irksome, but I knew that
they always had my best intentions at heart.
Remembering that was something I silently vowed to
work on changing.

'Nevertheless,' he continued, straightening himself up
as he did so, 'even through those hard times, I was
determined to achieve my ambitions. At heart, I was
always creative. My passion was music. It's what I woke
up for. I lived and breathed the guitar. Music was my
escape,' he explained, 'despite my Dad's constant
scrutiny and disapproval, I stopped caring. So what if I
was going to be a disappointment to him? He was a
disappointment to me. So, at nineteen, I abandoned the
need for my father's validation and joined Killer Venom.

'The song itself is about self-advocation,' he continued,
'it took a long time to walk away from that dark place
my childhood sent me to. But, in a sense, I'm glad I had
it. Or, at the very least, come out the other side of it a
better person. Should I ever have kids, I want them to
know that emotions are normal, tears show strength and
creativity is an incredible tool. Not only does it help you,
but it helps other people, too. And being candid about
those experiences is good for you and those around you.'

'Preach to that,' I smiled, briefly wondering if that was
the element I'd missed from my own book.

Believing in my abilities was something I also
struggled with at times, especially after Jake. He had an
impeccable way of whittling me down. And although I
felt like I'd done a good job at proving my self-worth
through solo travelling and relocating to London, all of
those things were physical – completely detached from

my inner-feelings. Ethan had observed all of his psychological cracks and worked towards paving them over. That was something I was still working on, which is why; perhaps, the story I'd already written had flunked. It needed more emotional strength and security for it to be truly felt; something that Ethan had in spades. And for that, I truly admired him.

'I think you're really brave to be that voice,' I tentatively composed, 'so many of us have these negative experiences, and it can be really hard to navigate a positive way out. But you've used your knowledge of that situation to help other people going through similar hardships. What you've done takes real fortitude, Ethan, and I wholly applaud you for that.'

A small arc emerged on his face as he watched me bring my hands together for a gentle clap.

'Thank you, Simone. However...' he began, inhaling and animatedly pointing both fingers towards the sky.

'That knowledge is absolutely nothing without wisdom. For as helpful as it is to know that tomato is a fruit, for example, wisdom is the important faculty that teaches us not to put it in a fruit salad.'

I couldn't help but laugh. It utterly fascinated me how far our conversation had spun out. Only someone like him could take such a heavy topic and lighten the load with a philosophical joke.

'You know,' I said, looking towards him in awe, 'you really are quite beguiling.'

For a moment then, I wondered if I should've chosen a different word. Who on earth uses *beguiling*, for crumb's sake? Nevertheless, he looked back at me with beaming eyes and moved in closer.

Damn, those pastel blues tripped my heart something rotten.

'Now, there's a first,' he replied, an air of coyness attached to his jovial confidence. 'That's got to be the first time anyone has ever described me as *beguiling* before.'

I bowed my head down, aware of the closeness and how much I liked it. Feeling a flurry in my chest was most certainly not a sensation I felt right to possess.

'Sorry,' I hurriedly apologised, coy from the intimacy, 'I have a rather strange vocabulary choice sometimes. I'm sure that my friends think I swallowed a dictionary as a child. Should I retract it?'

He laughed, shaking his head. 'No, please don't apologise. It's awesome.' He commended, sweeping stray pieces of his blonde fringe underneath his hat.

'You're a woman of many surprises, Simone. You shouldn't ever be sorry for that. And it's way too late for retractions - I'm making *beguiling* my new tag line. Also, may I offer you some additional brownie points for not correcting the way I said 'tomato' earlier either.'

Like I'd ever correct the way he said tomato.

To-May-Toe.

Toe-Mah-Toe.

His sounded so much better.

'Talking of surprises…' he interjected, pushing himself up off the green and stretching out his hand towards me, 'I want to show you something.'

Clueless, I stayed put and stared up at him.

'What?' I asked, confused. 'Where are we going?'

'Well,' he intoned, 'it wouldn't be much of a surprise if I gave that part away. But, I think you'll like it.'

A part of me instinctively trusted him. God knows where he was going to take me. And yet, I didn't even question it. There was something unwritten between us that just made sense. I felt like I knew him inside and out. However, nothing could have quite prepared me for what he was about to show me.

***

'How much further?' I whined, anxious as to where he was guiding me with his hands covering my eyes. 'We'll end up on the motorway in a minute!'

'You're nearly there,' he replied reassuringly, 'just a few more steps.'

'If I end up in the back seat of a car, know I have a good left-hook on me,' I jokingly grumbled.

His fingers nearly gapped enough for me to see the view as he sputtered with laughter. 'Oh yes.' he tittered, 'with all of that writing you do, I don't doubt the talent of your swing, Simone. But no, I'm not taking you to a car. I hope that doesn't disappoint you.'

'Shame,' I said, still walking blindly, 'I'd have quite liked to finally practice my secret MMA skills with a worthy candidate.'

A few more steps over lumpy terrain, and then I felt the path change into something smoother. Underfoot, I sensed the grass levels change from enveloping my trainers to them sinking in pitted pieces of dried mud. It was as if I'd walked onto a whole new landscape, and I sincerely hoped that once I opened my eyes, I wouldn't be completely lost.

'Okay,' he said, slowing my pace to a halt, 'you can open your eyes now.'

Steadying my gaze back into focus, I saw an overhead light shine onto something angled in front of me. My heart thumped at the thought that it really was a car boot.

How could I have been so foolish? Where do I run to? How do I escape?!

Thankfully though, it wasn't. And yet, the moment I saw what it really was, my heart nearly stopped beating entirely.

A black beast stared back at me. Silver discs reflected like teeth in the overhead lighting. My jaw dropped in fear.

'Surprise!' Ethan sparked, enthusiastically grabbing a helmet from behind a nearby tent and tossing it towards me.

I stared down at the carbon fibre weight encircling my hands.

'It's safer if you put it on your head rather than hold it in your hands, Simone,' he stated, already eagerly semi-kitted up in a matching black jacket.

A small gulp fell down my throat. I stared back at him. For once in my life, I was speechless.

'You…you want me to join you?' I asked shakily.

My trepidation was obviously amusing for him, because even through his shaded visor, I could see him grinning.

'Of course,' he chirped, helping pop the Stig-like helmet over me, 'it wouldn't be much fun without you.'

As a way of allaying my obvious fears, he soon told me that the bike was electric. Therefore, even if he chose to push it to the max, it still wouldn't go like the clappers.

'It may look fierce,' he commented, giving the side of the bike a little dust off, not that anyone could see it in the twilight hours, 'but it's pretty friendly really.'

A little smile escaped me.

'A bit like you then,' I piped before my mouth could stop the words from making their great escape.

He turned to face me; his head curiously cocked to the side.

'By which, I mean,' I stammered, attempting to quickly think on my feet for something that would explain, rectify, or reverse the embarrassment to the rather obvious connotations behind my declaration. 'In a human sense, a lot of people see tattoos and piercings - or in my case, eyeliner and funky-coloured hair - and think we're going to be intense, scary kinds of people. But, the truth is, underneath it all, we're total softies.'

Somehow, I doubted that what I'd said reversed the embarrassment. But even so, he nodded in agreement.

'You've got it in one, Miss Austen. Both my bike and I have that in common.' The light fell just enough for me to see him through the visor, merrily staring through the shaded view. 'So, are you ready for a ride? On the bike, I mean.'

Was it bad that I hoped he'd meant both? Yes. Yes, it totally was. I was in a relationship. I shouldn't have been thinking this way at all. No, I wasn't cheating. Well, not physically. Emotionally though…I wasn't so sure.

Does spending time with someone you like count as cheating whilst you're dating someone else?

No, of course it doesn't. It's not like feelings can be helped. Nor should they be suppressed, as we'd discussed earlier. In context, though, Ethan wasn't just someone I *liked*. He was, to me - if it can be expressed so candidly - sex on legs.

Every fibre of my body yearned to be near him; I couldn't deny it. There was an undoubted connection between us. Or, at least, there was from me to him. I couldn't be sure. Nevertheless, perhaps that was what cemented my reply to his question? Because without absolute certainty on whether this connection was reciprocated or unrequited, I decidedly shook the little nagging voice out of my head and proceeded to say...

'Absolutely!'

Without any further hesitation, he hopped onto the bike and patted the space at the back, ushering me to join him. Fear dissipated; I trotted over and bounded myself over the black ride like it was a horse, and then placed my arms appropriately around his waist. It's what I'd seen done in all of Katrina's soppy rom-coms, so I figured that was the correct protocol needed for this kind of moment. Plus, it was a good excuse to feel him up a little without it being considered pervy.

'Are you ready?' he asked, briefly turning to face me, our helmets reflecting in one another's like a scene from Space Odyssey.

'As I'll ever be.'

He quickly presented me a thumbs up before popping the bike into sport-mode. Then, as speedily as his thumb came and left, we began to accelerate around the empty grounds.

My fear once again grew with every bump in the terrain. The only source of relief for said fear was found in holding him tighter, which was, of course, completely involuntary. Nevertheless, I think he must have liked it a little, because he seemed to take every terrified squeal as a cue to pop the front wheel.

'I think I preferred it when I thought you were going to kidnap me in a car,' I cried, rather stupidly, in hindsight. We were probably only doing about forty miles an hour, but it may as well have been a hundred around that tiny patch of field. Each lap we circled seemed to merge together, and I was nearly almost one-hundred percent certain that we may end up back in 1985 alongside a DeLorean.

Automatically, I sensed the deceleration of the bike.

'Want me to slow down?'

'Please,' I mellifluously pled, trying to catch my breath back, 'just for a bit. Turns out there really is such a thing as too much excitement.'

He slowly decelerated to a complete stop and carefully pulled the bike up against a nearby fence. I inhaled briskly, as though I'd been holding my breath the entire time and only now remembered to let it out.

'Okay?' He asked, offering me his black sleeved arm for support as I attempted to get off the bike gracefully.

'Yes,' I bluntly replied before adding, 'just give me five minutes, and I'll be ready for round two.'

From the way I enthusiastically freed myself from the claustrophobic helmet, I think it was pretty apparent to him that round two was definitely not going to happen. Nevertheless, it didn't seem to offend him.

'Biking isn't for everyone, Simone,' he said, observing my relieved expression, 'it's all good if it's not for you.'

'Thank you, but I do feel like I'm letting down the rebel inside me, you know? She isn't afraid of anything.' I remarked, passing him back the dusty helmet.

'Didn't you once say that you'd been up the Burj Khalifa?' he quizzed, taking the helmet and then placing it on the ground. 'To go up the tallest building in the world on your own is pretty gutsy, Simone.'

I smiled - impressed that he'd remembered one of the many travel stories I'd shared with him from the first time we'd met.

'True,' I said, 'but that's different. It was all enclosed. There's a sense of safety inside a mirrored giant.'

He laughed at me then.

'Why are you laughing at me?' I asked, prodding him in the ribs.

'*Ow*,' he spouted in fake pain, 'you make me laugh, that's all. And I just think you're too harsh on yourself. You've travelled to all of these places and done all of these great things, including publishing your own novel - which I still want to read by the way - and yet, you're still putting yourself down. Why?'

We were both still unwinding from the previous giggles. But slowly, our emotions turned to a pensive place once more. This time, though, it was my turn.

'I guess. I just like to complete goals,' I admitted, sitting back down on the bumpy grass and looking up at the sky, thinking about the underwhelming sales of said novel and the dreams of venturing places I could ill-afford to visit. 'There are so many places I still want to travel and things I want to achieve, so I feel like a bit of a failure when I don't connect with something new.'

Ethan sat beside me. Once again, we both stared at the jet black sky above, its platinum stars shining down on us.

'I get that,' he assented, 'it's the price you pay for wanting to achieve things in life – for being an ambitious and creative person. The pleasure is in the pursuit itself.'

I nodded in agreement. Of course he knew this feeling.

'But you're not a failure, Simone,' he quickly interjected, shaking his head. 'Never think that. You can't connect with *everything* in this world. If we could, that'd make having strengths and weaknesses rather redundant, wouldn't it? That's why when you do connect with something or somewhere or *someone*, it's significant. It shows us that just because some things are rare to find doesn't mean they're impossible to discover, and I truly believe that's how each and every one of us navigates our own personal happiness.'

It was at that moment I could have sworn I saw a shooting star soaring above us. A fire burned inside of me. He really was unlike anyone else I'd ever met.

'With that in mind,' he said, whisking me away from another potential musing, 'let's go back to that list of yours. Tell me, what's your next travel goal?'

Taking no prisoners, the word mercilessly pushed its way out of me.

'Japan.'

Ethan's eyes suddenly lit up as brightly as the stars above us. 'Japan?' he repeated, 'I love it there.'

I elatedly turned to face him, strands of my hair gently blowing in the idle summer night breeze.

'You've been before?'

'Been?' he replied exuberantly. 'I used to live in Tokyo. It's a wonderful city - so much diversity and culture. I still have a few good friends out there, as well.

So when I can, I like to go back there from time-to-time.'

Wide-eyed, I sat like a child in awe as he filled my mind with pictures of all the places I'd dreamed of exploring – the gardens, the temples, all of the cultural delights, as well as the contemporary mesh of anime streets in Akihabara right to the Godzilla statue standing amongst the skyline in Shinjuku. It was the perfect tour.

'So, there's just a giant head towering over the cinema? That's so cool. I need to see this for real.'

'No doubt you will,' he said, smiling at me. 'I have a sneaking suspicion that, once you've made a decision about something, you're likely to go for it.'

There was a pause that hung in the air between us, much like the crescent moon in the sky above. A rush filled my chest. At that moment, I really did want to go for it. But, not in the way he'd meant.

After such a serendipitous night, the world felt like it belonged to only us. It was as though that spotlit field was a portion of reality that existed outside the realms of our own. Right there and then, all I wanted to do was lean in that bit further and feel his lips against mine, his touch exploring my body. My mind was racing; my heart was pounding. I was at my body's mercy.

And there was nothing I could do to stop it.

The Unstoppable Catalyst

Someone must have run me over multiple times because my head was pounding like hell. Just opening my eyes sent a merciless pain shooting through my left-hand side that made me clutch at my hair in anguish. I really should've taken a tablet as soon as it'd hit me. It was too late now, though. All I could do was hang tight until it decided to ease up and let me go.

In spite of the pain, I determinedly moved out of bed, trying to regain focus and start the day as I always did. But the more I adjusted to the morning daybreak, the more I flinched. I cricked my neck and let out a frustrated exhalation, looking around my room through squinted vision, only to suddenly realise I was alone.

At that moment, all signs of the pain in my head stopped, and I was utterly consumed by thoughts of the night before.

What happened? How did I get here? Did I really spend the evening with Ethan Brenner? Wait...Where is Ethan?

Casting my gaze to the bedside table, I spotted an out of place piece of paper. Eagerly, I reached for it, hoping it would somehow answer all the questions that spun round in my mind.

'Sorry to leave you without saying a proper goodbye, Simone,' it began, *'I don't want to go, but I have to get back to the field. You look so peaceful right now and I don't think it'd be fair to wake you. But I want you to know that I had a fantastic time with you yesterday. Perhaps, we could hang out again sometime? I'll even*

get you a special helmet for the bike, as I'm sure it's all your inner-rebel needs to shine. Anyway, take care of yourself, Simone and, next time, let's not leave our paths crossing up to fate x'

Underneath that last line was his number - Ethan Brenner's actual phone number. This had to be a dream.

'I saw your man-friend last night,' Mum suddenly sounded, loitering in my bedroom doorway, 'good-looking boy he was; very different from Matt.'

I could see where this was going.

'Mum, it's not what you think,' I pleaded, pulling myself upright to face her, my head's pound steadily returning. 'He just gave me a ride home. Nothing happened, I swear,' which, in all fairness, was true.

After that brief moment of weakness with Ethan, I managed to defy any stirring submissions and feigned tiredness instead. That's why he took me home. He point-blank refused to see me drive home tired. It was very kind of him, I thought. But mum seemed to feel differently towards the matter. Her eyes said words her mouth didn't. They emanated disappointment.

'I'm sure it didn't,' she said, monotonously, 'but that's not what concerns me.'

I gulped. This woman was not my mother. She was Mystic Meg, reading my mind.

Moving from the doorway, she sat beside me on the bed, tilting her head with an expression of worry and love all blended in one furrowed brow.

'Simone,' she began, 'did you know how much of a tearaway I was as a teenager?'

I shook my head, wondering where she was going with this trip down memory lane so early in the morning.

'Well, believe it or not, I was. I used to have your Granny Dawn running ragged after me. Constantly calling on her to fetch me from bars I shouldn't have been in, blind-drunk and clinging to the porcelain. I was a bit of a nightmare. Eventually, I grew up, though. Hard lessons taught me that who I was, wasn't going to get me very far. That's why I've felt so lucky to have you as a daughter. You've always been so well-behaved, so wise beyond your years – everything I wasn't.'

Feelings of confusion overwhelmed me. This was so unlike my Mum.

'But,' I interjected, sitting next to her, 'you always tell me off for standing my ground with Granny Dawn. I don't understand.'

A deep sigh escaped her. 'Oh Simone, sweetheart,' she said, stroking my hair, 'I just want an easy life.'

She bit her bottom lip.

'You know what you said about Andrew?' She continued, 'Well, you were right. Not fully. I do think he's lovely. But maybe that's because I just don't want any more drama? Growing up with Granny Dawn for a Mother wears you down a bit. That's why I rebelled so much as a youngster. It's also why I decided to be more lenient with my own children and allow them to express themselves and make their own choices. So far, I've been lucky. Even with your father's philandering ways rocking the apple cart. And yes, although I don't necessarily understand your choice in clothing or love of *screamy* music, I wouldn't have you any other way.'

Every word she told me sank in my skin like water, drowning me to silence. I'd never heard her speak like this before.

'What I'm trying to say, Simone, is that I don't want you to make the same mistakes that I did. You're wiser than I was. I think you know that what you're feeling, or not feeling, as it were, is wrong. Whether anything happened last night or not, your heart undoubtedly beats for another, and it's not fair to keep Matt hanging on in there for a love he can never have.'

It hurt to admit that she was right. For so long, I'd felt like my life had been on repeat - nothing notable happening, just living day by day to stay afloat. And during those times, I'd tried so hard not to acknowledge my resentment for it. I'd buried it deep, hoping that, one day, I'd forget it was there. But, just like the picture of Ethan at the bottom of my wonky wardrobe, I may not have been able to see it, but I would also never be able to forget it was there. I was a fool to believe that I could love another when my heart was already taken.

Our teary eyes stared at one another's. The revelation between Mum and me had reduced us both to something far too emotional for my liking. Nevertheless, I embraced her in a hug my arms so longingly desired.

'I'm a bad person,' I whimpered on her shoulder, the polyester of her dressing gown collecting my pitiful tears. 'I've tried so hard to love him, I really have. It's just not there though. He's a good guy, he does good things and looks lovely but, it's just…not enough.'

I could feel her nodding. Her ear brushed against my own as she did. All the while, she hushed me and reassuringly stroked my back.

'Your intentions are always good, Simone.' she softly intoned, 'I have no doubt about that.'

It was true. I did want to love him. But she was right in what she said. He deserved so much more than a half-hearted romance.

'Where's my car, by the way?' she queried softly, changing the subject's direction completely. 'Did it break down? Is it running okay?'

Without intending to do so, Mum suddenly reminded me that I'd turned my phone off.

Shit! Katrina's run.

Quickly rebounding from our hug to switch it back on, a surge of insistence coursing through my veins, I loaded my phone back to life.

'I need to ask Katrina how her run went,' I garbled, my head all over the place, 'I completely forgot about it.'

Scrambling with my phone, I waited for a moment until it reconnected with Mum's Wi-Fi.

'And yeah, your car is fine, don't worry,' I answered, in relation to her previous memory-jolting question.

'Ethan just gave me a lift home because I was too tired to drive last night.'

'Okay, as long as it doesn't need the RAC man to go and pick it up.' she said, her hand on my shoulder. 'Relax, Simone. I'm sure she doesn't expect you to contact her straight away.'

But I wasn't listening to her. I was altogether too determined to do the dutiful thing and message my supremely loyal best friend about the one thing that was most important to her. The one thing that I'd missed in order to fulfil some kind of teenage fantasy. All I wanted was a day without Matt and responsibilities and nagging. I just wanted to let my hair down, for a change. But the moment I saw thirteen missed calls and seven new texts,

I knew I would be paying the price for such emotional resplendence.

'Oh my God,' I said, my hollow voice disappearing as I stared at Mum's bewildered face.

'What is it?'

I couldn't believe what I was reading.

'Katrina's in hospital.'

PART 3

The Skyfall

My handbag exploded at just the wrong time, spilling my belongings across the hospital entrance – lip balm, phone, notebook – they all came tumbling out like the boulders in Indiana Jones.

'For God's sake!' I angrily spewed, trying to collect it all as the stampede of people carefully dodged them as well as me (the mad woman on her hands and knees chasing a hairbrush) in their passing.

The last twenty-four hours felt like an adrenaline-fuelled blur. As soon as I'd heard that Katrina was in the hospital, I felt sick with myself. *Was this a form of punishment for abandoning those I cared about for the sake of an evening of reverie?* My thoughts went back and forth like a swinging pendulum between the options as if someone else really could have control of my life, and everything I did was bound to some predestined result of something bigger. Now was not the time for an existential crisis, though. I had to get home.

In hindsight, it was a stupid idea to let Ethan take me home on his bike. Retrieving mum's car from the field meant appealing to Andrew's better nature and apologising, which really pained me to do because I still didn't feel he was right for mum and, honestly, he really was the most vacuous human I'd ever met. Nevertheless, he was kind enough to help me fetch it. It was probably more for mum's benefit than my own. But, he reminded me that no matter how bad things get between families, in times of crisis, "Families set aside their differences and pull together."

The fact that he regarded himself as "family" so swiftly worried me a pinch, but I had no other choice than to just leave it. He was doing something good, so I couldn't keep hating on him, even if his cooking was as vapid as his personality.

I caught my train home back to London by the skin of my teeth. Everything was a massive rush until the moment I sat on the train. Then, the longest hiatus came. Endless greenery followed me as I stared out of the window. My legs were restless and twitchy. All I could think about was Katrina, hoping she was okay. And yet, all I could do was sit and wait.

To fill my journey time, I made the necessary calls to find out exactly what happened. Tracey and Cherise were already with Katrina at the hospital, and Julian hadn't left her side. Hearing what they told me filled me with shock. The tears were falling from my eyes just thinking about my best friend, lying motionlessly next to them, whilst they retold the horrifying events of what had occurred less than twenty-four hours before.

Throughout the race, everything seemed to be fine. The weather wasn't too hot, considering it was June, and Katrina had been in better shape than I'd ever known her to be. As far as everyone was concerned, she was fighting fit. However, both Julian and I bore a guilty conscience. We both knew that wasn't completely true.

Now, more than ever, I was absolutely sure that Katrina's previous fainting episode was a warning of what was to come. We both should have listened to the voice that niggled inside instead of pretending that everything would be okay. We should have gone against Katrina's downplaying and said, 'No, the sugar isn't what's wrong here. Go to the damn doctors!' But neither of us did. Naively, we both accepted that she knew her body best.

But we were wrong.

They said Katrina had barely stumbled two steps across the finish line before her body suddenly went into cardiac arrest. It was at that moment, a nurse who had also participated in the marathon saw her collapse, and came straight over to perform CPR. Then, when the on-site first-aiders and medical support staff realised what was happening, they rallied in their numbers to take over. Katrina's heart had stopped beating for six whole minutes before they managed to pull her lifeless body onto a stretcher and finally take her to Hammersmith Hospital.

'We're lucky she's still alive.'

But Tracey's statement felt so far from the truth. It was all too much to take in. Never in my life did I think this would happen to someone so young, and in my heart of hearts, I still wanted to believe that, despite the terrifying incident, Katrina would be fine, she just had to be. There was nothing worse than carrying this internal weight in my chest. I just wanted to see her so that I could let it go, but there was only one way that I would know for sure.

By the time I'd hurriedly run off the train - my mountain of belongings swinging across my body, stymieing my speed – reached the hospital, collected the contents of my handbag from the hospital entrance and finally reached her ward, I was greeted by a sight so far from lucky.

'My God…Kats…'

Tears filled my eyes when I saw her unconscious body. She was hooked up to a whole host of monitors; no part of her was free of wires. She looked like she was being used as a human plug socket. It shocked me to see her in that way - my beautiful, best friend. The one who could outrun time, she was so fast. The one person I knew who could never stop going had finally just…stopped.

'How could this happen?' I cried, dropping my belongings at the foot of the bed and running to her side.

'The doctor called it 'Ventricular Fibrillation',' Julian flatly replied, still staring hopelessly at Katrina from the other side of the bed. 'The lower chambers of her heart were quivering. They still don't know why.'

I could barely see for the swell of droplets in my eyes. But I could see how bereft Julian looked despite them.

The warning signs were there. How could we have been so blind?

Suddenly, awash with worry, Julian reached for her hands and clasped them inside his own.

'We could've lost you, Katrina,' he snuffled, already in pieces at the thought, 'I'm so sorry.'

Silently, I tortured myself.

For that, we both were.

***

The days that followed passed by on repeat. Dawn fell to dusk in the blink of an eye, and yet, the lonely night's seemed to last forever.

Time stood still in our empty apartment in the twilight hours. The silence haunted me like an unseen entity, and I struggled to sleep. No matter how much I'd exhausted myself in the day; working in the shop and then returning to Hammersmith until visiting hours were over, my mind couldn't switch off. I couldn't remove the image of Katrina's motionless body out of my head. So I just lay in the pitch-black darkness of my room, staring at the ceiling, waiting for the day to come.

In times of crisis, though, families really do rally together, and by that definition, my family were also my friends. Which is why by day five of this interminable cycle, both Tracey and Cherise wanted to stay at the apartment - as did Seb and Tariq. Mum and Dad weren't able to be with me in person, but they figured out a way to set aside their differences and be there at the end of the phone. Having human company and my parents on good terms did help lift our spirits somewhat. Although we were still consumed with worry and stress, the moral support of the group made it a lot easier to stay strong. And since I was unable to take any time off work, that strength was something I desperately needed right now.

'I'm sorry, Simone,' Alexandra had said, 'but you're not the one lying in a hospital bed. No, I can't, and won't, have you off as well.'

Katrina was right. She was *Miss Trunchball*; heartless and callous - no, worse. She was a dragon. A fire-breathing dragon dressed in oversized teal skirts and crocs. How she could lack so much compassion, I couldn't understand. She acted as though I was asking for a jolly – it was unbelievable! Statements such as this proved why she'd never been gifted any, "World's Best Boss" mugs over the years. Her careless words spiralled around my head, sending me into a reserved apoplectic frenzy. I had to bite my tongue. I could ill-afford to lose my job, especially at a time like this. Nevertheless, working for such a curmudgeonly woman was becoming more than I could take.

'Don't worry, Simone. I'm here for you.'

And then there was Matt.

After everything that had happened over the last few days, my guilt levels were racking up higher than Tetris blocks. Of course, nothing physical had happened between me and Ethan, but mum was right - the feelings were there. Whether there was any poignancy to that or not, it wasn't fair of me to lead Matt on. Nevertheless, Matt's attentive (and rather obtrusive) concern for me was rather hard to either avoid or reject. He'd made his presence known and there was nothing I could do or say to stop it. As soon as we were within the walls of my apartment, all he wanted to do was "relax". How on earth could I relax? Everything in my little world was completely off-balance, I felt as though I was freefalling, and his credulous view towards the whole situation was not helping matters.

'But what can you do?' I snapped at him, my face crumpling like tissue. 'Being *here* for me isn't going to make Katrina any better, is it?'

Just like in the image of The Tower tarot card, I was plummeting from a great height, and soon, I was about to hit the ground and crash into pieces.

'You need to go.' The guilt was consuming me from every angle, and his besotted little face was only making it worse. I had to get him to leave.

'But Simone,' he pleaded, following me around the lounge of the apartment, 'you can't be alone at a time like this.'

214

I rolled my eyes, inhaling heatedly. 'What makes you think I need watching all the time? I'm not a baby, Matt. I can take care of myself.'

He paced after me; both of us looping the sofa as if it were a Maypole.

'Simone, I understand that you're stressed. Please, sit down. Let me help.'

Anger was rising within me like bubbles in boiling water. He wasn't listening. Worse – he was refusing to listen. Perhaps, he had my best intentions at heart, but I couldn't take it. I didn't want his consolation. He was killing me with kindness.

I silently reminded myself that I wouldn't be in this sorry predicament if it weren't for his incessant messaging that night at Download. If he'd just stopped pecking my head whilst I was trying to enjoy myself for the first time in what felt like forever, then I wouldn't have felt the need to turn off my phone in the first place. Ifs and buts may be something none of us can do anything about, but on this occasion, it served as the perfect fuel for my targeted rage.

'Oh, stop smothering me, Matt!' I screamed, flailing my arms. 'I don't want to sit down. In fact, do you know what I want to do? I want to listen to my heaviest of metal albums so loud that it would shake the walls down. I'm sick of Bach, and Mozart, and Chopin, and I'm sick of you telling me what to do and how to feel. You never listen to me. I'm always compromising for you, and yet, all you ever do is loll about, wasting your life away.'

I paused for breath, still shaking my head at the floor, refusing to look at his crestfallen face.

'My best friend is lying in hospital right now, and all she's ever done is given her all in life. She's never tried to change anybody. She's vibrant and outgoing, caring and fearless. Nothing stands in her way. But *you*,' I finally looked up at him.

'You do and give nothing but empty words. You're nothing more than a paper person. Now do what I want for a change and just go.'

Dumbfounded, he stared at me. The silence between us made it easier for me to hear his heart breaking. I couldn't take it.

'GO!' I yelled, pointing towards the door, my hand shaking in fevered anguish.

He let out an outbreath, bowed down his head and walked over to the kitchen worktop, picking up his jacket to cover the invisible wounds etched on his skin. Every word had cut him like shards of glass, and I was the one responsible for their indelible marks.

Unexpectedly, he didn't slam the door. But still, from the moment I heard it close, I cried my heart out.

***

A loose thread was coming away on the strap of my handbag. I couldn't help but pick away at it as a form of comfort. As though the incessant pulling would somehow remedy the torn-up emotions I carried inside. Everything had just become too much. I was struggling to cope. Even in a room full of people, I felt alone. Just me and the threadbare handbag balanced on my knee, sitting opposite my lifeless best friend.

'Do you want some tea?' Seb offered, gesturing a cup towards me. 'I know it's not as fancy as the stuff you usually have but, if you don't mind me saying, you look like you need it.'

I didn't even have the energy to roll my red eyes. Hospital tea was comparable to boiled dishwater. Of course I didn't want it. But instead, I simply took the cup from him with my free hand and mindlessly sipped on it.

'Thank you.'

I could feel his penetrative stare - him watching me whilst I watched Katrina, the intermittent beep of the monitors playing our soundtrack.

'Chick, I know that you're struggling right now and that confiding in me isn't something you usually choose to do,' he began, reaching for my hand that picked at the loose thread, 'but I can see you're not okay. Talk to me, sis.'

My heart leapt a jagged beat, as if it was attempting to break free from my chest. The caring side of my brother wasn't something I was used to. More often than not, sentimentality was a running joke between us. So to have this moment, a moment where his furrowed brow proved genuine concern, I was overwhelmed.

'Matt and I fought last night,' I confessed, sounding just above a whisper. Everyone else in the room had fallen asleep in their chairs. I envied them. *How could they sleep during a time like this?*

'What? Why?' Seb queried.

In my trance-like state, I wondered how best to explain to him the calamity of emotions bustling around inside.

'Because,' I began, still searching for an answer, 'I wanted to be alone.'

217

I went back to staring at Katrina and then scanned the room of sleeping bodies. Julian was leaning against Katrina, his top half on the bed and the bottom on the chair. Tracey and Cherise were head-to-head on the opposite side of us. Katrina's parents, Tricia and Paul, paralleled that image next to them. Tariq was slumped in the corner, sleeping on his hands and using a Psychologies magazine as a sheet for warmth. My lip began to tremble as I stared at them all.

'I'm a horrible person, Seb,' I said, turning to face him.

'Don't be silly, lovely,' he replied, squeezing my hand tightly, 'you're just having a tough time.'

'No,' I muttered, 'this is my entire fault.'

And so I told him the truth. I told him everything I'd kept hidden for so long - about the tarot reading and how everything Lilith predicted was coming true. The fear I'd had when Kats told me she'd fainted and that I'd said nothing. About my time with Ethan; the guilt for the torch I carried for him and the shame I'd felt for it. I told him about my indifferent feelings towards Matt, explaining my confusion for choosing a relationship I thought I was meant to have instead of fighting for the one I really wanted - even if its chance of becoming a reality was infinitesimal.

'And that's why I turned my phone off.' I trailed on, my beleaguered voice riddled with guilt, 'I just couldn't take anymore.'

'Oh, Simone,' He sighed, pulling me close until our heads mirrored those of the others in the room. 'You may be a bit of a dingbat at times, but this situation isn't your fault.'

I shook my head, not even contesting the dingbat statement, 'Seb, there may as well have been a billboard-sized sign in front of me, and I still would have ignored it. Of course it's my fault. I should have kept my phone on.'

'What happened to Katrina was out of your control,' he said, 'you've gotta stop blaming yourself. No one could have seen this coming.'

Except for Lilith - she did. She even said those very same words; words that would forever haunt me.

"Seeing it coming is not an option."

'As far as things with Matt go,' he continued, pulling me away from the past and back to the present, 'I know that if the shoe were on the other foot, and you had me crying on your shoulder like this about Tariq, you'd say it was obvious what choice I had to make.'

I nodded against him. Out of everything in my life that spun my head around, that was the one thing I finally knew the answer to.

'Plus, he's a bit weird,' Seb casually added, 'Ever since you told me that he plays Classic FM underneath his pillow at night, my whole opinion of him dropped quicker than a bar of soap in the shower. If that isn't a reason to get rid, I don't know what is.'

A freeing chuckle escaped me. 'It is weird, isn't it?'

All of a sudden, the handle to Katrina's room jerked down and the door began to open. Our now alerted heads raised in unison like meerkats in a field.

'Sorry to disturb you all,' the consultant said to us as he entered the room, 'I didn't realise everyone was asleep. My team just came to do some more checks.'

We all shuffled about in our seats as nurses made their way inside.

'Of course,' Tricia was the first to say, now wide-awake, 'we'll make ourselves scarce.'

'That's okay Mrs Stevenson.' The consultant continued, ticking papers on his clipboard, 'my team do need a bit of space, but two of you can remain here if you wish to.'

It came without question that those two people would be Katrina's parents, and rightly so. Nevertheless, I couldn't help but feel a little torn. In my mind, she was my family too. Ever since I'd moved to London, I'd barely had a day without her by my side. But now was not the time for petty quarrels. This was about what was best for Katrina. So, silently, we took our leave, and as the door closed behind me, I stared at my best friend through the separating glass window, praying for change.

The Bad Idea

For once, tea wasn't solving anything. I'd brewed myself an entire pot of calming herbs and placed it directly in front of me on the lounge table, waiting for the moment after I'd pressed a cup to my lips to feel a sense of relief. Multiple efforts were fruitless to my cause. I felt exactly the same.

Being alone in the apartment with only my rock power ballads playlist for company was probably the worst idea at this point. I was still feeling floored after I'd heard the consultants discuss the latest news about Katrina earlier that day. In fact, if I was being completely honest with myself, I already knew that a cup of tea was never going to touch the sides. But I wanted to try. It was Katrina's recipe, after all.

Inside every cupboard door was a note or two from her – little reminders dotted about the place about what foods do what and how certain botanicals can do this and that for the body. I liked that she left notes. Whether they were for her or for me, I loved to read them and learn from them. Today, though, that love broke me inside, as my mind constantly whirred with the reminder that she'd never write another one again.

Katrina's parents were the ones to break the news to us all. I don't think I'll ever be able to remove the image of Tricia's heartbroken features from my memory. She was so glassy-eyed when she explained everything, so matter of fact, as she revealed to us the desolate reality.

'There's no sign of improvement,' Tricia told us bleakly, 'every minute she's been in this comatose state, the less responsive she's become…They said it's because her brain was deprived of oxygen for too long after she initially collapsed.'

Tricia paused, her lips trembled as she contemplated the words she fought to keep inside, because once they'd managed to escape, she'd have to face something she could never take back.

'The tests they ran today confirmed that her brain is no longer responsive. The damage is irreversible…She doesn't even know we're here anymore.'

That's when she finally clutched onto Paul and broke down. Together, they clasped in a tearful state, realising the truth of the situation. Alongside the prospect of hope, Katrina may have been alive still, but she was already…gone.

Thoughts of the day hitting the sides of my head like a wrecking ball, I decided to raid the kitchen cupboards in search for something stronger than tea. The relentless memories were not going to release me unless I drowned them in a bottle.

Our cupboards were far too healthy. I shook my head as I looked at the endless offerings of nutritious wholefoods; opening and closing the doors as if something unhealthy would appear. What else did I expect from two women who worked in an Ayurvedic health store?

Where, *one* worked…

Eventually, after tireless rummaging and emptying, I found a few hidden wines at the back. No doubt they were birthday presents given many moons ago. They were probably off by now, but I didn't care. The edge was cutting me deep - I needed something to take it off.

Again, I dumped everything in the kitchen drawers onto the floor in order to find a corkscrew. If anyone had watched me, they'd have realised I was no connoisseur. I didn't know what I was doing. I just knew that I needed to drink. In my skewed perception, I thought that if I could successfully slip away for a bit, then the knowledge that my best friend was never coming back would too.

Dark red liquid filled my tea cup. I stared at it, wondering if I was the first person to have ever committed such a crime against drinks. Being classy with the appropriate glass was far from on my agenda, though. All I wanted to do was wallow in something red to smock the blue in my heart. So I retired back to the crumpled sofa, let myself sink into it, and drank the wine until I stopped thinking about the day's events.

Before that moment came, though, the thinking became worse.

It was hard to believe that Katrina was anything more than asleep. Her chest still rose and fell as though she were breathing. Her heart still beat as if it had something to live for. But it was all a mirage - an orchestra of movements and sounds conducted by machines. She could no longer breathe unaided. The ventilator was doing it all for her. Her life was supported by everything but herself.

After one cup, I poured myself another and put it down. Even mildly tipsy, I couldn't leave the flat looking such a mess.

I walked back over to the kitchen and began to clear up the clutter I'd tipped on the floor. Amongst all the spoons and forks, protein powders and granolas, I spotted an unfamiliar piece of paper. Clutching it, I remembered what it was.

'Ethan Brenner.' I said aloud and sighed. It was the note he'd left behind for me at mum's place. I bit the insides of my cheeks as I guiltily recalled my time with him.

Rising up and side-stepping the remaining mess, I took the piece of paper back to the sofa with me. For a while, I simply stared at the number at the bottom whilst drinking my second cup of wine. In hindsight, this was probably a bad idea.

**

'Whoa! What's the matter, Simone?'

It's an embarrassing fact to admit that the moment Ethan answered the phone, I started to cry. Not exactly the image I was going for. Instead of sounding effortlessly cool, I babbled like a fool, trying to hold it together whilst knowing I'd already fallen apart.

'I don't know what to do, Ethan,' I cried down the line, my laboured breath now catching up with my words. 'I…don't…know…what…to…do…'

In the virtual setting, his soothing voice cradled me. Although I didn't always hear what he was saying, just the sound alone managed to calm me down.

'Look, Simone,' he interjected, tears still rolling down my cheeks like raindrops on a window. I could almost envisage him putting his fingers through his hair as he spoke and then the other wiping away the sorrow from my eyes. 'The band is still in the UK right now and, well, tonight is free on our schedule. I'm not that far from the capital, so, if you want...I could come and see you? Just say the words. I'm only a bike ride away.'

I bit the insides of my cheeks again, wondering if this was all really happening. Perhaps, if I pinched myself hard enough, I'd wake up on the sofa, drool cascading my bottom lip and Katrina throwing a slipper at me. Then, I'd throw it back at her and tell her all about this crazy dream. I'd tell her about the psychic reading and the gig, and how my mind had concocted this ridiculously wonderful guy who could've only ever been a figure of my imagination. I'd tell her all about how I tried to thwart my cynicism towards romance by asininely dating Matt. Then, I'd reluctantly tell her about the pain I'd felt, believing that she was no longer here. I'd probably break down a little just at the mere thought. But she would hug me, tell me I was silly and that, luckily, it was only a dream.

I released my cheeks and realised that, despite my brief hopes, what was happening was so far from a dream. It was real. And since everything had already gone beyond pear-shaped in my car-crash reality, I decided that accepting Ethan's offer to come over couldn't exactly make things any worse. Or, so I thought.

***

Perhaps it *was* fate that kept our paths crossing. For every difficult bridge I had to face, Ethan seemed to be standing on the other side, waiting to take my hand. Once upon a time, if I'd seen something similar in one of the chick-flicks Katrina had put on, I would have mockingly commented that it was an utterly inane and implausible concept. Things like that never happen in reality. More often than not, two people who like each other don't have it so easy. I say, "easy". My life at that point felt very far away from that. But, as crazy as it all seemed, it was happening, and right there and then, knowing that Ethan wanted to see me again was one of the few things giving me strength.

Before the apartment button buzzed, I was licking bagel crumbs off my lips. In an attempt to sober up a little, I'd searched for the first dried good that caught my attention and ate it rapidly. Eating for hunger purposes was the last thing on my mind, but I couldn't see Ethan again looking a complete mess. I had to get my act together, at least a little bit. Plus, now the apartment smelt like buttery cinnamon and raisins, which had to be more inviting than stale sadness.

I breathed in and out, eyes closed, before composedly unbolting the lock.

'Hey,' he said, as I opened the door.

'Hi…' I sheepishly replied, still inwardly reeling from the embarrassment of calling him in floods of tears earlier on.

'So,' he began, after a few seconds of glances, 'your hallway really is lovely but, could I possibly come inside..?'

I jolted, realising that 'Yes, of course!' was the answer I quickly needed to say. So I pulled the door further open and let him in.

'Would you like a drink?' I asked as I closed the door behind him. 'Tea, coffee..?'

He mustered a little laugh, the one that etched a delightful slanted smile on his face.

'You really are so wonderfully British, Miss Austen.' he enunciated in his best English accent, whilst taking off his black jacket and placing it on a hook beside the door. 'Honestly, there's no need to go to any trouble on my account. Shouldn't I be the one making you a drink, anyway? Your phone call had me worried.'

His concern should have been what I noticed first, but it was actually the fact that he'd placed his jacket on the appropriate hook and not the worktop like Matt did. The mere act made me smile to myself.

'I'm so sorry about that,' I replied, pushing my hair behind my ears, 'I didn't mean to worry you. Honestly, I'm okay. Well, not okay. Obviously, I'm not okay. I feel like my life is crumbling around me, and there's nothing I can do to piece it back together. I'm so far from okay. But...' I realised my loquacious sentences needed to be cut short before I embarrassed myself any further. 'You've come all this way for a virtual stranger. The least I can do is make you a drink.'

He crinkled his brow. 'You're hardly a stranger, Simone,' he replied. 'I know we haven't known each other very long, but we've shared some quality exchanges. I'd regard you as a friend. However, I do know you Brits are very prim and proper and I want to respect that. So...maybe that label is a little forthright?'

'Oh,' I responded, now leaning my back against the arch of my newly un-crumpled sofa, smiling sweetly, 'friends is...good. I like that.'

Again, just like that day in the field when we'd both serendipitously bumped into each other, we stood there awkwardly observing one another like teenagers until he finally broke the silence.

'In that case, could I perhaps have a coffee?' he asked, already walking over to the kitchen corner, 'I'll make it, though. And, I'll make you a tea.'

'But,' I interrupted, watching him as he scanned my white cupboards, 'you don't know where anything is.'

He turned around and smiled. 'Point me in the right direction and I'll be well on my way. I promise I won't make your tea in the microwave.'

And so, even though loosening the reigns was a challenging concept for me, I let him make us both a drink. Another thing that surprised me about that moment; not only did Ethan seem to instinctively know where everything was, but he also didn't make a mess whilst doing it. For a rock musician, I half expected him to splatter the walls with tea and break my spoons in half. But instead, he was meticulously tidy. It was the most incredible thing I'd ever witnessed.

'Here you go,' he said, passing me a cup of French Earl Grey, 'I hope that it's done to your liking.'

That it was. Not too hot or too tangy, or over-brewed; just right. And, like he promised, he didn't terrorise me by microwaving it. However, despite enjoying my drink, I must have also been staring down at his coffee with utter disdain because the next thing he said was, 'Is coffee a deal-breaker to a tea lover?'

I looked up, taken out of my trance. 'No,' I stuttered, trying to think on my feet for words that were a little less monosyllabic and a little more interesting, 'I mean, it's a bit of a cardinal sin, but I can see past it.'

He laughed at that. 'What makes it *"a bit of a cardinal sin"* exactly?' he asked, air quoting the last bit of the sentence.

'Well,' I began, readying myself for a cerebral quip, 'it's a black coffee for starters. Milky coffee is one thing, but black? That's a whole other level.'

He raised an enquiring eyebrow from underneath his beanie. 'And why is that?' he questioned.

'Because,' I said, taking a quick sip of my perfect Earl Grey, 'only psychopaths drink black coffee.'

'What?' he belly-laughed at me, clutching at his grey shirt. 'That's crazy.'

'No,' I said, animatedly smiling back, 'it's true! There was even a study done on it that said so. I read about it online.'

'Oh,' he said, continuing to laugh, 'you read it online? Like, via a social networking link?'

I could see where this was going, '…Maybe.'

'Well,' he nodded jovially, 'in that case, it must be true.'

If anyone should ever ask, it was his own doing for the next words that I uttered as I nudged him with my shoulder. 'Just shut up and drink your coffee…psycho.'

He still tittered as he sipped. Both of us smiled at one another. For an ephemeral time, I forgot about the world outside. That seemed to happen a lot when we were together. But unlike the times before, in that moment of laughter, a cloudburst of reality suddenly came flooding back, and any glee I had then sank the watery depths below.

'Hey, Simone,' he said, placing his coffee cup onto the table, 'as much as seeing you smile is a great thing, there's obviously a lot of stuff on your mind. Talk to me, I'm here.'

I bit my lips back, hoping to hold onto the words trying to break free before they came out as a jumbled mess once again. This laughter was so freeing. I didn't want to be taken prisoner by my feelings again, but it was an inevitable sentence I'd have to endure.

'I don't know where to start,' I told him, 'there's just so much going on.'

His piercing sky-blue eyes solemnly stared at me from underneath a creased brow.

'Say the first thing that comes to your mind,' he said, placing a reassuring hand on my upper arm and rubbing it with his thumb. 'Forget about the flow of it and just let every word come as it does.'

And so I did, whether it made sense or was in any kind of logical order. And amazingly, he listened. Then, once I'd started telling him how I was feeling, the rest felt so easy to express. I'd not had that before. Maybe it was his unbiased presence working as some form of catharsis? Everybody else I cared about was far too involved with the situation. They all had their own feelings to deal with. It felt unfair burdening them with my woes when they already had so many of their own to contend with. I wanted to be strong for them. Turns out, though, being strong doesn't involve bottling up your emotions.

'Tell me,' I began, putting my now empty cup on the table next to his and turning to face him, 'why are you doing this for me? Yes, you can say we're friends now and that we've already shared a lot of deep thoughts etc. But, please don't take this the wrong way; this is by no means a criticism of your efforts - I commend your altruism. However, in essence, you still barely know me. So what's really made you want to come all this way?'

Ethan took a brief moment to think of a reply. 'Is it so hard to believe that I may like you?' he queried, emphasising the word *like* with his American inflection that made me feel a tad wobbly.

'A lot of people can like somebody,' I brusquely replied, shifting in my seat a little, 'but, I can't imagine any of my other male friends going to the same extent as you have tonight.'

He nodded, agreeing. 'Well, maybe I'm just an exception to the rule? Is that a bad thing?'

'Gosh. No!' I responded, quickly trying to explain myself more clearly, 'I'm just not used to it. That's all.'

Ethan keenly tilted his head. 'Are you saying that no one has ever sat and listened to you before..?'

'No, not *"no one"*,' I clarified, 'just not…a guy.'

I reminisced about all of the times I've wanted to get things off my chest before but never been able to. Of course, the girls always offered an ear to bend. But that's different. Women expect women to be emotional, and indeed, some men do too. I'd just not had the honour of meeting many of those types of men, and, out of the ones I did have in my little world, none of them saw me like that.

'I guess my male friends like the conversation to remain topical,' I explained, 'and that's great. But, sometimes I need to offload, you know? It's probably some of my own fault because I put up such a front - *I'm Simone, I'm hard-core and I don't care about all that mushy stuff.* So yeah, I guess, as a result, my male friends only seem to see me as *"one of the guys"*.'

My mind had completely erased Matt, how, I don't know. But as I confided in Ethan, I'd forgotten all about the forlorn man who I'd callously thrown out of the very same apartment just days earlier - the one who still deserved an explanation for my unfair asperity. Even with all of his faults, I really should have remembered that. If I had done, then, maybe it would have burst the virtual bubble Ethan and I were sat inside. Before it all went wrong.

'Well, I don't see you that way.' Ethan said, edging closer to me, '…I don't see you that way at all.'

At that moment, our eyes locked and my heart jumped so high that when it came back down, it sent a wave crashing through my chest. I stared at his lips and longed to touch them with my own. Now, no longer thinking about the world around me or the consequences of my actions, I finally did what I'd been yearning to do for so long…

***

Every defining moment in my life felt a lot like a photograph. Each one of them took only one fleeting second to capture, and yet, somehow, left behind an image that would last forever. The kiss with Ethan was one of those very moments.

It was like the whole world was celebrating the New Year in my chest. Rockets and Catherine Wheels charged through me. Crowds roared with cheer. It was incredible how something so gentle could cause such an explosion. Nonetheless, much like with New Year, the excitement had to dissipate at some point, and mine was the moment I realised what a terrible thing I'd just done.

I broke away from him.

'We should stop,' I said, suddenly riddled with shame. 'I'm so sorry.'

Ethan looked at me with understanding pastel-blue eyes. 'It's okay,' he began, straightening himself up after my wandering hands had previously unwrapped him, 'and look, I'm the one who should be sorry. You're feeling vulnerable right now. I should've known better than to kiss you.'

'You have nothing to apologise for,' I told him, 'I have wanted this for longer than you know.' My eyes focused on the room around me, and I began to shake my head. 'But now is not the right time.'

Guilt-ridden thoughts ambushed my mind as I stared at the apartment saturated with memories. This had been a place of love and laughter, anger and sadness, and now, it was a place where yet again I'd let myself become weak to fantasy. Only this time, I'd let myself succumb.

'Thank you for coming over,' I said, ashamedly bowing my head down, 'but I think it's best if you go back to the band now.'

Out of my peripheral vision, I saw him nod. This would be the second time I'd made a man leave the apartment that week.

'Sure,' he assented, slowly getting up from the couch and walking over to get his jacket.

I couldn't look at him. To do that would be to engage in an emotion I didn't want, and I already had so many of those. My mind felt like an overbooked hotel. I needed time to decompress, time to empty out everything that was filling it to the brim, so I could see things more clearly and feel things more freely. That, I knew, was going to take a while.

'If you ever need to talk...' he said from the open doorway.

Still on the sofa, I nodded back and briefly looked over at the man who'd changed everything. Not knowing if, once he closed the door behind him, our paths would ever cross again.

The Atonement

A very posh man was getting blown surprisingly hard on the television. As I watched it, I couldn't help but feel sorry for the poor guy. If the job involved reporting live from such windy sites, I'd hate to be a weather presenter.

'I wonder how much they get paid for doing that.' I said aloud, drifting my gaze back to Katrina in the bed, a part of me hoping she'd answer.

'Do you remember that time when you came home with your hair all soggy and crimped from the rain? It was the same day you brought back that weird pasta stuff to try.' I lightly laughed, 'It really did taste like straws.' The memory made me smile.

Her input was imperceptible. Most of the contributions came from the machines surrounding her, beeping away and monitoring repeated motions. I tried my best to fill in the gaps with the personality I knew so well.

'No, wait—' I suddenly recalled I was mistaken, 'The day you brought back that weird pasta was the same day I'd argued with my dad and Seb about my bloody relationship status.'

Those days felt like a millennia ago. Back then, nobody so much as caught my eye. Yet, for the best part of a year, I'd been in a relationship with Matt (wishing I could make it work) whilst secretly longing for Ethan (a person who seemed wholly unattainable). I felt like I'd aged ten years since then. Life had changed inexorably.

'How ironic,' I stated, recalling it all, 'From zero men to two in less than a year. When did I become so lascivious, Kats?' I shuffled in my seat and leant towards her.

'I never have told you about Ethan, have I? I wish I had before now. You'd probably have bitten my ear off about it, but at least you'd have saved me from making such a damned mess of everything.'

A lump of guilt slid down the back of my throat. Seb may have told me not to blame myself, but that didn't change the fact that I still felt like I owed Katrina an apology. I just hoped she could hear me,

'And that includes the mess of this. All of this.' The room seemed to engulf me. 'That day at the festival, Matt was driving me insane with messages. Every single time I had to turn my data on for the app, a flurry of nonsense came through from him...I had to turn it off. I didn't know that anything had happened to you for so long, all because my real boyfriend was sending me loopy and because, all of a sudden, Ethan walked back into my life. Honestly Kats, even now. I think back and I feel such a mixture of emotions.'

'A part of me loved that day more than anything. It was the best time I'd had in years. There's something about Ethan that's so wondrous. He makes me feel so alive—'

That last word cut me up into pieces, reminding me of whom I was telling this story of reminiscence to.

I reached for Katrina's hand and noticed that her pink nail polish had been removed. Even before a run, having a manicure was obviously still a priority for her. She'd have been so upset to see it cleaned off so badly. But, I guessed, she'd have understood the reasons why the doctors had to do it. They needed to see her circulation, after all.

'It's not fair that things had to happen like this.' I said, a chill running through me, despite the sun-bleached warmth pouring in from the adjacent window. 'You shouldn't be here like this.'

Today was the last day I'd be able to sit with my best friend before the machines keeping her alive would be turned off. I'd never experienced anything like this before, so I still didn't know the correct way to deal with it all. A part of me already acknowledged that Katrina was no longer with us and that this was, inevitably, the final necessary step to take. But the other part of me - the human part of me - simply wished to sit with my best friend and talk to her as if she were still able to hear me, filling her in on everything she'd missed. Katrina never did like to feel excluded.

Correct or otherwise, I held her hand and told her everything that had happened over the last few days.

'You'd be proud of me, though,' I said, trying to muster a smile. 'Despite everything feeling like the worst timing of all, I finally ended things with Matt.'

We often tell ourselves that something isn't the right time. Make excuses to delay ourselves from confronting the fear of it all. However, when situations like this arise, that entire concept goes out the window. Things couldn't particularly get any worse at this stage, so ending an already expired relationship seemed rather small fry. Plus, after what happened with Ethan just days before, I simply couldn't live with any additional guilt. So if there was ever a time to rectify situations, it was now.

Telling Matt it was over, however, isn't something I'll easily forget.

A small part of me had always suspected he was a bit of a mummy's boy, but the terrifying display he'd given really confirmed things for me. I'd tried my best to be delicate, especially with how I'd behaved towards him over the last few days (and, prior...) but even kid gloves were too strong a handle.

I remember feeling quite nauseous when I rang the bell of his family home; a grand old manor house that was still under renovation after five years of ownership. His mum, unsurprisingly, was the one who'd answered.

'Simone,' she'd buoyantly greeted, a glass of red wine in hand, 'we haven't seen you around in a while.'

And she wouldn't be seeing me much again after today, either.

I didn't like to be mean to Tonya, though. His mum had never been anything less than good to me. She'd even offered me an ear to bend at times. From what I could tell, Matt had inherited a lot of his naffer traits from his father, of which both Tonya and I inevitably bonded over. Her experiences and concerns were similar to my own a lot of the time. Nevertheless, unlike Tonya, I didn't have any plans to accept that way of living for the next thirty years.

'Hiya Ton,' I'd said back, 'is Matt home?'

'Yes, he's just upstairs. Do come inside.'

The liquid in her glass nearly spilt over as she'd used it to usher me through the door. I smiled guiltily, not that she'd have noticed.

The stairs that lead to Matt's room never seemed to end that day. They'd just continued to wind further and further around until my head dizzied and my breath jammed in my lungs. After what had happened with Jake

238

all that time ago, ending things was not an activity I was particularly fond of doing. But, a bit like pulling off a plaster, it needed to be done, and it needed to be done quickly.

Before I'd entered his room, I delayed things a few seconds more by knocking on the door. Then, once the grunt sounded, I walked inside.

'Hey Matt,' I'd said to the back of Matt's head as he'd continued to stare at yet another mindless YouTube video on his phone.

Upon hearing my voice, he then turned around.

'Simone! I...I wasn't expecting to see you.'

Placing the phone down on the floor, he'd stood up from his slouch bag and began to walk towards me. I guessed he wasn't sure exactly what to do, because he soon stopped and then took a seat on the edge of his messy bed.

I took it upon myself to sit next to him. 'I know. I just figured that it would be better to see you in person.'

His facial expression looked incredibly sombre and I couldn't help but notice how dishevelled he'd become. I was used to seeing his face. It surprised me how fast, and how badly, his stubble could grow. Patches of his skin were still clear of any facial hair. Even his follicles couldn't decide on his level of maturity.

'Matt,' I'd quickly jumped in before he could say anything, 'I am so sorry for the way I've been to you recently. The way I acted the other night wasn't fair. I shouldn't have taken my anger out on you like that. You didn't deserve it.'

'But—' I continued, 'it made me realise that this dynamic. Well, it isn't right.'

'What?' He'd interjected, shaking his head. 'No, Simone. You're allowed to be upset right now. I understand. What with everything that's happening, I am happy to give you space. Please,' his hands enclosed mine, 'don't say what you're about to say.'

Realising that this wasn't going to be easy, I took a deep breath and said, 'I'm sorry, Matt,' breaking free from his touch, 'but I think it's best for us to be apart.'

His eyes welled up as rapidly as an overflowing sink. 'No,' he'd cried, trying to clasp me back, 'you just need time. Simone, I promise you'll feel better on the other side of this.'

But he was wrong.

I moved away from him and stood up. 'Time won't change anything, Matt. I'm so sorry. I just can't do this anymore.'

I watched helplessly as the man I'd tried so hard to love began to beg me from his knees and encircle my legs in his long arms.

'Please don't go, Simone,' he'd snuffled, a mix of tears and nasal fluid streaming down his face. 'I can't live without you in my life.'

My heart should have been breaking. A part of it was. I was hurting someone I'd cared about. Aside from his flaws, he had been good to me as well. I tried to remember those times whilst carefully shuffling out of his determined grip.

'Matt, you need to let me go.'

He shook his head like a child.

'Matt, please. This isn't going to change anything.'

Finally, after losing the battle between his pleading eyes and my steely gaze, he let me go.

'Thank you,' I'd said, straightening up my clothes.

His snuffling became less exaggerated as he sat back on the bed, sulky expression lurking underneath his bizarre excuse for a beard.

'Can you at least do one last thing for me?' He'd solemnly asked.

I'd nodded back innocently. 'Sure.'

'Can you…Can we have one last kiss?'

My stomach knotted at the thought. *Was he for real?* This breakup was going in a far more cringe-worthy direction than I'd ever anticipated. As bad as I'd felt for ending things, there was absolutely nothing that would make me feel bad enough to submit to that request.

'No!' I'd yelled, insulted at the mere suggestion. 'It's over, Matt. Please!'

Not wanting to stay a moment longer, I began to pace my way towards the door.

'Fine, leave then!' He'd suddenly yelled, the dark side of his possessive designs finally revealing themselves. 'You never have done anything I've asked, anyway. You still talk to Harry, despite me telling you how upset it makes me to see another man make you laugh more than I do. You still listen to rock music, even though I've told you countless times that it makes me worried for your mental wellbeing. And then, you even go to a damned festival surrounding it. God knows what kind of wretched tearaways you've been with during those times. I've tried to trust you, Simone. In spite of everything you've put me through; I've allowed you to be independent. Most women would love a man like me – a man who takes care of them like I do. But you,' he

241

snarled, 'after everything I've forsaken, this is how *you* treat *me*?'

I stood in an aghast silence as he'd spat the last words out at me.

'You can go fuck yourself.'

From my position in the doorway, I'd said nothing. Everything he'd said didn't require any justification.

It was time to leave.

As I'd fled the scene, quickstepping down the never-ending stairs and out of the front door, I don't think I even took a breath. I'd only realised once I was back outside that I could let out the plug of air blocking my throat.

I should've been furious. Perhaps, I should've felt upset, too. But instead, once I'd released that clog of air into the London sky, I smiled. No part of me even felt an ounce of guilt anymore. His resentful outburst made sure of that. It confirmed everything that my soul suspected to be true. Matt wasn't good for me. He wasn't the one. And for that realisation, I was truly thankful.

'So yeah, it's finally over.' I said to Katrina, closing my rather odd breakup story. 'And even though I know I'm not faultless in all this and took way too long to actually take your advice; I don't feel like too much of a bad person. Not as much as I did before, anyway.'

The TV above us continued to display more weather reports. I never could understand why we needed so many in one go. Looking out of the window was all the validation I needed to prepare myself for the day ahead. And, let's face it, this is Britain. It's probably going to rain. It wasn't, however, raining on the day I relayed more of the week's stories to Katrina by her bedside.

'Oh, and I think Dad has finally lost the plot,' I divulged, 'as a way of trying to cheer me up, he sent me a remote-controlled Lamborghini. I know he's obsessed with cars, but jeez…Can you seriously imagine me racing that thing around our flat?'

'Nevertheless, it did present me with an opportunity to speak to both him and mum about a few things…'

After ending things with Matt, I'd decided to celebrate my newfound freedom with a chocolate doughnut at the Belsize Bakery. More often than not, if I'd gone there with Seb, I'd have simply watched him fill his hollow legs with sugar-laden treats, wondering where on earth he put it all. The only sensible reasoning I could deduce was that my watchful eyes consumed all of the calories on his behalf. However, on this particular day, I'd decided to throw caution to the wind and enjoy those calories myself for a change. If my thighs were going to start rubbing together, I wanted to at least play an active role in their creation. Plus, those doughnuts were worth every bite.

'So good,' I'd mumbled, ridding dots of chocolate sauce from my chin, 'so messy, but so damn good.'

'Good to see you eating, blossom.' Dad said to me from across the table, stirring his hot chocolate. 'Your mother and I have been worried about you.'

It was Kats who'd helped me see the light about my family initially. All of our conversations long ago showed me that a reluctance to let others be themselves was stymieing my own happiness, which is exactly why, upon receipt of the toy Lambo, I'd organised a day to see my Dad.

'Not being able to be with you recently, to support you…' he babbled. I watched eagerly as he fumbled for the number that could help him get in touch with his emotions. 'Well, it's not what any parent wants to do – to be separate from their child in their time of need.'

I'd shrugged my shoulders whilst swallowing the last delicious bite of the best doughnut in the world.

'Neither of you exactly live around the corner,' I'd said. 'Just having you both at the end of the phone has been enough.'

The truth was so far from that statement, though. There was nothing I'd wanted more than to be the little girl inside and have both my parents hold me like they used to; like back in the days when we were an actual family, living under the same roof, before it all went wrong. But I didn't want to expose this truth. There was no getting those days back, so there was little point in attempting to recreate them.

'Sure, and we both know you're very independent, Simone,' Dad stated, staring at me over his towering hot chocolate glass, 'but, things right now aren't exactly the same as usual.'

Sometimes, I was glad he wasn't an emotional person. At times like these, especially. Crying in public definitely wasn't an action I wanted to engage in, and luckily for me, Dad's way with words kept me far from achieving that.

'Fiona—I mean, your mother is sorry she couldn't join us,' he'd added, apologetically, 'the bank wasn't exactly obliging.'

My mood was dampening, but I nodded decisively and smiled anyway.

'It's fine, Dad,' I'd replied, thinking of a way to soften my terseness until finally deciding on the words, 'I'm glad you're here.'

He'd smiled at that.

There was a stark contrast between the last time we'd sat here together and this day.

It was quite hard to forget how much resentment I carried towards my Dad for his infidelities. The fact that he wasn't even with the woman he tore our family apart over made that feeling weigh even heavier on my heart. However, after everything that had happened over recent times, all I wanted to do was finally set that anguish free. Having a grudge towards someone is like letting them live rent-free in your mind, and there wasn't enough room left in mine to accommodate that.

'How's Mayzie?' I'd asked, trying to reroute the subject from such heartfelt avenues.

Dad's eyes widened. 'Oh Simone, she's an absolute beauty!'

From that point onwards, I could have left the room several times and he wouldn't have noticed. It reminded me of a joke I'd once heard, about a policeman asking a man who'd lost his wife to identify her. His description was, of course, rather vague. But, when the policeman then asked him about the car he and his wife were driving before she'd vanished, the husband could go into intricate detail.

Dad then began to show me several pictures and videos of him and Mayzie.

'Jeremy Clarkson was bang on the money,' he commented, observing the plethora of MX-5 footage he'd captured with gooey eyes. 'Nothing else puts as much of a smile on your face. It's such an enjoyable car to drive. Just look at her. Isn't she a great little motor?'

Usually, I'd have wanted to roll my eyes and poke some satire into the conversation. But on this day, I simply couldn't do it. Instead, I submitted a rather surprising response of, 'She really is quite something.'

All of a sudden, as if by necessary force, a memory pushed its way into our cosy little scene. It transported me back to the moment Katrina spoke words of wisdom: *'If you hold onto this feeling and something bad happens to someone you care about, will you, in five years' time, regret showing love to that person despite their flaws, or losing them having said nothing?'*

That was when I took hold of Dad's hand.

'I'm happy that you're in a good place now, Dad. And, I…I just wanted to say that I'm so sorry again for what happened last time we were here. I never properly apologised for that.'

With his free hand, he turned off his phone.

'Hey,' he'd said softly, 'don't worry yourself, blossom. What kind of Dad would I be if I didn't take a little crap from my kids every so often, anyway? Plus, I should've known better than to push you into finding someone. You're an adult now and capable of making your own choices. Plus, I've recently learned that being single is quite enjoyable. Your mother, for example, would have never let me buy Mayzie if we were still married.'

We both smiled a smile of mutual understanding. Everyone else had now moved on with their lives. It was about time I did as well.

After mine and Dad's heart-to-heart, I'd decided to strike whilst the iron was hot and call mum, too. I hadn't exactly been the most accepting of her relationship with Andrew, and although he was never going to be what I envisioned my mum to be with, I had to accept it. Just like with Dad and his adoration for cars, whether I thought it was ludicrous or otherwise, I had to accept that was his choice. Maybe I'd never understand them, but for the sake of peace, I knew that they had to live their own lives and make their own judgements, just like they'd finally allowed me to do.

All I wanted my family to know was that, despite the challenges we'd faced and dramas we've created, I loved them – even Seb. And so, I'd decided to spend the rest of that afternoon making sure they knew that. I'd also managed to power-walk my way around most of central London as part of the process, which hopefully put some of the calories from that devilishly delicious doughnut to good use.

'Did you know that Seb took great pleasure in taking the piss out of my heartfelt speech?' I said to Katrina, wrapping up the second story of the week whilst straightening out her bedsheet. 'Honestly, he can be so hit and miss that brother of mine. But hey, what else should I expect from a human cheese string, right?'

As I stared back up at the TV, the news had been replaced by a period drama. A blonde-haired woman wearing rags fled across the scene and into a darkened tepee. She looked flustered, but slowly started to calm down when another woman from inside the tent called her to take a seat at a cloth table. From what I could tell, the woman who was beckoning the dishevelled woman with an alluring finger was a fortune teller. I cleared my throat and bowed my head down upon the sight of it. I had only wanted to relay the week, but at that point, I knew that I'd have to revisit a past much further away.

'Do you remember when we went to that psychic switch? And, I told you that it was a load of hooey?' I tilted my head guiltily, 'Well, I may have mildly exaggerated.'

'Of course, I still wasn't sure at the time whether she was legitimate. Some things she'd told me seemed rather innocuous, whereas others…' The memory still sent shivers down my spine. I shook my head in disbelief. 'She just couldn't have known them. And yet, somehow, she did.'

A silence hung in the air between us. Even though I knew Katrina probably couldn't hear me, I still wondered if her soul could somehow instinctively take it all in. If the year was anything to go by, I wasn't discounting the possibility.

As I was about to break into another lengthy speech, a nurse came in to check Katrina's stats. I meekly smiled at her and tried not to inhale. This particular nurse had a distinctive scent that I couldn't quite shake off. It reminded me of a customer who'd regularly visited Botanique and, although this particular lady always spent an absolute fortune on beauty remedies and bathing treasures, it didn't change the fact that she still smelt like she didn't use any of them. I'd tried not to judge, but the waft could sometimes be so overpowering that both Katrina and I would go in and out of the back just to breathe. As I remembered it and looked over to my motionless friend, I wished we could recapture that moment. She made me laugh so much. I'd miss that.

I already did.

The nurse left without saying a word, and, as soon as she closed the curtain, I opened the window.

'Right,' I puffed, taking my seat back next to Katrina, 'now, where was I? Oh, yes – the psychic.'

Out of everything I wanted to share with Katrina that afternoon, it was that I was sorry for everything. I was sorry for poo-pooing the psychic, for not heeding the warnings she'd given me, or for the warnings Katrina's body had, and I was sorry for not supporting her and missing her big run for the sake of a festival.

'I know you said it was okay and that I could go, but—'

My mouth stopped talking at that very moment. It was as if a gentle finger had placed itself on my lips, calmly gesturing that what's done is done. I imagined it to be Katrina, as though she were standing right in front of me having this conversation.

She always used to express that I should have more fun - *live a little* - and that she never could understand why people felt that abstaining from fun put them on a moral high ground. It was not the way she lived her life, nor did she want to change that. And so, even if she had wanted me at the run, this thought reminded me that she'd also wanted me to live my life, as she did hers.

Throughout our friendship, I'd learned that what we valued wasn't the quantity of time we'd spent together, but the quality. We were two very different people who lead two very different lives, which is why when those paths did coincide at work or at home or on a night out, it was special. Neither of us needed to be stitched at the hip to know that we cared for one another. The strength of our bond wasn't tied to that.

In my silence, I looked over at Katrina one last time, trying to envisage what she would tell me if she were standing beside me.

'You know me, Sims. I tell it how it is. If I don't like something, I'll tell you. If I do, I'll tell you. And I was pretty open in telling you to inject some more excitement into your life, which is why I told you to go to Upload festival, or whatever it's called. Of course, I would have loved to have seen you at the run. But, as far as I knew, we were going to see each other the next day, anyway. It was no biggie. Plus, I'm a firm believer that everything happens for a reason. You needed that gig as much as I needed that run. Imagine if one of us had sacrificed that? What happened would still have happened, but neither of us would have anything good to take from it. In this life, Simone, we only regret the things we haven't done.'

Whether I'd concocted that speech in my head or Katrina had somehow told me herself, the sentiment sat with me. It was true, when we look back at our lives and all the good and bad choices we've ever made, we only ever truly regret the things we never did - the projects we never finished, the places we never went to, the people we let slip away. And yet, when I thought of mine and Katrina's friendship, I had no regrets. The only thing I did regret was that it had to end so soon.

I inhaled as I reached over to stroke her long dark hair, smiling at her. The afternoon sun had dipped away and cast a faded shadow across her face. In her own way, she looked rather peaceful.

All of a sudden, an unexpected tear rolled down my cheek. More were piling up behind my eyes, but I managed to keep the rest in check whilst I said the one last thing I wanted my best friend to know.

'I love you so much.'

The Light

The hands of time couldn't have moved any slower than they did that morning. They'd barely lifted a finger as they stretched from one minute to the next. Sometimes, I could swear that they'd even reversed five minutes. Not that I was one for wishing time away, but I was very much aware of the little time I had to get from work to the hospital once my shift was over. And if the woman at the till planned on spending any longer paying me penny by penny for her foot cream, I'd be too late to see Katrina.

'Thirty-nine, forty…Or, was that fifty?' She stared at the row of coppers with perplexity. 'Oh, I think I best count them again to make sure.'

I looked back at the clock and noticed that time seemed to have done a quantum leap. Ten minutes ago I'd had twenty minutes until I could escape, and then, all of a sudden, I only had five.

'It's fine, don't worry,' I stated, swiping the coins off the counter and into my hand, 'I'm sure we won't miss ten pence.'

The woman's eyes bulged. 'But I would feel awful if I'd short-changed you,' she declared, her stunned expression remaining affixed.

'Please, don't.' I said, closing the till. 'The items are all overpriced, anyway.'

That statement didn't seem to help, but detecting my curt manner, she nodded and made her way back onto the bustling streets of Oxford Circus.

Again, I looked at the clock and began untying my apron before even taking in the time. One minute to two. That was good enough for me. I never left early, but on a day such as this, I was certain that even Alexandra couldn't be that cruel.

Between the members of Katrina's family and friends, we'd all reluctantly agreed that today would be the last day the machines would stay on. The decision itself still didn't feel real. Everything had changed so quickly in such a short space of time, and even though I'd seen her every day and was wholly aware of what had happened, I still wasn't fully prepared for the moment it would arrive. All I knew was that I needed to be by Katrina's side. Because that's what best friends do - they stick by each other, even if it's going to be the hardest thing in the world to do.

'See you tomorrow, Alexandra.' I called, whilst signing out my name on the timesheet.

Alexandra came out from her lair, I mean, office, and stood behind the till.

'Thank you, Simone,' she said softly. 'And if you don't feel up to coming in tomorrow, please let me know. I understand this is a hard time.'

I glanced up at her from the customer side of the till with surprise. Seeing her compassionate side wasn't something I was used to. Until then, I didn't even know she had one.

'Thanks.' I replied, slowly putting down the pen and putting on my lacy fingerless gloves. 'I appreciate that.'

It may have only lasted a millisecond, but we both shared a smile.

'Bye,' I said, half raising my hand in a bid of farewell. She nodded back in acknowledgement, and I made my way towards the glass door of freedom.

Out on the crowded asphalt streets, a fierce gust of wind took me by surprise. It was almost as mighty as the one I'd seen that weatherman experience on the TV. Of all the things I expected from the weather, that was the last thing on my list for June. My hair was now splaying wildly and I could barely see the tube entrance for it. I fumbled around for my phone, hoping that my fingers could seek out which slot my Oyster card was in where my eyes couldn't. Through windswept strands, I saw the blue checkpoint sign marking, "Oxford Circus Station" and hotfooted down the steps.

Now safe within the underground, the only things left to battle against were time and tourists. Of course, in the height of summer, in the middle of the day, in the busiest part of the metropolis, my chances of winning that battle were slim to none. But I was determined. My phone said it was only ten minutes past one, so I still had time. All I had to do was get on the next train.

The red Central Line hovered above the barriers in front of me. I quickly navigated my way towards the least crowded one and smacked my Oyster card down, waiting for the longest second known to man before it finally let me through.

It was fortunate that I knew the tube stations like the back of my hand; even with hordes of commuters blocking my view, I was certain of my route. The journey should only take thirty minutes, and that's if I decided to leisurely pace my way to Hammersmith Hospital once I'd reached East Acton. Obviously, I would be running like the wind instead. That was the plan, anyway.

On the platform, I caught my breath and stared up at the sign above which stated that the next train would be arriving in one minute. The time was now seventeen minutes past one.

Before I could even finish putting my phone away, the train pulled up and opened its doors to reveal a packed carriage full of sweaty people all huddled together. As a rule, that would be the kind of carriage I'd prefer to avoid. But, desperate times call for desperate measures, and in my book, today was one of those times. I held my breath, as if it would make a difference to my size, and wedged myself in by the doors, which soon closed sharply behind me.

It was so unbearably hot on the tube that I had to take off my lacy gloves. They seemed like such a good idea first thing in the morning, but now I was suffocating in a sweaty sardine tin, their attachment to my fingers was no fun whatsoever. I actually began to yearn for the surprise wind outside. However, I was counting my lucky stars regardless. Despite the odds, I was going to make it.

For the first few stops, everything seemed normal. Aside from learning how to breathe in such a crammed carriage and wishing that I had a bottle of water to cool me down, I was relieved to know that I was going to be there in time to be there for Katrina. This time, I wasn't going to let her down.

Out of the blue, the train began to slow down. We'd already gone past the last stop, so I initially assumed that we were slowly approaching the next. But, instead of the train windows unveiling a stretched white platform, everything outside remained black.

It must be a traffic light; I silently reassured myself. Other passengers continued to stand with their noses in the free newspapers or with their eyes towards the plethora of adverts overhead. No one seemed concerned at first, but after several minutes of standstill went by, that soon changed.

'Apologies for the delay,' came the tube driver's voice through the speakers, 'unfortunately, we have encountered a minor technical failure. Please rest assured that we are doing everything we can to fix this, and appreciate your patience.'

A resounding chorus of agitation syncopated through the carriage. Some people merely sighed, others began to cuss; I, however, was now unreservedly in a state of internal panic. I was so close and yet so far. Nothing was meant to get in the way of me being there for Katrina and yet it seemed as though this was fate's way of punishing me for my previous failings. This was the price I was going to pay.

Hot, stressed and fearful, I manoeuvred my hand into my bag to reach for my phone. I needed to let someone know that I was going to be late. Maybe then they would hold on a bit longer? That was my hope. But, the big cross hovering above my phone's signal bars told me otherwise.

'Fuck, fuck, fuck no!' I wailed, already feeling on the edge of tears. 'This is not happening.'

The temperature inside was climbing, and multiple beads of sweat began to run from underneath my fringe. Other people were becoming distressed and irritable, whining every minute as to why we hadn't had any other updates from the conductor.

'What on earth is going on?' one woman huffed, talking to anyone who'd listen. 'Are they even doing anything to fix this?'

Standing opposite me was another woman who looked as though she were about to collapse.

'I don't feel right,' she gurgled, swaying ever so slightly. 'I need to stand by the doors. Please,' she begged. 'I need to stand by the doors.'

Men in suits anchored their torsos so she could pull herself through. There was absolutely no air anywhere, but being inches closer to a potential escape must have had a psychological impact, as once she'd slumped herself beside my feet, she seemed to calm down.

'Are you okay?' I asked her. She nodded, glazed eyes fixed to the floor.

Half an hour went by before any further information was given. It honestly felt like a lifetime. Eventually though, the driver alerted a sea of worried faces on what was to happen next.

'Despite attempting to get the train moving again, unfortunately, this hasn't been successful. As a result, I'm afraid we are all going to have to walk half a mile down the tracks towards Shepherd's Bush. Please kindly follow the directions given by the staff in your cabin.'

People's faces were awash with a mix of horror and excitement. The tourists, mostly, saw it as an exciting opportunity. A couple of them even began to start taking selfies and filming it. Everyone else, however, couldn't have felt more differently.

By this point, all I could do was cross my fingers that everyone at the hospital would wait for me, knowing that I wouldn't miss my chance to say goodbye to Katrina without good reason. I tried not to think too hard about it. I tried not to see Tricia and Paul's angry faces as they thought of their beloved daughter's useless friend who couldn't even be there for her one last time. I tried not to imagine the scene of doctors filling up her room, turning off the alarms on her machines and removing her breathing tube. I tried desperately not to think about the entire scene but simply couldn't help it. Katrina was my best friend, and all I could think was that she deserved so much better than me.

Hundreds of passengers were now stretched out in front of me, like human dominoes, through the dark tunnels. It was the most bizarre experience. Any other time, I'd have probably just put my iPod in and listened to some music whilst pacing from plank to plank down the dimly lit track. Today though, I could only feel resentment for the situation. On all of the days this could have happened, why did it have to be today, and why did it have to be now?

With every step, I watched through sweaty eyes to see whether my phone signal would change. It must have been thirty degrees down there, and even though the train staff were doing their best to keep our spirits lifted, nothing was detracting from the weight I felt in my chest. Time was soaring past as I effectively stood still, waiting for tourists to quit taking pictures in front of me and for bilious people to quit stating that they were "going to die" if they didn't get out soon. I tried so hard not to react to that statement. Instead, I simply walked. I walked and walked until, eventually, I would be where I needed to be - at my best friend's side.

***

By the time I arrived at Shepherd's Bush station, it was absolute bedlam. Crowds overran the station and paramedics rushed to the aids of those who'd collapsed from the heat. I didn't know where to look. I may have been on the other side of one nightmare situation, but I knew I still had a whole other yet to face.

Since realising that there was no way I was going to make it to the hospital by two o'clock, I'd stopped looking at my phone. If I did, I knew I would have simply burst into tears or, most possibly, gone into a flight of rage, cursing the world for its cruelty. But there was nothing I could do to change what had happened. All I could do was focus on the present moment, so I instead put every effort into getting myself to the hospital as quickly as possible. Just because the machines had been turned off didn't mean that it was over. There was still a small chance that Katrina was still alive. In my heart, I wanted to believe that.

With a newfound adrenaline coursing through me, I pushed my way through the station crowds and dashed to the outside, hoping that one part of the day might still be on my side. Luckily, as soon as my sneakers trailed the kerb, a taxi was there waiting.

'Hammersmith Hospital, please,' I said, piling myself into the back of the black cab. 'As quickly as you can.'

***

Finally, time was on my side and so was the driver, who raced through the city streets as though his cab was on a PlayStation game. In and out he dodged the rush hour traffic, showing no mercy to the roads of the metropolis. After such an intense afternoon, I nearly threw up in the back seat. Yet somehow, through sheer grit and determination, I managed to hold it back. Nausea may well have accompanied me on my journey, but there was no way I was going to acknowledge its existence.

It was only upon sight of the sculpture at the hospital's main entrance that I realised I'd been holding my breath. I let it out as soon as the taxi pulled to a halt, quickly passed my money through the internal window and then headed towards the doors.

Inside the building, I bolted at lightning speed towards Katrina's ward, the flicker of hope still burning strong in my heart. I darted up the stairs, to the left and to the right, avoiding the lift at all costs. I wasn't going to give technology any further chances to thwart me. And then, as I approached Katrina's wing, I began to slow down my pace.

The hall felt long and empty, extending just like those never-ending tunnels. There wasn't a person in sight. It was quiet - too quiet. And as I slowly turned the last corner to her room, holding my breath once more, I suddenly realised why.

A doctor had his hand placed on Katrina's wrist, his eyebrows were furrowed in mute concentration, and I watched on interminably as he gathered his words together. He then gently placed her arm back down by her side and saw me in the doorway, my mouth quivering in fear of what he was about to say. Sombrely, he finally admitted them.

'I'm so sorry.'

My heart split in two the moment I knew hers had stopped beating. No matter how hard I'd raced against time to see her, hoping somehow fate would pause from cutting her life short, I was too late. She'd already slipped away, and knowing that I'd only missed it by minutes shattered me like glass.

At the end of her bed I collapsed in a heap on the floor, a crumbling mess of a woman, shaking to my very core. I don't know what words escaped me. All I can recall are the mix of disbelieving *no's* catapulting out of my scratched throat and the floods of tears pooling their way down my face. Despite the machines being turned off hours before, her soul desperately clung to the precipice of life, waiting for me to say goodbye. But I'd failed her once again.

My mind was full of pain, and yet, it was almost empty at the same time. Waves of despair washed everything else underneath, with only the rapid waters filling my mind and collecting behind my eyes.

'This isn't real,' I wailed, staring at my best friend who lay before me as though she were simply asleep. 'You've got to wake up, Katrina. It's time to wake up...Please.'

As I moved in closer, I reached across to stroke her skin. She was icy to the touch. Her lips had already started to turn a pale shade of blue, and as I took in the sight of her, my teeth chattered as though it was me who was frozen. My breath disjointedly rattled out of my chest. All in that moment, everything suddenly became clear.

Despite hoping that a miracle would take away the pain and give back what had been stolen, it wasn't going to happen. Because that's what it was - Katrina's life had been stolen. Her unique spirit, her passions and dreams, her quirky habits; every single thing that made her, her, was gone. She had now faded away into a world unknown, and no matter what I or anyone else had hoped for, nothing was going to change that. Her soul had succumbed to the light.

The only thing left I could hope for was that she was finally at peace.

The Last Goodbye

TWO WEEKS' LATER

There was something mysterious placed underneath my knee that I daren't look at. My mind concocted many an unwanted image of what the tiny object could be, but rather than be brave and discover what on earth had stuck itself to my tights; I thought it wise to continue doing my makeup in the smudged round mirror balanced on the windowsill instead. Of course, I expected nothing less from a student house.

 Most teenagers, once released from home and into the wild, will live accordingly. I did, however, find it a nice gesture of Seb to let me stay at his place the night before the funeral. He lived closer to the church than I did and, quite surprisingly, Seb couldn't bear the idea of me staying alone in the apartment during a time like this. Apparently, Tariq had recently told him there was a psychological reasoning behind the notion of being stronger together. He said that it was foundational to humans and that painful experiences worked as a type of "social glue" in creating solidarity. And so, whether it was down to Seb's own morals kicking in or Tariq's Derren Brown-*esque* influence, it led me to sleeping in the spare room of the five-bedroomed student house they shared. How, I wondered, everyone there could obtain a degree and yet still not have mastered the art of vacuuming, I would never fathom. Nonetheless, I was incredibly grateful for the company, which is why I decided against complaining, and also why I chose to let

263

whatever had attached itself to my knee remain as it was; a mystery.

As I adjusted my black choker, my phone buzzed beside me. It was Harry, saying that he was thinking of me and that if I needed to talk then he would be there. I raised my eyebrows a little and tilted my head.

Maybe pain really did work like glue? Everyone was sticking by me – even my seemingly impassive male camaraderie. It was rather heart-warming to say the least. On the other hand, my head was already quite full that morning, having only enough space for the thoughts on Katrina's speech.

Initially, I'd written it not knowing what it was. I'd just started thinking about Katrina's passions and peeves after looking at her little kitchen cupboard door notes, and then suddenly felt the urge to write it all down. Ten minutes later, the pen fell out of my fingers and onto the notepad's open page. I was only ever going to keep those words to myself, but Tricia unexpectedly stumbled upon them when she'd come over to the apartment to discuss plans for the funeral. And, even though my initial assumption was to apologise, she'd proved insistent that I read it at the service. After everything that had happened recently, she knew that my care for Katrina ran deep.

Now, next to my phone, those very feelings lay.

I gulped a little as I stared at the words that expressed them, making me realise that I needed to loosen my choker a little. As I unfastened the chain and looked at the pages, I wondered how I was going to even get past the first sentence without falling apart. I wasn't sure if I had the strength. Revealing my innermost thoughts wasn't something I was used to, but I would do anything to express my adoration for Katrina. Wherever she was now, I wanted her to know that she was loved.

A gentle tap sounded on the room's chipped blue door.

'Everyone's downstairs, just so you know,' Seb said, slowly walking in, 'are you ready to go?'

I'd never seen him wear all black before. For me, wearing black wasn't such a shock to the system. Everyone was used to seeing me in dark colours. But Seb was a personified glow stick. He didn't *do* dark colours. So seeing him today, dressed from head to toe in black and white, was very surreal.

'Nearly,' I replied, eyeing up my brother's well-turned-out suit. 'You look smart, Seb. Though, I think Kats would have probably found it a tad weird to see you without your standard psychedelia.'

'My psyche-de-what-now?'

I shook my head, smiling to the side. 'I just think you should put on a dot of colour.' Looking around for something that he could add, the perfect accessory caught my eye.

'What about this?'

On the bedside table was a neon green wristband used to gain entry to the nightclub in Camden we all used to go to. Just seeing it brought back all the memories so crisply; it was as though they'd only happened yesterday. Smiling at the recollection, I picked it up and passed it over to Seb.

'Katrina would have liked this,' I stated, fastening it around his wrist. 'Plus, it signifies good times. We have to cherish those.'

His bottom lip turned inwards as he nodded, looking mournfully down at the little green strap.

Observing his saddened appearance, I reached for his suit's sleeve and lightly smoothed his arm with my thumb. It was never going to be an easy day, but it was one that we both had to face, and as long as we had each other, I knew we'd be okay.

'Hey,' I uttered comfortingly, now squeezing his hand, 'it'll be alright. I promise.'

He looked up at me with hopeful eyes and slowly bobbed his head.

'Now, come on,' I continued, attempting to provide the motivational platform we both needed to stand on, 'let's give her a send-off to remember.'

***

Outside the church was an overspill of penguins. At least, that's what it looked like as we approached it from Tracey's car.

'Gosh. What a turnout.' Cherise said, soaking up the Antarctic scene. 'I never realised she knew so many people.'

Mesmerised by the sight, I nodded in agreement. 'Neither did I.'

As we entered the church's circular car park, I was surprised when Tracey suddenly pulled the car to a stop.

'Can you guys make your way from here?' She asked thinly. 'At the best of times, I get nervous parallel parking, let alone with so many people around and in a bloody doughnut-shaped car park.'

266

Without so much as even a jeer, Cherise, Julian, Seb and I carefully exited the little Yaris and began to pace towards the sea of suits.

In front of us, the afternoon sun shone through the garnet trees and spilt onto the ground like golden pieces of glitter. Experiencing nature's unrefined beauty was a rarity in the city, so beholding it on a day like this brought a sense of ease to my heart. With every step I took closer towards the crowd, I simply breathed in, remembered Katrina's bonny face - especially the way she used to leap ahead of me anywhere we went - and, for her sake, carried on.

'I'm so glad you could all be here,' I heard Tricia say to some of the guests as she and Paul took each of them hand by hand. 'It would mean such a lot to Katrina to know you'd come.'

One of the older men brushed his hand gently through the air. 'Miss Stevenson was an exceptional pupil,' he declared, 'to teachers and students alike, she left an indelible mark behind. On behalf of the whole college, being here today is to pay homage to all that she gave us.'

The first of many tears emerged in Tricia's eyes in that moment.

'Thank you so much.'

For a while, we simply observed the herd of people taking turns to pass on their condolences. From old teachers to previous bosses, anyone who was anyone in Katrina's life had come to pay their respects. That was when I saw something that took my breath away.

'Is that...' I pointed towards the church's arched doors, 'Alexandra?'

Seb tutted at the unmistakable sight of her. 'So it is.'

A second of absorbed silence passed before he added, 'I wonder if she'll catch on fire the moment she sets foot in the church?'

I scoffed, before giving him a gentle nudge, 'Shh. This is a holy place. Don't want the man upstairs to hear you.'

He merely shrugged at that, 'Only saying what you're thinking. Katrina would've said just as much.'

It was true. She did call her *Miss Trunchball* for a very good reason. Even so, I didn't want to further advocate any mockery, just in case.

'Indeed. Oh, look. Tricia and Paul are both free now. We should go and speak to them before the service begins.'

I pulled Seb by the hand and mustered an awkward wave in their direction.

'Hello you two,' Paul said, with a smiling mouth and downturned eyes. You could see this was hard for him, for both of them. Seb, recognising this, went straight for a hug.

'We're here for you, all day, whenever you need us.'

Tricia and Paul both smiled as they tapped him gently on the back.

'Thank you, Seb,' Tricia said kindly. 'Katrina was so fortunate to have had friends like you.'

Noticing that our turn to talk had finally arrived, Cherise, Julian and Tracey began to walk over too. Of course, after myself and Seb, Julian was next to come in for a hug – a slightly more gentle one.

'Thank you for coming, Julian.' Paul said, squeezing him encouragingly on the shoulder. Both men, upon release, wore matching sombre expressions. 'Katrina was right about you. You're an upstanding young man.'

'Certainly,' Tricia concurred, 'I know that today is going to be hard. Katrina played a very special part in all of our lives. Which is why, like Seb said, we want you to know that here for you, too.'

We all nodded in silent agreement before the vicar came over.

'We are ready to begin.' The nodding turned into inhalation. *Breathe in...breathe out.* Pleasantries aside, the real task had only just begun.

***

In the centre of the great vaulted room was the smallest box I'd ever seen. Seb and I both gripped each other tightly when we saw it, knowing what was inside. My breath juddered out like a car engine in the snow.

Inside that tiny box covered in flowers, we both knew, was Katrina. To this day, I don't think I'll ever get over how she could have been in there. Her character was larger than life itself – how could they have contained it in such a small wicker casket? For a moment, none of us could move. Our eyes had stopped our feet from walking. But we had to keep going, and we had to do it quietly. This day was not about us.

We all took our seats on the front row, with the rest of Katrina's family. Julian sat next to Paul, who sat beside Tricia, who sat beside me, Seb, Tracey and Cherise. From that point, the rest of the congregation poured in through the doors behind us. But we could only hear their subdued steps. Turning around isn't something you do once you've taken your seat and I couldn't risk

269

looking up at the casket again without fear of tears. So instead, I decided to reach for the order of service booklet and look at Katrina's smiling face on the front cover, delicately tracing the tiny timeline of her life underneath with my finger. It didn't help prevent the tears.

I then felt a reassuring hand squeeze mine. Through waterlogged eyes, Tricia and I both looked at one another with knowingness. Being strong sometimes meant letting it all out. But despite the truth of that, I still had a job to do.

Once everyone had taken their seats, the vicar took his place at the podium and began with the eulogy.

He shared her life story with us in a mere ten minutes, offering a lot of religious prose to pad it out. In my mind, I didn't feel that it did my friend justice. Her spirit was vibrant, her love was endless, and she deserved more than some spiel of Godliness. One more hymn soon followed, and then it was my turn to change that.

'Please take your seats once more,' the vicar said, as the shuffle of bodies returned to silence. 'We now have a reading from one of Katrina's closest friends.'

He gestured toward me.

'Simone Hartley, would you like to say a few words?'

The whole row smiled at me and Seb gently squeezed my arm. Their comfort was reassuring, but I was still absolutely terrified. My biggest challenge was not the speech itself; it was having to walk past the casket with my best friend inside. No matter how much I wanted to hold it together, I knew that just looking at it would send me tumbling down. And for the sake of doing Katrina justice, I had to stay strong. It all rested on me now.

Slowly, I rose from my seat, speech in hand, and walked towards the podium.

It was the most unusual place to be. The arched ceilings towered above me, the sea of suits watched on with broken features, and I looked down at my piece of paper, taking one last deep breath, preparing myself to say exactly what Katrina would have been thinking.

'Katrina would have hated this,' I echoed to a now slightly surprised audience. 'Seeing all of her friends and family with the number eleven etched between their eyebrows would have driven her crazy.'

I let out a little laugh thinking about it, remembering how her encyclopaedic knowledge of skincare and supportive nature was so cleverly intertwined. And that, if she'd ever caught me frowning, she'd remind me just how many muscles it took to look miserable. There was no way she could ever advocate such misuse of facial movement.

'We all knew Katrina didn't like to see people sad. She'd always be the first to provide a shoulder to cry on. But with that comfy headrest also came the price of a reality check. As if she'd ever let you leave a room without the casual reminder that, yes, she loved you but, no, you still need to have a word with yourself. Nevertheless, she somehow managed to strike the perfect balance between lending that sympathetic ear whilst providing a good boot up the rump.'

The room laughed through silent tears that strolled down their faces. Every person was sharing this same reminiscence about the beautiful woman we'd grown to know so well.

'Katrina,' I continued, looking up towards the monumental height of the church ceiling, 'you taught me more than you'll ever know. Without you, I wouldn't be where I am today. Your unerring confidence and positive view of the world made me realise so much about life. It's a fantastic place, full of wonder and magic – even when it doesn't seem like it. But people like you are the ones that inject that magic. Your vision and infinite passions made this world a better place, and your friendship made me a better person. Never again will I look at life with my eyes half-open. All of the memories I carry of you will make sure of that.'

The next lines in my speech were always going to be the hardest to read.

'With that said, saying goodbye isn't really an option. For as long as I remember you, Katrina, and those that love you remember you too; you'll always live on. Even new experiences will still have room for your unforgettable presence. So instead of saying goodbye to you by conventional means, I'd like to say this instead…Goodbye is not forever. Goodbye is not the end. Goodbye is just a way of saying *until we meet again*.'

A gulp suddenly blocked my throat and made it hard to speak, causing tears to well up in my eyes like an overflowing bath.

'I love you, Kats,' I sobbed, clutching the podium until my hands turned red. 'I'm going to miss you every day.'

***

The rest of the service blurred in with the familiar trickle of notes that played in the background. For so long, I'd been in love with that famous Goo Goo Dolls song, especially since Katrina and I had watched the City of Angels together. That memory now, however, felt like a lifetime ago, and today, hearing the poignant track did not leave me feeling in love, but rather, in two minds.

'Ashes to ashes. Dust to dust.'

One by one, we each took a step towards the open ground and allowed it to swallow our pensive collection of soil. Throughout this time, I could still hear nothing else around me, only the heartfelt lyrics encircling my mind.

In the midst of those inaudible soundwaves, my life flashed me by. Every memory, belief, feeling, wish...regret, they all returned in floods, bringing tears to my eyes with each heart-wrenching reminiscence. And, although it pained me to remember all the chances I'd taken for granted, the moments I wished I could live again - just once, even for a single minute - it made me realise something far, far bigger:

'Second chances aren't always an option, and no matter how much you will it, nothing can change the past.'

Unlike in the famous film this song was made for, we don't have a choice on whose shoes we walk in. In reality, we have to live through the pain with gritted teeth in order to learn how to smile again.

'In the hope of resurrection unto eternal life...'

On this plane, everything is impermanent. Between life's good and bad spells, in truth, there is only the here and now. Time keeps on ticking whether we like it or not, and I was slowly learning how to no longer take this desolating, and yet beautiful, concept for granted.

'Amen'

***

Sandwiches have never been more unappealing than they were today. Each floppy white triangle had been stacked on silver trays and slathered over by the other attendees. I could not comprehend how anyone could eat on a day such as this. And yet, still, I perfunctorily added three to a paper plate alongside a meagre piece of Victoria sponge, and taken it to one of the outside tables to stare at.

'How's the egg and cress?' Tracey asked, rubbernecking my redundant offering of food.

I shrugged my shoulders, 'Have it.' I said, pushing the paper plate towards her, 'I don't even know why I took it. I'm not exactly hungry.'

She picked up the flaccid sandwich with slight uncertainty and began to pull off chunks between her finger and thumb.

'I liked your speech, Simone,' Julian piped from the opposite end of our wooden table. 'Hearing about the things that made Katrina who she was as a person and how she'd impacted all of our lives was a great touch.'

Offering a slight smile, I replied, 'Thank you. The eulogy didn't exactly showcase her as an individual, in my opinion, so I'm glad I did it.'

Tracey covered her mouth as she interjected, 'It was really brave, Simone. I couldn't have done it.'

'Me either,' Cherise agreed.

Seb humbly placed his arm around my shoulder.

'Katrina would have been so proud of you, Sims.'

A blush began to colour my cheeks. 'Honestly, guys, I just wanted to relay the good things about Katrina - who she was, and what she did, and how those things shaped our experiences together. She brought so much joy to my life - all of our lives. It seemed only right to share that.'

A brief stillness intercepted the table. There was nothing more in that moment than the low afternoon sun touching our backs and a gentle breeze stroking our skin. Even with masses of chatter surrounding our table, in our little bubble, there was only us.

'Can I say something?' Tracey asked, breaking the fleeting melancholy. She barely waited for our response before emphatically adding, 'I think we should all share something we love about Katrina.'

Four pairs of eyes looked at one another in silent agreement.

'Yeah, okay. That would be lovely,' I voiced on behalf of us all. 'You start, Tracey. What was your favourite thing about Katrina?'

For the first time on this tragic day, I witnessed the emergence of smiles. We were all about to walk our most-cherished routes down memory lane, and that prospect alone brought a newfound enthusiasm to the rickety table.

Tracey, who was first to explore, returned the half-eaten egg and cress sandwich to the paper plate and shuffled upright on the bench seat, ready to share her story.

'Okay, so we all know how much Katrina loved to help out, right? Well, she was the one who actually helped me buy my Yaris…'

Surprised at this fact, we all stared at one another in a mirrored fashion.

'Katrina knew about cars?' Julian asked, obviously oblivious. In fairness, I was the same but definitely wasn't going to let on.

'Oh my, yes,' Tracey exclaimed, 'well, she knew how to see through the sleazy guys at the dealerships, anyway. Honestly, we must have circled like, five different ones that afternoon? On and off the train we were. It was a right mission. But, she was so dedicated to helping me find the right car, and, eventually, we did.'

Tracey turned away from the table to admiringly look at her beloved red Yaris sat in the pub's car park.

'Had Yoshi three years now and still going strong. Every time I sit inside him, I think of her.'

A waitress came over at that very moment to clear the empty glasses and plates on our table. She couldn't have looked more confused by what she'd just overheard. Without context, that sentence must have sounded incredibly bizarre. But we all knew she was talking about the Yaris, and as long as we knew, that's all that mattered.

'You learn something new every day,' I said with a grin. 'Okay, what about you, Cherise?'

Cherise's eye's flicked up, rifling through her memory bank for the ultimate Katrina story from her extensive collection.

'So many to choose from,' she said, now placing her hand underneath her chin and looking downwards at the edge of the table. 'Well, there was that time I fell down the stairs—'

A giant snort escaped Seb's nose and caused me to jump.

'Oh gosh, yes,' he uttered with glee, 'I love this story.' Another bemused expression was cast across the rest of the table.

'How can you love a story about someone falling down the stairs?' I retorted.

His hand brushed away the question mark floating in the air above us. 'It's the way she tells it, Sims – pure gold. Anyway, sorry Cherise, my lovely - do pray tell?'

She laughed a little, 'It's okay, Sebby. Right, so…the day I fell down the stairs was a pretty average one. It was my day off and I'd decided to clean the house, as you do. The morning had been pretty successful. Everything looked clean, sparkly and tidy, just how I like it. But, as I was taking the vacuum up the stairs, I saw an invading piece of fluff on the step. *How dare it be there!* I thought. After all the bloody elbow grease I'd put in that morning, how did it even get missed? Anyway, rather than pick it up like a sensible person, I decided to set the vacuum on it - big mistake. The suction was so strong that I ended skidding on the carpet and sliding down backwards on my arse. The best bit, though, was that the hoover itself actually did the same thing. Bolt upright, it suctioned every step as it cascaded its way down to my slumped body at the bottom. It was like something from a comedy.'

As the image of this played in all of our minds, a big chortle spread across the table.

'That would have so gone viral if it had been caught on film,' Tracey giggled. 'But wait - how does Kats come into this?'

An explanatory index finger popped out from Cherise's hand. 'Well, I obviously had to tell someone about this incident. Plus, my butt was a little sore from the ride, so I thought I'd message Katrina about it first and foremost. Unlike you guys, she's always been more sympathetic.'

'I would have been sympathetic,' I interjected, hoping for some kind of acquiescence. But instead, I was greeted with the complete opposite.

'Sims, I love you and all that, but let's be honest now. You're way more likely to take the mick than offer your sympathies in a situation like that.'

She was right...

'Okay, fine. That *may* be true. So what did Kats say when you told her?'

'She was very understanding, of course. Her concern outweighed any giggling.' Cherise shot us some jovial daggers at that point. 'I told her that I'd scraped the back of my legs and bottom. Well, I moaned that I had. The pain just got worse as the day went on, so strange. Anyway, before you know it, she's standing at my front door with a little care basket of Ayurvedic skin lotions. It was so unexpected. But that's exactly what she was like. She'd do anything for anyone.'

None of us could argue with that fact. Katrina's altruism always surpassed expectations.

'I couldn't agree more,' Julian concurred, 'she was the same when it came to helping me organise events at the club.'

This was one story, I remembered.

'I put her through so much Rod Stewart music whilst trying to sort out that singles night. I truly believed his songs would set up the ideal playlist. Not too soppy, not too samey. I wanted us to stand out from the other clubs. Poor Katrina, though, she really didn't share that vision. Thank God she didn't. Without her input and patience, that night would've been a complete disaster. She saved the day. I remember what she said when I told her that, actually. *Get me a little red cape and just call me Supergirl.*' He laughed reverently at the memory, as did we. 'I wish I'd bought her that red cape. She saved me in so many ways…More than she'll ever know.'

'That was Kats all over,' Seb added, finger wistfully tracing the side of his glass, 'she'd do anything for anyone and never once complained about it. Without her, I'd have never been able to fully embrace my identity.'

My eyebrows rose at the revelation Seb was hurtling towards our table.

'She was the first person I came out to. I still remember how easy it was to finally admit the words that had been caged up inside me for so long. It was actually at your apartment, Simone. You weren't there. I can't remember where you were… I guess you may have been working a different shift or skulking around London with your noisy music at the time.' I rolled my eyes at that remark but continued to listen nonetheless. 'But yeah, I was feeling proper torn up about things. My last year of college was an absolute nightmare and, obviously, living at home was about as much fun as being slapped in the face with a mackerel, so I needed some space. I needed time to get my head straight, ironically. Katrina though, yeah, she just made me feel so welcome, so at ease. We sat together, drinking hot cocoa, and she said to me: *Baby Seb, you should embrace all that you are. Be the person you want to be. You deserve to be happy, and know that those who love you will only ever want that too.* And that's exactly what I did.'

He paused briefly before conclusively adding, 'So, now you all know who to finally blame for all of this colour.'

As it turned out, my best friend brought a lot of colour to people's lives. Whether it was a small dot or an almighty rainbow, Katrina's actions proved just how big an impact a little kindness could have, and in this black and white world with its dashes of grey, we needed more people like her. She was special.

'When they made her, they truly broke the mould.'

The last nod of the night to Seb's words instigated a toast.

'Here, here,' I said, raising my glass. 'To Katrina - the woman who broke the mould.'

In unison, our glasses harmonised a chorus of clinks, and in tune to that gesture, we looked up towards the sky and altogether said, 'To Katrina.'

The Final Outcome

'*Can you seriously imagine me racing that thing around our flat?*' were my famous last words today, as I mindlessly steered the toy Lamborghini Dad had given me around the apartment.

Although there was nothing more ridiculous than the sight of a fully grown woman playing with a little yellow Lambo and watching it career into every table leg as though that was part of the challenge, I still couldn't seem to see anything else but Katrina. Whether it was in the kitchen making her staple protein granola breakfast, flopping on the sofa in the lounge with her long hair resting over its arm, or determinedly wandering in search for her morning cappuccino on the counter. In my mind's eye, I'd see her there, and every time I did, my heart would sink.

Daily life was manageable in the places where I didn't expect her to be there. But, of course, when I was somewhere she would usually accompany me; a weight would sit in my chest and instantly choke me to tears. Distracting myself wasn't working all that well, so I tried to pretend that she was simply on holiday instead. That way, it would be easier to cope. Only, denial has an annoying habit of letting down its guard and inviting the truth inside. She was gone, and unlike a holiday, I had to accept that she was never coming back.

With that said, if you had asked me the year before whether I believed in fate or the afterlife, I'd have expressed with absolute fervency, "*Of course not. What poppycock!*" But, after everything that had happened since then - all of the situations I couldn't put down to mere coincidence - I was beginning to believe that there was more to life than what we could merely see with the naked eye alone.

Perhaps losing someone close makes you vulnerable to those beliefs as a means of self-comfort. Revisiting memories of loss is far easier to bear when you think that their soul is still out there, somewhere. So, although the idea of spectres and symbols still seemed fairly farfetched, there was now a small part of me that believed in the notion of a realm beyond our own – a place outside of time and space, where those no longer with us are happy.

I tried to imagine this realm like a window, just a pane of glass separating this world from theirs. One day, I would see my best friend again on the other side of it. With that image in mind, I envisaged her hand meeting mine as I pressed it to the air. God, I missed her so much. Nevertheless, as much as all I wanted to do was confine myself to a hollowed existence, Katrina's friendship served me as a very important reminder.

One: That connection is important. Kindness can be found from all kinds of relationships, helping restore our faith in others, provide structure, and keep us strong. More than anything, we need kindness within our team, so that we have a better chance of hitting a homerun when life throws its curveballs. And, two: that nothing lasts forever. Whilst rewriting the past is not an option, it is up to us how we use those experiences to narrate our future. For now, as hard as it was to do so, I had to remember that.

At that very moment, I heard a loud bang in my bedroom. I jumped ever so slightly at the sound of it and placed the remote control down on the sofa. Cautiously, I walked towards the door to find out what the culprit was behind the noise.

As I entered, the little Lamborghini conked against my foot. Nothing else, from what I could tell, seemed out of place. But, as I looked around in search of an answer, I suddenly saw it. The newspaper clipping with a tribute to Katrina had fallen off my corkboard.

Her smiling face stared back at me. The picture they'd used was a selfie she'd taken just before the marathon. She looked so happy, so vibrant, so full of life. It's hard to believe that the same lively character had crumpled to the ground like tissue paper at the end of that very race. I choked a little, re-reading it. No matter how many times I'd scanned the little article, the quote from her parents always got to me.

"We're devastated without her. Inside and out, she was the most beautiful girl. Life won't ever be the same without Katrina's uplifting presence in it. Our only solace for the pain is knowing that she helped save four people's lives."

Right to the end, Katrina's selflessness was unparalleled. If only she'd known that even her last decision - to donate her organs - had given those four people a new lease of life.

Out of the corner of my eye, I noticed a hypnotic contrail from a passing plane outside my window. For a brief time, I captivatedly watched on as white ribbons twirled in the city sky. Perhaps it was naïve of me, but I wondered if, somehow, Katrina had heard my very thoughts.

And so, as a means of observing that hopeful notion and everything her friendship stood for, I decided to make myself a new pact.

Keep on living.

Ethereal Epilogue

TOKYO, JAPAN
One Year Later

Autumn sprinkled tawny-gold colours onto the passing trees. Crimson leaves nestled in-between and waved back in imperial glory, each one gloriously saluting me as I walked through the gardens. Saying it was beautiful would be an understatement. The feeling it delivered was breathtaking, and my heart skipped a beat with every inch I absorbed of nature's seasonal palette. Standing in the midst of such elegance reaffirmed to me that, despite all the odds, the decision I'd made was the right one.

Losing Katrina was, without question, the worst thing that could have ever happened to me. Even with all the warnings, I still didn't see it coming, and I hated myself for being so blind.

There'll always be a part of me that'll blame myself for her death. Maybe, if I'd been more focused on what was real and not waylaid by my emotions, I would have been able to save her. For the months after her passing, I'd allowed this thought process to engulf me. Inside my torn apart heart, I couldn't ever imagine being happy again. But somehow, in spite of all the sadness and despair that dwelled within me, I found light through the darkness.

Life taught me an invaluable lesson the hard way, but I realised that the only way to learn from my mistakes was to keep moving forward. As much as it burned inside me to know that Katrina and I will never ride the waves together, or meet our soulmates to have the double wedding she'd always dreamed of, I also didn't want to waste any more time living life in slow motion.

Katrina was never one for regret. Regret is reserved for the things we never did but wished we had, for the words we always wanted to say, but instead, chose to hold them forever captive inside our hearts. Thinking that is what irrevocably opened my eyes. I didn't want to spend another day acting like they were infinite. Life could stop any minute and I wanted to live mine knowing - should it come to a sudden end – that I left this plane doing the things I'd always dreamed of.

On this liberating day, I was freed from the pain that had tethered my soul to such anguish - to the responsibility for a life I couldn't get back. After all this time, I finally knew what I had to do.

So, instead of burying my head as I walked the asphalt streets of London, I smiled at passers-by. At work, I took it upon myself to not only learn more, but to also stand my ground more. To my friends and family, I reminded them all on a regular basis how much they meant to me, enjoying them cringe with love as I did so. And, of course, I decided to be brave and dedicate time to my true passion – writing, perfecting the art of patience, whilst doing so. However, out of all those actions, I soon realised there was still one important call I needed to make…

The truth is; I don't think anyone ever expects these things to happen in their reality. To most of us, it's the kind of story that only exists in soap dramas and box office movies, so we never fully prepare ourselves for it.

But even if those stories are fictional ones, their foundations are based on events entirely possible.

For better or for worse, life can change at any given moment - and not always when we expect it to. These are the kinds of physical experiences that can impact profoundly on the heart, and change a person's entire outlook on things. This is why, as a consequence of everything that had happened, the next step in my journey landed me six-thousand miles away from home.

Tucked behind the Sumida River, sat on a bench inside Tokyo's Kyu Yasuda Garden, I began to write down the foundations of a life story about a girl who'd taught me far more than I could ever pen down on paper – Katrina.

A gentle breeze swept up my chin, and I stared as the scarlet-scattered path danced around me. The merriment of people passing through immersed themselves in the same simple pleasure, from a flora of histories past, and I couldn't help but wonder if my best friend was there with me. If somehow, the whispers in the wind meant that she could see me now. And, if so, whether she'd be proud that I finally did what I set out to do so long ago.

'Thank you, Kats,' I whispered to the rustling trees, 'I owe you everything.'

A solitary tear emerged, but I quickly wiped it away, bookmarking the page of my little notebook with the treasured photograph of us at the same time. This was a happy moment. I didn't want to cry.

According to the rule of Tarot, 'The Final Outcome' refers to the end result of your reading, based on the rest of your cards in the spread. This was mine. This was the ultimate consequence from a very long and unexpected period in my life. Lilith was right - I'd know when my new beginning was when the time came. And as I got up from my spot on the bench and started to walk across the path, heading towards the red-armed Azumabashi Bridge with its view of the towering Skytree reflecting in the waters below, I felt the dividing threshold between my old life and the new. This was the first chapter of my new story, and it began the moment he turned around.

'Hello, Miss Austen.'

THE END

How These 7 Japanese Concepts Inspired "A Cosmic Chance"

Whether it is in the character's topical interest or by observation of circumstance, Japanese philosophy heavily underpins many aspects of Simone's story, and its presence there aims to teach us a few things about emotions and wisely applying them to the world around us.

The following 7 concepts are ones that prove most poignant within this exploratory narrative.

1) Ikigai (生き甲斐) – Literally: "Value in Living:" Meaning: "Individual's reason/purpose for being"

Composed of the words *iki* (meaning "life") and *gai* (which describes value/worth) Ikigai is a term with derivatives set in the Heian period (794 to 1185 – back when Buddhism, Taoism and other Chinese influences were at their height) In those days, *kai* (meaning "shell" – where the word *gai* originated) were deemed as highly valuable items. As time went on, the phrase "ikigai" was neologised and, inevitably so, went on to express the idea behind the "value in living".
It's all about perception. Life is ever-flowing, and it's important to know how to swim with its current. Being mindful of that will undoubtedly aid fulfilment in the journey.

Simone's constant curiosity for finding her place in the universe is a perfect demonstration of Ikigai. It is the search many of us face when evaluating our lives. Amongst her convivial comradery, she remains the only one against the idea of love, for example; putting it last on her list of things to do. Her abstemious attitude reflects her thinking that the most important things in life are on a more philosophical level, and that achieving them requires no distraction. However, she does harbour a secret longing for love, unbeknown to her friends. But this could only with a likeminded other - who she doesn't believe exists. Alas, in a world where she feels isolated in that way of thinking and where no experiences offer her the truth she seeks, she struggles to find life's value. Ultimately, she attempts to fit in with the crowd and inevitably falls into the relationship trap; stuck with the *oh-so* vanilla, Matt. This is when her self-awareness of purpose kicks in. At this moment, she feels completely and utterly lost. She realises she's submitted herself to fall in line with societal expectations, rather than her own, all because she didn't believe it was tenable. As the story evolves, she takes back the reigns on her own independence - slowly accepting that it's okay to do so - and no matter what occurs from that point onwards, Simone accepts that the choices she made were her own. Good or bad, those experiences would have happened irrespective to her decisions, and, in the end, it's that knowledge which provides her a sense of comfort in the identity she's now settled into.

2) Mono No Aware (物の哀れ, もののあはれ) – Literally: "The pathos of things" Meaning: "The poignancy and sadness of ephemera; a wistful emotion to the beauty of impermanence"

Originating from the words "mono" (thing) and "aware" (pathos) the question of sadness comes from an awareness of its transience. Take the fleeting appearance of cherry blossom in the spring, for example; its exceptional beauty can also elicit sadness. However, this knowledge is also what heightens the pleasure we take when admiring its beauty in the moment.

Most notoriously represented with seasons in Japanese culture, but can also be extended to life in general. In the story, the beauty of friendship is demonstrated in this way, as well as transient, yet poignant, moments in life that last forever in our hearts. None of us know how long anything will last, and we also cannot take for granted whether we'll be fortunate enough to experience them again, which is why there is such an emotional weight within Simone's narrative. From her meeting with Ethan to when her best friend, Katrina, tragically passes,

291

everything that occurred came unexpectedly, and both carried beauty within their sadness, and vice versa.

3) Koi No Yokan (恋の予感) Translation 1: "The mutual feeling upon first meeting someone that you could both inevitably fall in love" Translation 2: "A reciprocated and innate knowledge of connectedness with another soul"

Interestingly, this contemporary notion of romance, most often affiliated with origins in Shōjo Manga, has a particular resonance to both young and old alike. But, unlike *Hitomebore* (which translates as "Love at first sight") *Koi No Yokan* highlights an emotion within the sphere of love that hasn't yet been written in English.

The phrase as a whole regards love (koi) being something that can potentially be predicted (yokan) and whilst there are a few interpretations given for this "untranslatable" experience, the most agreeable aspect of it is that the premonition of love reciprocally occurs between two people upon first meeting.

Ethan and Simone are the idyllic example of this untranslatable Japanese phrase. Upon first meeting at the Koko, it was evident that there was an attraction. However, although Simone enjoyed Ethan's company and felt completely safe in his presence, as the night goes on, she becomes unsure as to whether this was completely unrequited. Due to a run of bad luck in the romance department in the past, suddenly, her mind runs amuck with anxiety. In the blink of an eye, the whole situation is turned on its head, and as a means of self-protection, she keeps her guard up and her heart locked up tight. Thankfully, though, fate was determined to push them back together, and when the time was right, they would meet again. Ethan's repeated presence and the time they shared together helped allay Simone's fears, and she began to realise that she wasn't imagining things. Ethan felt the same way. This was more than simple attraction. This was a connectedness of souls, and it was felt it from the moment they'd met.

4) Shōganai (しょうがない) – Literally: "It can't be helped/accept your fate." Meaning: "Because we cannot influence every variable in life, we must learn to accept them and move on."

When faced with adversity or injustice in our path, it is important to maintain a dignified approach. This is because not all situations are within our control, and the sooner we learn to accept that certain things are beyond our reach, the sooner we'll establish emotional equilibrium.

For some, it can prove a rather overwhelming place to be and completely knock us off-balance, but the ultimate aim of the Zen Buddhist philosophy, *Shikata ga nai* (or, *Shō ga nai,* as it's also known) is to teach us that these difficult times are a natural part of life and that acceptance of them will fair us greater than avoidance.

Simone's existential crisis in love and in life weighed heavily in the beginning. She is dissatisfied with where her world is headed. Everything seemed predictable and pointless. What she wanted versus what she had rendered her lost in her own mind, and she desperately sought to figure out a way of changing things. As a result of that irritation, she inevitably took some of the special things for granted and misused her emotions. Foregoing her own worth meant that she forsook others, too. For example, even though Matt was evidently not right for her (and was not the best boyfriend, either) situations became heightened because she delved into a relationship she never truly felt. On the surface, it was unfair on him, but it was also unfair on her. Sadly, it took the unexpected passing of her best friend to teach her this important principle. Metaphorically speaking, Simone finally understood that she could not control the ocean of life, moreover, her only job was the learn how to ride the waves. Ultimately though, by accepting this notion, she found strength and inner peace.

5) Nanakarobi Yaoki (七転び八起き) –
Literally : "Fall down 7 times, stand up 8"
Meaning: "When life knocks you down, stand back up; What matters is not the bad that happened, but what one does after."

Once the importance of acceptance has been recognised, the next life lesson to learn is to never give up. When you have a goal, promise or wish in need of fulfilment, perseverance and resilience are two traits that need to be mastered. Dedication to those behaviours is what plays the rudimentary part in achieving ultimate success. Nevertheless, there is a chance that the many knocks in life will send your off course in your journey and you may even believe that you've reached the end of the road. This is where Nanakorobi Yaoki comes in.

This popular Japanese proverb, which is often expressed through the medium of the historic Daruma Doll, reminds us that the pitfalls and bumps are a just small part of a very big road. We must keep moving. There is no other motivation to succeed, except our own power of will.

Having the courage to carry on, even when times are impossibly hard, is an important sentiment of Simone's story. She could have easily succumbed to the inviting darkness during these difficult times. But the story aims to show that happiness can be found by turning that negativity around. Of course, sadness is still involved and allowed. There is no shame in exploring those emotions. It is, however, through all the explorations of worry and fear that working out a way to change things for the better can be found. Similar to the philosophy of Nanakarobi Yaoki, Simone intrepidly realises the importance of time and how easily it can either pass by in a state of inertia or transform entirely, depending on one's actions. This is why, after everything that happened, Simone finally sets out to visit Japan, and at long last re-establishes her connection with Ethan.

6) Yūgen(幽玄) – Literally: "An unspoken connection with the world." Meaning: "An awareness of the universe that triggers an emotional response too deep and powerful for words"

By understanding the seven aesthetic principles for achieving Wabi-Sabi (see below) and engaging with them and the arts regularly, it is possible, according to Zen Philosophy, for appreciation to develop into the deeply profound state of awareness known as, Yūgen.

To try and explain this ideal, think of this: nothingness is not a celestial chasm. Now is a transient state. There is no "perfect" construct. Life is, and ever will be, a place of potential, mutable and fallible aspects...and that's what makes it so wholesomely charming. That is the universe; imperceptible, untouchable and unreachable - everywhere and nowhere. When this powerful state of Yūgen is felt, words need not apply.

This is something Simone learns to master, as she slowly finds herself through her experiences with others and in her own wants, fears and strengths. For someone so young, the many vicissitudes in her journey inevitably enable her to understand and grow as a person. She becomes wiser, more self-controlled and, as well as this, more accepting of the negative emotions she has to endure. As a result of this, she also realises the beauty and the necessity in all of life's mutable offerings, and becomes at one with the universe both as a whole and in all its intricacies. Thus, achieving a fundamental state known in Japanese as, **Wabi-Sabi** – "imperfect, impermanent or incomplete beauty."

7 Principles of Wabi-Sabi

Fukinsei (不均整): asymmetry, irregularity

Kanso (簡素): simplicity

Koko (考古): basic, weathered

Shizen (自然): without pretence, natural

Yūgen (幽玄): subtly profound grace, not obvious

Datsuzoku (脱俗): unbounded by convention, free

*Seijaku (静寂): tra*nquillity, stillness)

7) Natsukashii (懐かしい) – Literally: "Fond reminiscence"

Deriving from the verb *"natsuku"*, meaning, "to keep close and become fond of" – indicates joy and gratitude for the past. Whilst being nostalgic in English is often associated with a sombre emotion, in Japanese, it is linked with a rather contrasting feeling. For example, if something is to be considered Natsukashii, it should enable the individual to recall happy memories; it's used when something evokes fond pastimes, such as a song or location. This is because many of our most cherished stories are from places we've been to and shared with those we love. In Japan, to experience this type of nostalgia is a solid reminder that you are fortunate to have had those experiences. The fact that you cannot return to them is what, ultimately, makes them all the more poignant.

At the end of the story, Simone finally embarks upon her journey to Tokyo, and, in contrast to her time in London when she bleakly stared out at the charcoal Thames or watched the rain pouring from the window, she instead sits in tranquil Japanese garden, absorbing the colours around her, and remembers her best friend, Katrina. Although Simone deeply misses her, it is their friendship and Katrina's encouraging disposition during that time which brought her to be where she is now. She realises how fortunate she was to have her in her life, and as she writes about her best friend, she recalls the gratitude for her and for everything she gave.

AUTHOR'S NOTES...

"Essentially, none of us really know our reason for being here. High and low we search, back and forth we travel; exploring different paths and choosing from a variety of options – none of which are marked as the "right one" – and simply living in hope that one day, one of those choices will make sense. And yet, still, the map of destiny is unclear. Your existential meaning is so ambiguous. In spite of ceaseless efforts, you lose faith in trying to find it, and instead, you simply just...carry on."

*"Humans are creatures of habit; living on repeat is ultimately all we really know. Our certainty of what to do in a situation relies heavily on how it makes us feel, based on prior knowledge of potential outcomes. Perhaps then, with that in mind, that is all our purpose really is – to live a life that makes us **feel** good?"*

"If you think about it, your whole world can be completely transformed by something as simple as a word. All it takes is a moment, then, suddenly, the atlas of your future is as clear as the big blue marble you see beneath the wings."

"Magic is the art of fate - creating visions of kaleidoscopic colour from life's hidden truths. Nothing you see makes sense. Until finally, it all comes together..."

ACKNOWLEDGEMENTS

First and foremost, huge thanks go to YOU, the reader! Your support and enjoyment of this book makes all this possible and enables more stories to be written, so thank you.

Another chunk of gratitude goes to Sam Rosser, my copy editor and fellow lover of rock music. You were the first person to read this story the whole way through, and your aptitude and belief in the narrative gave me the confidence to put it out there. Thank you so much for that.

Of course, many thanks has to go to my close family and friends who lived through/suffered the pain of me discussing this story night and day. Mum, you made a great guinea pig when I read snippets out to you over a cuppa. Having you be open enough to listen to it, commend its good parts and pick me up on any flaws was the kind of critique I truly needed (even if I *occasionally* jumped to the defence…) Either way, despite appearances, I did value your input and always will. Thank you for always being there.

As for the friends who I sent the story across to (Simon, Kirsty, Hannah, Phoebe, Lisa, Vikki etc.), apologies for not forewarning you that it would make you cry, but I'm still so pleased that it did. I'm not a sadist, honest! I'm just thankful that the story elicited the desired emotion and that you all enjoyed reading it. Thank you so much for that support.

To the friends of mine who have such wonderful personalities that I simply had to *mildly* steal them in order to create these characters (you've probably guessed which ones possess your traits). But, as my suitcase says, *"Careful, or you'll end up in my novel."* The warning is there in technicolour, so you can never say you missed it.

And lastly, to the events and the people who inspired this story, but will probably never know how their presence evoked something so special. As a result of knowing you and experiencing these times, I grew as a person. Good, bad or fleeting, I feel stronger for having met you and gone through all that I have. Now this story is forever immortalised, should you ever read it, I hope that you realise how deep my gratitude flows. Thank you.

BOOKS AND BLOGS

*If you enjoyed this book, you may also enjoy my debut novel, **Picture-Perfect** - a story of self-empowerment through adversity, and love through courage. Available as both an eBook and paperback from Amazon, Barnes & Noble, BookBaby and many more online retailers.*

*You can also read similar articles online via my Thought Catalog page, or on the main website, **sachakurucz.com***

LET'S GET SOCIAL

Facebook @sachakauthor

Instagram @sachakuruczauthor

Phoebe,

What a pleasure it is
to be able to call you a
friend. You truly are an
exceptional young woman.
But as much as I know you
love being on-the-go, I hope
you'll find some time to take 5,
brew some nice tea & enjoy a
bit of light reading. As always,
thank you so much for your support.

Sacha
xXx

Printed in Great Britain
by Amazon

68353605R00180